A PLACE OF
ACCEPTANCE

To Sharon —
I'm so glad we're
neighbors! I hope you
enjoy my second novel.

Julie

A PLACE OF
ACCEPTANCE

A NOVEL

JULIE BELL

Tate Publishing & Enterprises

Published by Tate Publishing & Enterprises, LLC
127 E. Trade Center Terrace | Mustang, Oklahoma 73064 USA
1.888.361.9473 | www.tatepublishing.com

Tate Publishing is committed to excellence in the publishing industry. The company reflects the philosophy established by the founders, based on Psalm 68:11,
"The Lord gave the word and great was the company of those who published it."

Book design copyright © 2011 by Tate Publishing, LLC. All rights reserved.
Cover design by Amber Gulilat
Interior design by Christina Hicks

Published in the United States of America
ISBN: 978-1-61346-036-8
Fiction / Christian / Western
11.06.20

For my sisters, Mindy and Kasey. I treasure your love and friendship. I'm so blessed to have you in my life. I love you both very much.

PROLOGUE

Frankfort, Kentucky, 1871

The gavel came crashing down with a resounding clang on the judge's desk. Rigby's heart stopped, and his breath caught in his throat as he waited for the verdict.

The deep, clear voice of the judge spoke the inevitable word that Rigby expected. *Guilty.* Murmurs of satisfaction rose from the crowd that had gathered to witness the event. The men who had destroyed so many lives throughout the years were finally captured and facing the consequences of their lives of crime.

Sweat poured down Rigby's face as he stood next to his father and three older brothers, twisting his cap in his hands, awaiting the sentencing.

The judge sat for only a moment before he looked them all in the eyes and spoke with great authority.

"Buck, George, Bob, and Cotton, you have been found guilty of murder, robbery, and kidnapping. You are hereby sentenced to death by hanging."

They made no comment but only eyed the judge with hatred. Rigby stood with uncertainty. His name was not mentioned with the others. He glanced up at Buck, his father, who angrily glared back down at him then turned questioning eyes to the judge.

"Rigby," the judge began, "you're a very unusual case. After taking into consideration the circumstances in your situation, I feel that a different sentence is warranted. You will, and should, be punished for your role in the crimes. However, seeing as you did not choose a life of crime for yourself, I will spare your life. You are hereby sentenced to spend the next ten years of your life in prison. Court is adjourned."

The judge's gavel came down one last time in conclusion; then he rose and left the room.

Rigby stood wide-eyed. He could not believe his ears. His life was to be spared! A surge of relief flooded his being, and he breathed a prayer of thanks.

He turned as Buck grabbed for him in anger.

"They are making a mistake with you," Buck hissed furiously at his youngest son. "You will never amount to anything."

"You're wrong, Pa. God has given me another chance, and I won't let anyone down. Good-bye, Pa," Rigby said sadly as he watched his father and brothers being led away. The deputy took Rigby's arm and guided him toward a waiting guard who would escort him to the prison.

CHAPTER 1

Darby, Kentucky 1881

Dr. Howard Clarke whistled brightly as he walked briskly toward the train station. Today was the day that his niece, Dana, was to arrive in town. Dr. Clarke was nearly bursting with excitement. Dana recently finished her training as a nurse in Richmond, Virginia, and was on her way to Darby to work at her uncle's practice.

"Mornin', Levi," Dr. Clarke called as he waved hello to Levi Thomas, the owner of the general store and mercantile. Levi was sweeping off the front porch and waved back.

It was still early in the morning, but the small town of Darby was already coming to life. Business owners were opening up shop, women were bustling through town on their way to the general store, children were running around the schoolhouse playing, and Dr. Howard Clarke was happily making his way to the train station.

Dana Clarke was his brother's girl, and Dr. Clarke had only seen her a couple of times. He didn't make the trek out to his family's hometown of Virginia very often. He was thrilled to learn that Dana was going into the field of medicine. The need for another doctor in Darby was growing, and as Dr. Clarke was in his late fifties, he was at the point where he needed some help.

When he learned that Dana had finished her nursing studies, he immediately wired his brother to see if Dana would like to work in Darby. She quickly took him up on the offer, saying that she would be more than happy to oblige.

Dr. Clarke glanced at the pocket watch that he pulled out of his vest pocket. *Eight twenty-five a.m. The train should be here any minute.* Dr. Clarke walked up on the platform and waited for signs of the train. He was too anxious to sit, so he merely paced back and forth in anticipation of the train and the arrival of his niece.

After about ten minutes, which felt more like an hour to the excited doctor, a whistle was heard in the distance, and Dr. Clarke began to feel the rumble of a train. The train slowly made its way into the station and finally squeaked to a halt. Dr. Clarke nervously twisted his hat in his hands as he watched the passengers descend. So far there was no sign of his niece. Of course, he didn't even know if he would recognize her. The last time he saw her she was ten years old. That was nine years ago.

Finally, a stunning young woman, who appeared to be unaccompanied, stepped lightly down from the train. She had thick, dark hair that was swept up with a few stray curls that fell against her face, deep blue eyes, and a sparkling smile. Behind her, Dr. Clarke noticed a young man with a beard and unkempt hair step down. Dr. Clarke could have sworn that he recognized him from somewhere but couldn't quite place him. As Dana looked around expectantly, Dr. Clarke moved forward with a tentative smile.

"Uncle Howard?" she asked, the smile never leaving her face. Dr. Clarke nodded as Dana threw herself into his arms.

"Oh, I'm so glad to see you, Uncle," she gushed as she stood back to look at him. Howard Clarke was a handsome man for his age with dark hair that was only graying at the temples. Dana thought it made him look dignified.

"I can't tell you how happy I am to have you here." He released her from the hug and held her at arms length. "My, but you've grown. How was the trip?"

"The train ride wasn't bad, except that I was so anxious to arrive I didn't really have time to enjoy the scenery." She chuckled.

"It's such a pleasure to have you here, my dear. You're an answer to prayers. In my old age, I'm having trouble keeping up with all of the patients."

"Oh, Uncle, you exaggerate!" Dana couldn't see her uncle as old or needing help.

"Oh no! I didn't even think to bring the buggy. I'm afraid I walked. It's not a long walk, of course, but you must be terribly tired from the trip, and I never stopped to think of that."

Dana grinned. "Uncle, after that long ride cooped up in a train, I'll enjoy the walk," she said, her eyes dancing merrily. "Trust me."

"Very well, Dana. I'll have your luggage sent for this afternoon," he said as he turned her toward the town.

"Thank you, Uncle."

"Well, my dear, welcome to Darby." He gestured to the town with his arm. Dana took a moment to take in the town that her uncle called home. The town was small and quaint with many businesses lining both sides of the street. There were trees and flowers throughout the town. Dana was pleased with what she saw.

"Oh, Uncle, it's simply charming!" She looped her arm in his, and they walked from the train station at a leisurely pace. Dr. Clarke took time to show her the town. He pointed out the general store, the hotel and restaurant, the bank, the livery, various other establishments, and finally the church and schoolhouse that stood off by itself at the far end of town.

"We had to build a new church and schoolhouse because the old one burned down ten years ago," he recounted to his niece, who listened attentively. "In fact, an outlaw set the schoolhouse on fire with the schoolmarm inside. Fortunately, Caleb Carter, a local ranch owner, saved her seconds before the building came crashing down. They ended up marrying." Dr. Clarke watched as his niece's eyes turned dreamy.

"How romantic," she murmured.

"Well, here we are." Dr. Clarke stopped in front of a wooden, two-story building. He steered his niece inside. "This is my office." He took her through the front waiting room and showed her the patients' rooms in the back. "My apartment is up here," he said as he led the way up the stairs. They stopped in front of an open door. "Here is the room that I set up for you." He smiled at his niece, who turned and threw her arms around his neck.

"Thank you, Uncle. The town is just perfect. I love your office, and the room is perfect. This is all so wonderful."

She released her hold on her uncle and walked into the room that was to be hers. It was small but comfortable. There was a small bed, dresser, and a washstand.

"I'm sorry there aren't any curtains or fancy things suitable for a woman," Dr. Clarke apologized. As a lifetime bachelor, he never had frills or many colorful things in his home.

"Don't worry about that. I'm sure I can spruce the place up in no time." She walked toward the window and gazed at the scene in front of her.

"This room has the best view in the place," Dr. Clarke said with satisfaction as he came up behind her. Dana's room was on the backside of the house, so her view was not of the town. She looked out to see a meadow filled with blooming wildflowers.

"It's beautiful. Oh, Uncle, I just know that I'm going to be very happy here." She turned and flashed him a beautiful smile that showed off her straight, white teeth. As soon as her uncle left the room, she bowed her head to send a quick prayer of thanks up to God then immediately set to work unpacking.

Rigby stepped off the train behind the most beautiful woman he had ever seen. She was a smiling vision.

He shook his head. Never mind all that. He had business to attend to. Being back in Darby was nothing short of nerve-racking for him. He stood on the platform to the train station and looked around. The town hadn't changed much. There were a few new buildings here and there, but aside from that, everything seemed to be the way it was when he left.

Someone with a large suitcase walked in front of him, and he took a clumsy step backward. He lowered his head and discreetly tried to look around to see if anyone recognized him. Of course no one did. He had changed from a boy to a man in the years he had been away. He gripped the one small bag he had with him and set out for the only place he knew to go to—the Blue Star Ranch.

Ten years was a long time. Rigby Buchanan, once forced into a life of crime by his family, was finally free. He worked hard in prison, mostly laying tracks for railroads. It was hard, backbreaking work that changed the sixteen-year-old boy into a man. He grew into a large man with a broad chest and corded muscles that rippled through his arms. Appearance was never a priority for him in the last ten years, and as a result, his hair was long and unkempt. He had a full beard that covered his face. He knew that no one in Darby would recognize him. No one, that is, except Alicia Carter.

Ten years ago, his family had kidnapped Alicia Carter. The kidnapping was part of a bank robbery, which left the bank owner, Mark Brewer, paralyzed. During Alicia's captivity, Rigby developed a friendship with her and eventually helped her escape. Rigby and his family were arrested and put in jail in Darby while they awaited their trial. During that time, he came to know the Lord as his personal Savior with the help of Pastor Tyler and Caleb Carter, who soon after became Alicia's husband.

Rigby continued to walk toward the ranch where Alicia and Caleb lived. He had no family or friends and nowhere else to turn. Alicia was the only person he could think of who might possibly find it in her heart to help him. After all, she was the one who pleaded with the judge to spare his life. Rigby topped a small hill, and his breath caught at the sight of the Blue Star

Ranch below him. Caleb Carter owned the largest horse ranch in the territory and a great deal of property.

Rigby broke out into a sweat. He didn't know what he would do if they didn't help him. Or worse, if they told the other towns-folk that he had returned. He figured they wouldn't take too kindly to a former outlaw returning to their neck of the woods. He wiped his sweaty palms on his pant legs, took a deep breath, and started toward the ranch.

CHAPTER 2

Alicia hummed to herself as she hung laundry on the line behind the house. It was a bright, spring morning, and she felt good. She had much to be thankful for. Caleb had given her a good life with a sturdy roof over their heads and three beautiful children. Her two boys were helping their father out on the range checking the fences. Her youngest, four-year-old Daisy, was playing outside.

Daisy was a high-spirited young girl, much like her mother, as Caleb liked to say, who loved the outdoors. She could spend all day outside playing with Rebel, the old German shepherd. The family loved that dog—especially Alicia. Rebel helped save her life when she was kidnapped. Sadly, Alicia understood that Rebel was getting along in years. She and Caleb had talked before about getting another puppy for the children, but the timing never seemed right. Her thoughts continued to whirl as she worked steadily on the laundry.

Daisy sat nearby, watching her mother. She pulled on Rebel's ear then pulled his tail and giggled. Fortunately, Rebel was a calm dog who took it all very good-naturedly. However, Daisy had been taunting him all morning, and he was beginning to get fed up. He got up and trotted into the front yard away from the four-year-old's fingers, and she gleefully trailed along behind him.

Rigby watched from a few feet away as a small child and dog made their way into the front yard. He watched them both lie down in the dirt and smiled at what a precious sight the two of them made. He walked up slowly, so as not to startle the little girl.

"Excuse me, little girl?" he asked kindly. Daisy blinked then let out a loud shriek. Rebel immediately came to attention and began to growl at the stranger.

"Whoa there, boy," Rigby said as calmly as he could as he backed up. "I won't hurt anybody."

"Daisy!" Alicia cried as she ran into the front yard. She quickly assessed the situation and scooped up her frightened daughter. Oh, how she wished Caleb was here! Who was this strange man? Fear crept its way through her, and she backed up, putting distance between herself and the stranger. Rebel stood his ground, snarling at the man who threatened his family.

"Alicia," the man said in a deep voice.

"Who are you?" Alicia demanded, her tone not at all friendly.

"I guess you don't recognize me. When I left, I was only sixteen years old."

Alicia squinted at the stranger as his identity began to dawn on her. *It couldn't be. Could it?*

"Rigby?" she asked hesitantly. She did a quick mental calculation in her head and realized with a start that ten years had indeed passed.

"Yes, ma'am."

"Daisy, honey, go into the house, please. I'll be right in." Alicia set the child down and watched her make her way up the front steps and into the house. "It's okay, Rebel," she said. The dog relaxed but continued to keep a watchful eye on the stranger.

"Rigby Buchanan. I wondered if we would ever see you again. How are you?" she asked as she extended her hand to the young man. He gratefully accepted it and smiled.

"I'm fine, ma'am." He nervously twirled his hat in his hands. "I just got out of prison. I had nowhere else to go, you see, so I thought I'd take you up on your promise and come back to Darby."

Alicia thought back to the time over ten years ago when she told Rigby that if he was given a second chance at life and wanted to come back to Darby, she and Caleb would do everything in their power to give him a fresh start.

"Rigby, I'm so pleased you decided to come back," Alicia said pleasantly. She leaned over, about to give him a hug, when her nose was assailed with the stench of a man in desperate need of a bath. She raised an eyebrow and looked him over. His clothes were filthy. *Probably the only ones he has,* she thought ruefully.

"When was the last time you had a bath?" Alicia watched him continue to twist his hat in his hands uncomfortably, refusing to make eye contact. "That long ago, huh? Well, what you need is a bath and a hot meal." *A shave and haircut wouldn't hurt either.* "Why don't you go down to the creek and clean yourself up? Then come back to the house for a good home-cooked meal."

"Thank you, ma'am." Rigby was visibly relieved. Alicia's heart went out to him. She wondered when the last time was that he had a decent meal. Poor young man with no family and no home. She hoped that Caleb would be able to help him out.

At suppertime Caleb came riding back. Their two sons—Cameron, who was nine, and William, who was six—were riding proudly with their pa. Cameron was growing up and becoming a big help to his father. Young Will was still more of a hindrance than a help, but he loved to go everywhere with his father, and Caleb was happy to oblige.

After Caleb and his sons stabled the horses and got cleaned up, they entered the house to be greeted by the delicious aroma of fried chicken.

"Mrs. Carter, you are such a good cook," Caleb said as he came up behind his wife and put his arms around her. He greeted her with a light kiss and sat down at the table.

"Actually, Caleb, may I speak with you for a moment outside? Cameron, watch Will and Daisy for a moment, please. And don't leave the table. We'll be right back." Alicia quickly ushered her husband outside through the kitchen door.

"You just can't resist me, can you?" Caleb teased as he put his arms around his wife.

"Now, Caleb, be serious for a moment," she whispered as she removed his arms from around her waist. "We have a visitor."

"Who is it? Mark and Claire?" Claire was Caleb's sister, and her husband, Mark, was one of Caleb's closest friends.

"Not exactly."

Caleb's eyes narrowed. "Rigby Buchanan showed up in our front yard this afternoon. He was just released from prison, and, as he has no other connections, he took us up on our offer to help him. Poor boy. He was in desperate need of a bath and a good meal. He's staying to supper, and I thought you might like to talk to him." Alicia watched as Caleb nodded thoughtfully.

"Well, what do ya know?" he said. Caleb knew deep down that one day Rigby Buchanan would be back. He had felt it from the moment they extended the offer ten years ago. The look of gratitude in Rigby's eyes had told Caleb all he needed to know.

"He's waiting in the living room for us to call him to supper. I wanted you to know and not be taken by surprise. Oh, and by the way, I let him borrow some of your clothes. His were threadbare and filthy."

"Well, let's not keep our guest waiting."

The couple went back inside. Alicia served up the chicken as Caleb went to get Rigby. He walked into the living room, and Rigby quickly stood from the armchair he was seated in. Rigby's nerves made it difficult for him to look Caleb in the eye, but when he finally did, he saw the same thing he saw in them ten years ago. His eyes were warm and gentle, letting Rigby know that he need not be afraid.

"Rigby," Caleb began as he shook hands with the younger man, "Alicia told me you were here. I'm so pleased." Caleb saw all of the tense muscles in Rigby's body begin to relax.

"Thank you, sir."

Caleb took a quick assessment of the man standing in front of him. "I can't believe how well my clothes fit you," he said in surprise. Caleb was a large man, tall with a broad chest and shoulders. The clothes were almost a perfect fit on Rigby.

"I grew a lot in prison, sir, what with all the labor we had to do." Caleb nodded and led Rigby out of the living room.

When they walked into the kitchen, Alicia was amazed at the transformation. She had supplied Rigby with scissors and a razor when he went down to the creek, and the difference in him was unbelievable. He was clean, with short hair and a neatly trimmed, full beard. He actually looked quite handsome.

"Children, we have a guest tonight. This is Mr.—"

"Jones," Rigby supplied, cutting Caleb off. Caleb looked at him curiously. "Dakota Jones." He glanced at Caleb and Alicia and silently begged for them to go along.

"He'll be having supper with us tonight," Alicia finished.

"Well, let's bow our heads." Caleb watched his family and their guest bow their heads and then began in a reverent tone. "Lord, we thank you for this meal you've seen fit to bless us with. And thank you for our company tonight. In Jesus's name. Amen."

A chorus of amens was heard before the children began reaching for food, and the boys began to excitedly tell their mother all about their day out with their pa. Alicia listened attentively all the while keeping an eye on Rigby. She half expected him to have crude manners after spending ten years in prison and eat noisily and sloppily, but he did neither. He was polite and neat. Alicia was impressed. She couldn't wait for the time later tonight when the children were in bed and the adults could finally talk openly.

It took a while, but eventually all of the children were put to bed and resting comfortably. Daisy was the hardest to get to sleep. She still fought sleep and wanted to stay up with her parents. Alicia quietly tiptoed down the steps and into the living room where Caleb and Rigby were waiting.

Caleb sat in an easy chair with his legs propped up on the ottoman, perfectly at ease. Rigby, on the other hand, sat on the edge of the sofa fidgeting, clearly nervous and uncomfortable. Caleb wondered if it had anything to do with the new name he insisted on. At last, Alicia stepped into the living room and took her seat in a rocker next to Caleb.

"Well, Rigby, I wondered when we'd see you in these parts again," Caleb began. "We're glad you've come back. Why don't you fill us in a little on the last ten years?"

"Yes, sir." Rigby cleared his throat and twisted his hat in his hands. Alicia looked on compassionately. The poor young man seemed lost and frightened. She remembered a time when she too appeared at the Blue Star Ranch feeling desperate and alone.

"Well, sir, they released me from prison a few days back." He paused to clear his throat. Caleb and Alicia patiently waited for him to continue.

"I spent the last ten years of my life in prison doing hard labor. Mostly I was laying railroad tracks. It was hard work. But I never forgot what you and Pastor Tyler told me about Jesus and that he loves me. I gave my life to Christ while I was still here in Darby in jail. But then you know that already." He paused for a moment then stood and began to pace.

"I promised myself from then on that I would do right by God and that I would make up for my past. God gave me a second chance at life, and I don't intend to waste it. That's why I thought of you and Alicia, sir. You know I ain't got no family, no home, no job, no nothin' really. I was hoping you two might help me get my life back together." When Rigby finished, he sat back down on the edge of the sofa and looked anxiously first at Caleb then at Alicia.

Caleb rubbed his hand along his jaw line thoughtfully. He knew deep inside that God had a plan for this young, former outlaw's life, and he felt pleased to get to be a part of it. Of course he would help Rigby out. God calls us to help our neighbors, and Caleb intended to do just that. He looked to his wife, who smiled reassuringly at him. He knew that she hoped they could help Rigby as well. Caleb met Rigby's expectant gaze and spoke.

"It'd be our pleasure to help you out, son. We told you that you were welcome back here, and we're very glad that you took us up on our offer. But I have a question for you. Why did you ask my children to call you Mr. Jones?" Caleb wasn't pleased with the way Rigby blurted that out at the dinner table, leaving him and Alicia no choice but to go along.

For the first time that night, Rigby began to look somewhat sure of himself. He had expected this question from Caleb, and this was one thing he was standing firm on.

"Sir, the people in these here parts know who I am. They know the name Buchanan, and they know the part I had in the crimes that my family committed. I don't think they would take too kindly to me being a member of their town. I want to change my name, sir. I've done a lot of thinking on it, and I think it's the only solution. No one will ever really give me a chance if they know who I am. But I'm a new man. I left here a boy about to be tried for crimes and have come back a hard-working, God-fearing man, and I aim to prove myself to the townspeople of Darby without prejudice. I'd like to be known as Dakota Jones." Caleb and Alicia listened attentively, but Rigby continued as if he wasn't sure if he was getting through to them just how important this was to him.

"Please. In the Bible, Saul changed his name to Paul after he found the Lord and began his life as an apostle. I want to do the same. I'm no longer Rigby Buchanan, former outlaw. I'm startin' a fresh life, and I think that calls for a new name."

"You know, Caleb, it might be a good idea for him to use a different name and get a fresh start," Alicia chimed in. She looked at her husband then back to Rigby. Caleb agreed.

Rigby made a valid comparison. God turned Rigby's life around and changed him to a new man the same as he did for Saul. It seemed the only thing they could do to ensure that Rigby had a real chance at making a life for himself in this town. He knew the townspeople wouldn't be pleased to know that he was back. He shuddered to think what some of them might do. Justice had been served on Rigby, but some people thought that they were above the law and would take matters into their own hands where he was concerned. Caleb didn't want that to happen.

"Fine. Dakota Jones it is. Welcome to Darby, Dakota." He grinned as he extended his hand to the young man.

"Much obliged." Dakota gratefully shook his hand and smiled—his first real smile in years.

"Well, we may as well start calling you Dakota and getting used to the name. We mustn't slip in front of the children. They pick up on *everything*," Alicia whispered conspiratorially to Dakota.

"Dakota, do you remember my sister, Claire, and her husband, Mark Brewer?" Caleb asked.

A shadow fell over Dakota's eyes, and he hung his head. Thanks to his family, Mark Brewer was permanently paralyzed and was in a wheelchair.

"Yes, sir," Dakota answered with his eyes still down.

"Look at me, son," Caleb directed. Dakota slowly raised his eyes to meet Caleb's compassionate smile. "God has forgiven you of your past, Dakota. He's given you a second chance. You can't dwell on the past or what your family did. You'll never forget all that happened, but you have to learn to forgive yourself as well. You can apologize to Mark when you see him, and then you must move on. We'll leave the past in the past." Caleb was firm, and it was exactly what Dakota needed to hear.

But Dakota didn't miss the part about apologizing to Mark.

"Sir, if I apologize to Mark, then he will know who I am," Dakota admitted hesitantly.

"Dakota, Alicia and I are willing to keep your secret from everyone but Mark and Claire. They are good, honest people who will be more than willing to keep your secret and help in any way they can. I am going to tell my sister and brother-in-law, but aside from that, your secret goes nowhere else. Agreed?"

Dakota slowly nodded. He really didn't have a choice.

"No one will recognize you, Dakota," Alicia put in. "You look so different all grown up. And with the beard, no one would know it was you. I don't think you have anything to worry about."

"I agree," Caleb put in.

"I've also noticed," Alicia added, "that your speech has improved remarkably since you left. How did that happen?"

Dakota shook his head, a slight smile playing on the corners of his mouth. "My cellmate was a former professor. To be honest, I think he was a little out of his mind. Well, we spent a lot of time together, and he would correct every mistake I made. I got to where I didn't talk the way I used to much at all."

"Well, I think it makes you sound very refined," Alicia said.

Dakota smiled shyly and averted his eyes. He wasn't used to compliments.

Caleb stood and moved to the fireplace, where he rested his arm on the mantle. "Now, let's talk about what you can do in this town. Is there anything that you're interested in or any skills that you might have picked up?"

"No, sir," Dakota admitted. "I don't have any skills, but I'm a hard worker and very strong."

"Well, then, I've got a proposition for you. Why don't you stay on here and work as a ranch hand for a while? At least until you figure out what it is that you want," Caleb suggested. "There's a bunkhouse close to the barn where the ranch hands stay, and Oscar, the cook, makes sure the men stay well fed. What do you think?"

Dakota's face brightened. He was finally free and getting a new start at life with a good job. He would have a roof over his head and food to eat. What could be better?

"Sir, I don't know what to say." He tried to stem the tears that threatened—tears didn't seem manly to him—but he was too overwhelmed to stop them. "Thank you," he managed.

"Good. Well, son, let's go get you settled." Caleb moved from the fireplace toward the door. Dakota followed, anxious to prove himself as a good worker.

CHAPTER 3

Dakota quickly proved to Caleb and the other ranch hands what a hard worker he was. He was working from sunup to sundown. Caleb tried to tell him to take it a bit easier, but then Alicia reminded him that that was probably the way he was used to living. As the afternoon drew to a close a few days later, Caleb returned to the barn to untack and brush down his horse. As he approached the barn, the sound of voices inside stopped him, and he leaned up against the door to listen.

"Do you see that cat up in the loft?" he heard young Will ask.

"I certainly do," a deep voice answered. Caleb recognized it to be Dakota's.

"And do you see how fat she is?" Will continued.

"She's not fat, Will," Caleb heard his oldest son, Cameron, correct in an impatient tone. "She's going to have kittens."

"I was going to tell Mr. Jones that!" Will whined. Caleb snuck a peek around the corner to see Will stomp his foot and stand with his hands on his hips. Dakota scooped up the young boy and carried him up the ladder into the hayloft.

"Does she have a name?" Dakota asked quietly.

"No. I reckon no one's ever given her a name."

"Do you think we should?"

"Yes!" Cameron chimed in as he climbed up the ladder behind them.

The three laid on their stomachs in the hay, watching the cat lazily sleep and occasionally swish her tail.

"How about Dynamite?" Will asked.

"What kind of a name is that?" his older brother demanded.

"Well, when she has her kittens, she'll explode—kind of like dynamite." Dakota hid his face in his arm so the young boy couldn't see his laughter.

"That's silly," Cameron felt the need to say.

"Well, that's a good suggestion," Dakota interrupted, trying to stem an argument between the brothers, "but seein' as she's a girl cat, I figure she might ought to have a more girly name." The boys nodded thoughtfully, and Dakota enjoyed watching the wheels turn in their heads. They took the job of naming the cat seriously.

"What about Pearl?" Cameron finally broke the silence. "Her fur is sort of the color of pearl."

"I think that's a great name. What about you, Will?"

Will looked a little put out that they didn't use the name Dynamite, but he readily agreed that Pearl was a better fit. The three made their way back down the ladder, and Dakota was startled to see Caleb standing there.

"I'm sorry, boss," he stuttered, clearly embarrassed. "We were just—"

Caleb raised his hand to cut Dakota off. "No need to apologize, son. You don't have to work yourself to death every moment. It's nice of you to spend some time with my boys. And Pearl is a fitting name," he added with a wink.

"Do you like the name, Pa? I thought of it," Cameron said proudly. His father's attention and approval was the most important thing in Cameron's little world.

"I did like it. I also liked Dynamite," he added as he tousled Will's hair. "All right, go on inside and get cleaned up. Uncle Mark and Aunt Claire are coming for dinner."

The boys leaped for joy as they ran toward the house. They loved spending time with their uncle, aunt, and cousins.

"We'd like you to join us," Caleb said as he resumed brushing his horse. Dakota stood uncertainly.

"I don't know."

"Come on, Dakota. Another one of Alicia's home-cooked meals will do you good. And Claire is bringing over her famous apple pie."

Dakota hesitated. He knew that he needed to apologize to Mark Brewer. And he knew he couldn't keep putting it off. The Carters had extended their hospitality to him, and he didn't want to refuse them.

"All right," he conceded.

"Good," Caleb said. "Don't worry. It won't be bad. I know they'll be as glad to see you as we were."

But Dakota wasn't so sure about that.

Later that evening, Dakota walked up from the bunkhouse to the main house. He had cleaned himself up in the creek and put on his dark denims and a freshly washed button-up plaid shirt. The day after he arrived at the Blue Star Ranch, Alicia insisted on taking him to town to get some new clothes. At first Dakota was resistant, but in the end he knew that he didn't really have a choice. He was in desperate need of new, clean clothes.

His steps slowed as the sound of laughter floated out the windows. He stopped at the bottom of the porch steps, trying to get up the nerve to go in. He hadn't seen Mark or his wife since the day of the trial in Darby ten years ago. More laughter wafted down to his ears, and he took a deep breath and slowly made his way up the steps. He knocked on the door quietly but firmly.

"Hi, Mr. Jones," Cameron said as he swung the door open to allow Dakota to enter.

"Hey there, buddy." Dakota tried to keep his voice light. His heart threatened to pound out of his chest.

Cameron grabbed him by the hand and led him into the living room.

"Uncle Mark, Aunt Claire, this is our new friend, Mr. Jones." Mark wheeled over to him, and the sight put a knot in Dakota's stomach. His family had put Mark there.

"Good to meet you." Mark offered a handshake, which Dakota returned.

"Same here, sir."

"Dakota's our newest hand," Caleb supplied as he came out of the kitchen and walked over.

"We're so pleased to meet you." Claire rose from the sofa and walked over to the men. "Caleb can always use an extra hand around here. I declare, this place grows so fast one can barely keep up."

"My sister exaggerates somewhat."

"You're too modest, Caleb," she responded then excused herself to help Alicia in the kitchen. Caleb motioned for Dakota to sit down, and the three men settled in to talk. Though, Dakota spent more time listening than he did talking. He halfheartedly listened to Caleb and Mark discussing the latest town business.

"Did you hear that the Heards moved out of the area?" Mark was asking.

"I heard that. Sad thing too. The children sure do enjoy Mrs. Heard teaching Sunday school."

"Pastor Tyler came by the bank today, and I asked him about who was going to teach Sunday school, and he said that some people might rotate but that no one wants to commit themselves to the job."

Caleb rubbed his chin. "Surely there's someone out there. I'm sure we'll find someone soon."

The ladies called everyone to supper, and Dakota sat back in awe as he watched the two families interact. The children were talking over each other, each seeking a captive audience. The adults smiled and laughed, admonishing the children to take turns speaking. The atmosphere was warm and relaxed. As much as Dakota enjoyed the home-cooked meal, the food suddenly became tasteless as a wave of some unknown emotion rushed over him. He couldn't quite pinpoint it. Sadness? Loneliness? Perhaps. Looking around the table, Dakota realized there was one thing he wanted more than anything else in the world: a family of his own.

The sound of Emily's coughing caused Claire to put down her fork and turn eyes filled with concern on her youngest daughter, who was a year older than Daisy.

"Are you all right?" she asked as she gently patted the child's back. Emily nodded pitifully. "Here, honey, drink some water."

"That cough doesn't sound good," Alicia remarked.

"I know. It came on in the middle of the night last night, and she's been coughing like that off and on all day." Emily took a few sips of the water and was able to resume eating. Claire watched her closely with a glass of water always on hand, but she didn't have another bout of coughing during the meal.

"Uncle Mark, can we play the rolling game tonight?" Will asked around a mouthful of food. Mark looked over at his youngest nephew, who momentarily forgot to finish chewing while he was waiting for his uncle's answer.

"Honey, it's not polite to talk with your mouth full," Alicia reminded her son. Will noisily swallowed the rest of his food, causing the adults to put their napkins up to their mouths to hide their amusement.

"Well, now, I don't know," Mark answered with a mischievous gleam in his eye. The children loved to sit on his lap while he rolled them in his wheelchair up and down the hallway as fast as he could go.

"Oh, please!" Daisy added.

"Yeah, it'll be fun, Uncle Mark," Cameron joined in. Mark looked around the table at the children, who sported anxious looks on their faces.

"Oh all right," he consented with a grin.

The children let out a chorus of cheers.

Alicia looked around the table and offered second helpings to those who were running out. Caleb helped himself to more mashed potatoes, his wife's specialty.

"Rig—" Alicia began then caught herself. Dakota's eyes flew to her, and Caleb glanced over at her as nonchalantly as he could. "Dakota, would you like more potatoes?"

Thankfully, no one else seemed to notice the slipup. "No thank you, ma'am," Dakota answered quietly.

After dinner, Alicia and Claire shooed the children outside to play while there was still some daylight left.

"May I interrupt you for a moment?" Caleb asked as he stuck his head in the kitchen doorway.

"Certainly," Alicia said as she wiped her hands off on a rag, and she and Claire followed Caleb into the living room. Alicia's eyes roamed the room, landing on an obviously uncomfortable Dakota. His posture was tense, and he kept wiping his sweaty palms on the front of his thighs. Caleb took a seat next to him and put his hand on his back.

"We have to tell you the truth about our new hand," Caleb said, speaking toward Mark and Claire. "About a week ago, he came to us. But Dakota Jones isn't his given name."

Claire raised her brows questioningly.

"It's Rigby Buchanan."

Claire sucked in a breath as her hand flew to her mouth. The muscles worked in Mark's jaw as he processed the information.

"You both know that we extended an invitation to Rigby before he left that he could come back to Darby and we'd try to help him get a fresh start," Alicia said as she walked over to Dakota and laid her hand on his shoulder. "We're glad he took us up on the offer."

"As part of getting a fresh start, he's changed his name to Dakota Jones. We told him that we would tell no one aside from you. We trust you'll keep the secret too," Caleb finished.

Claire couldn't believe what she was hearing. Never in a million years did she think he would actually return to Darby. Claire's wide eyes held fear, but only for a moment before she regained her composure and smiled. If Caleb and Alicia trusted him, then she did too. "Of course we'll keep the secret." She turned to Dakota and smiled. "You saved my sister-in-law's life, after all."

Dakota's shoulders sagged in relief. His eyes flickered over to Mark, who was still working on accepting the information. Dakota had no doubt that his return would be the most difficult for the banker. Dakota slowly stood and walked over to Mark. He sat down in a chair next to Mark and forced himself to make eye contact.

"What my family did will always haunt me. I'd like to apologize once again, Mr. Brewer."

Mark's eyes began to soften. He had long ago given his handicap over to the Lord.

"Call me Mark. And thank you," he said with a nod as he looked Dakota squarely in the eye. "It's in the past, and we're moving on. Now, who's up for a game of checkers?" The collective breath everyone seemed to be holding during their interaction was released, and Dakota and Mark played the first game, while the women went to finish in the kitchen.

That night as Dakota lay in his bunk, he lifted up a prayer of thanks that God allowed the Carters and Brewers to help him begin anew.

The next afternoon, Dana Clarke was putting away medical equipment in her uncle's small office. After only two weeks in Darby, she was settling in quite nicely. During her first week, her uncle took her with him on his rounds through the town, which gave Dana a chance to get to know the people. They all seemed to accept her with open arms; everyone knew that Dr. Clarke needed help as he was getting older.

Dana turned as a knock sounded at the door. She held the door open as Claire came in with Emily.

"Hello," Dana greeted warmly. "What seems to be the problem?" Another round of coughing shook Emily's little frame, and Dana helped guide her to the patient table. "I think I know what the problem is now," she said kindly to the little girl. "Just sit right up here, and we'll make that mean old cough go away." She helped Emily get settled on the table then turned to her mother.

"I'm Dana Clarke, Dr. Clarke's niece." She extended her hand. Claire took it in both of hers.

"I know. We're so glad you've joined our community."

"I'm afraid that I've met so many people lately that I don't remember everyone's names."

"I'm Claire Brewer, and this is my youngest daughter, Emily."

"Does she have any other symptoms besides the cough?"

"No, and it just started night before last. It comes and goes, but it's getting progressively worse."

Dana nodded as she moved toward the medicine cabinet. She opened the door, revealing bottles of various shapes and sizes with small labels on them. She scanned through them before she selected the one she wanted.

"Do you see this, Emily?" she held up the bottle as she walked over to the little girl. Emily nodded. "This is special syrup that will help ease your cough. Here now, why don't you take a little for me?" Dana took a spoon, filled it with the liquid, and gently put it in Emily's mouth. Claire put her hand over her mouth to stifle her amusement when Emily's nose crinkled up.

"It doesn't taste good," Emily said when she finally swallowed.

"I'm sorry, sweetie, but it will help you feel better. Take this syrup"—Dana turned to Claire and extended the bottle—"and give her a spoonful twice a day. The cough should be better in no time."

"Thank you very much, Dana." Claire helped Emily down from the table and walked over to the door. She turned the handle then stopped and turned around. "Would you and your uncle like to join us for dinner tonight?"

"We'd love to," Dana answered enthusiastically.

"Wonderful. We'll see you then." Claire closed the door behind her, and Dana let out a contented sigh. She resumed cleaning and putting away the medical equipment as she hummed a little tune. The town of Darby was growing on her more every day.

CHAPTER 4

The morning sun shined in the through the window, and Cameron squinted against its brightness as he slowly opened his eyes. He jumped down from the top bunk and shivered as his feet hit the cold floor. He walked over to the window and looked out. It had rained for the last three days, and the sun shined brightly, beaming promise and hope down on the land. The raindrops on the blades of green grass seemed to dance in the sunlight.

Finally the rain had stopped. Cameron knew his parents were grateful for the rain. There were many farmers in the area whose livelihoods depended on it. But as a nine-year-old boy, Cameron was grateful for the respite. He hated to be cooped up indoors or constantly washing off before coming inside because he was covered with mud.

He wanted to spend the day outside. And he wanted to spend it with his new friend, Dakota Jones.

Cameron raced to get ready and then ran down the steps. As he hit the last step, he collided into something solid. He looked up to see his father's face. Caleb's eyes held amusement, but his face was stern. Cameron looked down and shuffled his feet.

"What have we told you about running in the house?"

"Not to," Cameron answered softly, his eyes anchored to the floor.

"What if that had been Daisy at the bottom of the steps instead of me?"

"I'm sorry, Pa."

"It's all right. But try to remember next time." Cameron finally looked up at his father, who smiled warmly at the boy. Cameron's heart lifted in his chest. The one thing he hated most in the world was his father's disappointment.

Caleb took Cameron's hand, and they walked out to the barn together. They each grabbed a rake and began cleaning out the stalls and putting down fresh hay.

"Pa," Cameron began tentatively, "I was wonderin' if I could go fishin' today?"

Cameron never took his eyes off his father as he watched him stop and prop his arm on the rake. "Well, I don't see why not after you get your chores done." Cameron shifted his feet and gave no response. "Somethin' else on your mind, son?"

"I want someone to go fishin' with me."

Caleb felt sure he knew where this was leading. "Who?"

"Mr. Jones." Cameron looked away, clearly afraid that his father would tell him that Dakota was too busy.

"You know that Dakota has work to do today," he reminded Cameron.

"Yes, but it's Saturday, and you always let the hands go early on Saturdays."

Caleb looked down into his son's optimistic eyes. While he and Alicia made sure not to spoil the children, there wasn't much that Caleb wouldn't do for them.

"All right," he conceded. Cameron jumped up and let out a whoop. Caleb chuckled. "Easy there. You'll have to check with Mr. Jones first and make sure he doesn't have other plans." Cameron turned to run out of the stables and toward the bunkhouse.

"Don't be late for breakfast!" Caleb called after him.

Later that afternoon, Dakota, Cameron, and Will set out for a good fishing spot. The three saddled up the horses because Cameron boasted of a good fishing hole that was on the other side of the property. The horses trotted at a leisurely pace, and Dakota listened patiently as Cameron and Will pointed out various trees and flowers along the property. It was nothing that Dakota didn't already know, but he pretended that he was hearing the information for the first time and that he was fascinated.

They finally arrived at the fishing hole and baited their hooks. Cameron was right. It was the perfect fishing spot. The creek opened into a nice-sized pond, and the area was cool and shady. There was a tree behind Dakota, and he leaned back against it, pulling his Stetson down over his eyes. It was a peaceful afternoon, and he sat lazily listening to the sounds of the gently moving water.

"I got one!" Cameron's excited voice roused Dakota, and he sat up with a start.

"Reel 'er in gently," he advised as he came to stand behind the boy. Cameron expertly brought in the fish, and Dakota whistled.

"What a beauty. Nice job, Cameron." The boy beamed at his praise.

"Ma and Pa will like having this for supper," he said proudly. Dakota turned to Will, who seemed to be put out with his brother's success.

"Now it's your turn," Dakota said as he tousled Will's hair.

"I can't catch a fish that big," he pouted as he crossed his arms over his chest.

"Sure you can. You just need to give it some time."

Will still sported a pout as he walked away.

"Where are you going?" Dakota called.

"Just over here," Will answered. He remained within sight, and Dakota sighed. He kept an eye on him while he and Cameron continued to fish. Dakota watched the little boy as he kicked some rocks.

"He always gets like this when I catch something," Cameron said as he baited his hook and threw it out again. "Don't worry about it." Dakota's eyes switched back to Will, whose arms were still crossed as he continued to kick at the ground.

"We'll give him some time to cool off," Dakota said as he and Cameron threw their lines back into the water. For a while, nothing could be heard but the sound of the breeze rustling through the trees, gently moving water, and an occasional bird flying through the air. Dakota tipped his head back and closed his eyes, enjoying the feel of the warm sun on his face.

A blood-curdling scream jerked him back to reality. He threw down his pole and ran over to where he had last seen Will standing. He stopped short when he saw the child lying on his back, propped up on his elbow. Panic and pain were written all over his face.

Dakota's eyes landed on two bite marks on Will's leg. Just in front of Will a snake was poised in the air, fangs bared, ready to strike again.

Before Will could even blink, Dakota had his pistol out of the holster and shot the serpent through the head. Both remained still as it continued to writhe. Dakota got a good look at the reddish brown snake with crossbands that stretched across its back that looked like little hourglasses. The snake's vertical pupils confirmed it. Copperhead.

Once Dakota was sure that the snake was no longer capable of attacking, he scooped up the trembling young boy and ran back to the horses. He set Will down under a tree and forced himself to try to think clearly. What was it that he was supposed to do when someone was bitten by a poisonous snake?

Cameron, who had remained a safe distance away, ran over and took his little brother's hand, trying to console him.

"It'll be okay, little brother," Cameron said as he brushed back Will's hair from his face. He looked up at Dakota with wide eyes. "Mr. Jones, what do we do?"

A flashback of his days laying tracks for the railroad suddenly popped in his mind. He and some other prisoners had been working all day to lay tracks when suddenly one of the men hollered. Dakota, like all of the other prisoners, ran to see what had happened. The prisoner had been bitten by a rattler.

Dakota squeezed his eyes shut, straining to remember as clearly as possible what happened next. Someone called frantically to the guard to help, but Dakota remembered with disdain that the guard merely looked on with a smirk on his face. What did he care if one of the prisoners died? Dakota shuddered as he remembered the fear that sliced through him when he realized at that moment that no one cared whether he lived or died. He shook his head and tried to focus on the memory.

The prisoner lay in agony. Everyone was aware that he only had minutes left. But then another guard, clearly with more compassion, dropped to his knees next to the prisoner with a knife in his hand. He sliced the wound and began to suck the venom out. But Dakota's memory didn't stop there. There was something else that was done. After he tried to get the poison out, he created a poultice for the wound.

"Mr. Jones," Cameron called feverishly when Will's little body began to convulse.

Dakota shook his head and realized he was out of time to think. He had to act. He sent up a quick prayer for guidance.

"He's in shock," Dakota said as he got down on his knees next to Will. He quickly unbuckled his belt and tied it tightly above where the snake had bitten to try to stop the flow of venom as much as possible. "It'll be all right," he said soothingly.

Cameron had his arms wrapped tightly around Will's shoulders.

"Try to relax, Will. You're going to be fine," Dakota said softly. He turned his back so the boys wouldn't see him as he eyed his knife nervously. Should he try to cut the wound? Did he have any other choice? The venom was spreading with every passing moment.

Dakota took a deep breath. What other option did he have?

"Will, I have to try to get out the poison as much as I can so I can get you to the doc's. Turn your head away and lay very still." Will was numb and merely did as he was told. Cameron's eyes widened as he saw the knife, and he tightened his hold on his brother.

"God, help me," Dakota whispered the prayer as he quickly cut between the two snake bites and saw blood begin to pour from the wound. Will let out a yelp and began to cry. Cameron held him and shushed him as Will's cry became louder. Dakota leaned over, put his mouth to the wound, and sucked in. He spat the blood out and quickly repeated the process several times.

"Lay still," he ordered as he ran to his saddlebag. Within moments, he returned and applied a paste of some sort that Cameron watched him hastily put together.

"What's that?" Cameron asked.

"It's a poultice of bark and gunpowder. It will help until I can get him to Doc Clarke's." He scooped up the little boy, who had stopped crying but was still trembling. Will looked up at Dakota with terror in his eyes that nearly melted Dakota's heart. He gently eased Will onto the horse and swung up in the saddle behind him.

"Cameron, I need you to do something for me." The boy nodded and looked to Dakota expectantly. "I'm taking Will to the doc's. Take the other two horses back home, and tell your parents what's going on." He tightened his grip around Will as he dug his heels into the horse's flank and spurred him into a gallop toward town.

The ride was rough, and Dakota tried to hold Will as still as possible. Will whimpered in pain, and the sound tore at Dakota's heart. His horse couldn't carry the two of them any faster. Dakota prayed that they would get to Dr. Clarke's in time.

About a mile outside of town, Dakota felt his horse stumble and with horror realized that the horse was not going to be able to regain his balance. The horse lurched forward, and Dakota held tightly to Will.

Everything happened in a blur. The trees, leaves, and grass were nothing but blobs of green and brown. The horse landed hard, throwing the riders off. Dakota pulled Will against his chest as he flew backward toward the swiftly approaching ground. Dakota tried to straighten his feet but soon realized his mistake as his weight landed on one foot and then his back was thrown against the ground at a speed that took the breath out of him. Will was safely on his chest, and it took Dakota several moments before he could regain his senses.

He finally was able to catch a breath, and as he tried to raise himself into a sitting position, he winced as pain seared through his ankle and up his leg. He gritted his teeth and forced himself to sit up with Will sitting in his lap. His back ached from the impact of the fall, and his foot was in terrible pain. He looked down at the boy and noticed that his eyes were closed.

"Will," Dakota said frantically. Will moaned, and his eyes fluttered open for only a moment before he closed them again. Dakota put a hand to the boy's forehead and realized that he was running a fever. Fear tore through Dakota. He absolutely had to get Will to the doctor.

"God, I can't do this alone. Give me strength," Dakota prayed quietly. He took a deep breath and used every ounce of strength to stand.

A groan escaped from Dakota's lips as unbidden tears formed in his eyes. His swelling ankle screamed at him. Dakota bit his lip and squeezed his eyes shut. He reopened them and took a step forward. He nearly lost his balance and started to tumble forward. He held tightly to Will and was somehow able to right himself. He took another step and another. His ankle was so weak and he was in so much pain that Dakota nearly went out of his mind. It was all he could do to hold his own weight, much less the weight of the boy he carried.

Finally, after what seemed like hours, Dakota looked up and was relieved to see the town come into view. Looking back, Dakota knew that it was only by the grace of God that he was able to get himself and Will back to town on his ankle.

"Doc!" Dakota yelled as he burst through the door carrying a whimpering Will. He nearly sank to the ground. He couldn't take another step. Dr. Clarke came from a room in the back of the building and hurried toward them. He took the boy out of Dakota's arms, and Dakota grabbed the doorframe, leaning against it to try and hold himself up. He took a deep breath and tried to stop the dizziness that threatened to engulf him. Dr. Clarke gently set Will down on the patient table.

"What happened?" Dr. Clarke asked as he rolled up his sleeves.

"Snake bite," Dakota said weakly.

Dr. Clarke looked over at him, and Dakota mouthed the word *copperhead*. Dr. Clarke's eyes widened a bit. "I tried to suck out the poison, and I put a poultice on it." Dr. Clarke nodded.

"Dana," he called for his niece. Dakota looked up as the most beautiful woman he had ever seen gracefully descended the stairs. Her dark-brown hair flowed just past her shoulders, and her blue eyes were mesmerizing. For a brief moment, their eyes locked, and Dakota forgot about the pain ripping through his ankle. Her eyes were a deep, bright blue. Dakota had never seen eyes like them before. She looked like an angel.

For a split second, Dakota couldn't remember why he was there. He snapped back to reality when the beautiful woman called Dana spoke.

"Oh my," she said, concern lining her voice. She went to the washbasin, washed her hands, tied on an apron, and took her place next to her uncle.

"Dakota," Dr. Clarke addressed him, "would you please wait in the waiting room just across the hall?" Dakota nodded, and as he limped out of the room, Dr. Clarke stopped him.

"What else happened?" His eyes flicked to Dakota's ankle.

"My horse tripped on a root and took us all down with him. I hurt my ankle really bad."

"I'll take a look at it as soon as I'm done here," he answered as he shut the door to the patient room.

Dakota sank gratefully into a chair in the waiting room and tried not to think about the throbbing in his ankle. He wondered instead how little Will was doing. A copperhead bite could be fatal. He shook his head as if to remove that horrible thought from his mind. He tried to reassure himself that Will would be fine.

He also couldn't get his mind off that angelic creature. When he first saw her, he thought she looked familiar, and it suddenly came to him. She was the one on the train he rode into Darby. He thought she was attractive then, but in seeing her up close, attractive didn't begin to describe her beauty. The thought flitted through Dakota's mind that he might be able to speak to her one day, maybe get to know her better. But almost as soon as the thought materialized, he brushed it aside. What would a beautiful woman like her want to do with a ranch hand like him? Thoughts of Will and Dana continued to bombard him, and he finally put his head in his hands and began to pray.

The door to the doctor's office swung open, and Dakota looked up. Caleb and Alicia rushed in. Dakota tried to stand and winced as he sank back down.

"Cameron told us what happened," Caleb said. He had his arm around Alicia's waist to support her. Her face had drained of color upon entering the doctor's office. Dakota's heart went out to the worried mother. "What kind of snake was it?"

"Copperhead."

"Oh no." Alicia covered her mouth with her hand and sank into a nearby chair. Caleb rested his hand on her shoulder.

"Has the doctor said anything?" Caleb inquired.

Dakota looked toward the closed door and sighed. "Not a thing."

Caleb took a seat next to his wife and put his arm around her. Caleb noticed that Dakota was trembling.

"Are you okay, son?" he asked as he put a hand on Dakota's arm. Dakota looked down and realized his arm was shaking. Dakota explained everything that happened, ending with the horse fall and getting back to town on a hurt ankle. Try as he might, Caleb couldn't stop the tears from shining in his eyes.

"Thank you, son."

Dakota nodded humbly. The three of them sat silently, each sending prayers of mercy to God on behalf of a poor little boy who had an encounter with a venomous snake.

After what seemed like hours, Dr. Clarke finally emerged from the patient room. He wiped his hands on a cloth as he entered the waiting area where the nervous parents quickly rose from their seats. Dakota remained seated but looked on anxiously.

"How is he?" Alicia asked. Everyone noticed the tremor in her voice.

Dr. Clarke looked at all three adults and let out a deep breath. "He's going to be just fine." He looked over at Dakota. "Your ranch hand saved his life."

Alicia's hand flew to her chest. "Thank you, God," she whispered. She turned to Dakota and put her arms around him, pulling him into a hug as tears ran down her face. She finally released him and dabbed at her eyes with a handkerchief. "Can we see him?"

"Of course. Right this way." Dr. Clarke led them into the room where Will was resting comfortably. "I gave him something to help him sleep so he wouldn't feel as much pain," Dr. Clarke explained.

Alicia moved to her son's side and stroked his forehead. He looked so young and helpless lying there. "Thank you, Doctor," she whispered, her voice thick with emotion.

"Much obliged," Caleb said as he shook hands with the doctor.

Dakota glanced over at Dana, who was cleaning up, and she smiled slightly at him. His heart hammered in his chest.

Dr. Clarke turned. "It's your turn now." Dakota hobbled over to another patient table and sat down. Dr. Clarke gingerly felt his ankle, and Dakota bit his lip to keep from moaning in pain. "Well, I'm glad to say that nothing is broken. You have a very bad sprain. You need to stay off this ankle for at least a couple of weeks. Come back and see me in two weeks, and we'll go from there."

With that, Dr. Clarke handed Dakota what looked like two long sticks. "They're called crutches," Dr. Clarke said to answer the questioning look on Dakota's face. "They'll help you walk until your ankle heals."

Caleb helped Dakota down and get settled on his crutches. Then he paid the doctor and they all left for the ranch.

Once everyone was gone Dana asked her uncle the question that had been burning inside her.

"Who was that?"

Dr. Clarke looked knowingly at his niece. No one could miss the awestruck way that Dakota looked at her, nor the fact that Dakota was a handsome young man. "He's the Carters' new ranch hand."

Dana mouthed the word *oh* as she finished cleaning up. When she came down the stairs and first saw Dakota, she felt something strange inside her. She felt fluttery and suddenly a little unsure of herself. When their eyes met, it felt as if her legs wouldn't support her weight anymore. His penetrating gaze seemed to see right into her soul, and it took her breath away.

She was usually levelheaded, and these feelings left her a little shaken up. No man had ever made her feel that way before. She shook her head, silently rebuking herself for feeling such nonsense.

But she couldn't help but wonder when she might see him again.

CHAPTER 5

The next day, Sunday, the Carters invited Dakota to join them for church. All of the ranch hands were welcome to go with them, but those who did choose to go usually went by themselves. Dakota jumped at the chance to go with them to church, and Caleb helped him into the Carter wagon. Dakota laid his crutches next to him, and Daisy curled up beside him. He was anxious to see Pastor Tyler again. He knew that the elderly pastor wouldn't recognize him anymore, but Dakota wanted to see him nonetheless. He knew that one day soon he would be revealing his true identity to at least one other person in town—the pastor.

As the wagon ambled along the dirt road toward town, sounds of discontent could be heard coming from the bed of the Carter wagon.

"I don't like church, Pa," Will complained. "Not anymore." He shifted positions and crossed his arms. He had the same face on that he had when he was pouting at the fishing hole.

Alicia turned in her seat. "Why is that, Will?" she asked patiently.

"With Mrs. Heard gone, there's no one to teach Sunday school anymore," Cameron supplied. "It's boring in the big church with the grown-ups."

"Yeah," Will agreed, barely looking over at his mother. The frown was still plastered to his face.

"And she promised she would teach us to sing 'Jesus Loves Me,' but she left before she did." Daisy's lower lip began to tremble, and Dakota prayed she wouldn't cry. He couldn't stand it when that precious child cried.

Caleb continued to look forward as he held the reins but spoke over his shoulder. "We understand how you feel. And hopefully it won't take long to find another Sunday school teacher. But until then, you'll have to stay in big church with us. And don't forget what it says in the Bible. It says enter into his gates with thanksgiving and into his courts with praise.'"

As the oldest, Cameron most readily accepted this. Caleb and Alicia knew it was harder for the younger children, and they prayed that it wouldn't be long until they found a new teacher.

Dakota sat quietly listening to the whole exchange. He glanced over at Daisy, who was still upset, and said quietly, "I can teach you the song."

Her eyes flew to him, and a smile broke on her face. "Really?" she squealed.

Dakota looked uneasily at Caleb and Alicia as if realizing for the first time what he had just said. Their eyes reflected surprise and something else he couldn't quite place. Approval?

"That would be wonderful, Dakota," Alicia said encouragingly.

Daisy clapped her hands in delight. "Oh thank you, Mr. Jones."

Dakota took a deep breath and then began, "Jesus loves me; this I know…" Alicia and Caleb exchanged a glance. His deep baritone was soothing to listen to, and they were surprised at the pure quality of his voice. Once he was done, he shrugged slightly.

"You have quite a voice, son," Caleb said. He looked over at Dakota and gave a brief nod.

"Will you sing it again?" Daisy asked. "I want to learn too."

Dakota spent the rest of the ride to the church teaching Daisy to sing "Jesus Loves Me."

They arrived to church on time, and as they pulled up to the church, Dakota felt his stomach begin to turn. What if people recognized him? What if they asked a lot of questions? He swung his legs around to the edge of the wagon, placed his crutches on the ground, and eased himself down. He stood staring at the small, white building. Then he felt a hand on his shoulder.

"I know you're nervous," Caleb spoke softly for Dakota's ears only, "but you don't need to be. No one will recognize you."

Dakota nodded, grateful for the reassurance. Caleb led his family inside, and Dakota followed. They moved toward the front of the church and sat in the normal Carter/Brewer pew on the left side. Dakota looked around, but he didn't see many faces he recognized, nor did he see anyone looking at him strangely. He breathed an inward sigh of relief.

He glanced over toward the door, and his pulse began to quicken as he saw the doctor and his niece enter. She stood in the doorway for a moment, and the sight caused Dakota's mouth to drop. She was wearing a pale-blue dress that accentuated her deep blue eyes, and the sun shone in from behind her. An angel.

Dakota caught himself shamelessly staring and turned away in embarrassment. He hoped no one had noticed. His palms began to sweat as he heard the doctor's voice right behind him. As it turned out, the Clarke pew was right behind theirs. Dakota shifted uneasily as he heard Caleb talking with Dr. Clarke. He turned around when he heard his name.

"Nice to see you here," Dr. Clarke said as he patted Dakota on the shoulder.

"Thank you, sir," he replied. He chanced a glance at Dana, who gave him a warm smile. He mumbled a brief hello and quickly turned back around and tried to still his racing heart.

At one point, Dakota glanced around and saw several children just like the Carters who would obviously rather be in Sunday school. He noticed their constant fidgeting and their parents reminding them to pay attention and not cause a scene. The children looked bored and uncomfortable. Dakota, like the other adults in the room, lifted a prayer to ask God to provide a Sunday school teacher quickly for the children of Darby.

After what seemed like an eternity to Dakota, the congregation finally stood to sing the last hymn. He had found it hard to listen to the sermon, but he tried his best to focus and not think about the angel seated behind him. The church building had become awfully stuffy since Dana Clarke came in.

Caleb led his family back down the aisle and stopped at the doorway to greet the pastor on the way out.

"Another inspiring sermon," Dakota heard Caleb say. He looked behind him to see that Dr. Clarke and Dana were still in their pew visiting with several members of the church family. Dakota figured that, being the doctor and nurse, they had to know everyone in town.

"And this is our newest hand at the ranch, Dakota Jones." Dakota started when he heard his name and turned to find himself face-to-face with Pastor Tyler.

"Glad to have you," Pastor Tyler said as he shook Dakota's hand. Dakota studied him carefully, and while kindness shone in his eyes, there was no recognition. Dakota felt his muscles begin to relax as he thanked Pastor Tyler and reiterated what a good sermon it was. *The parts of it I heard*, he thought wryly.

As they exited the church, Dakota began to head for the wagon. He stood waiting for the family and was surprised when only Caleb joined him. Caleb reached into the wagon and pulled out a picnic basket. Dakota raised his brows in surprise.

"We're having a picnic today," Caleb told him. "It's such a beautiful day. It's traditional on nice days to stay for a picnic after church." Dakota looked around at the bright blue sky and breathed in deeply. It was a nice day to be sure.

"We've packed plenty. Come on," Caleb said as he turned to start walking. Dakota smiled and tried to keep up with Caleb's pace as best he could on his crutches as they made their way to the open field next to the church building and set up their picnic.

Caleb threw two large blankets down. He and Alicia settled onto one, and Caleb chuckled when he realized that he and his wife had the whole blanket to themselves. Dakota was surrounded by their children, who took up the entire blanket and were talking a mile a minute to him. Caleb almost told his children to give Dakota some space, but as he watched them, Caleb realized that Dakota was grinning from ear to ear and enjoying every minute of it. So he leaned back on his elbow while his wife prepared plates for everyone.

He looked around and felt a wave of gratitude wash over him as he looked at the people in his town fellowshipping with one another and enjoying the bounty that God had blessed them with. Plenty of food, a clear blue sky, shade from nearby trees, family and friends. What more could they ask for?

"Mind if we set up next to you?"

Caleb squinted against the sunlight as he looked up to see his sister and her family standing there.

"You better," Caleb answered. Bethany and Emily ran to the blanket that Dakota shared with the Carter children and squeezed in. "You'd better lay one of your blankets over there to give them more room." Caleb laughed as he watched all six of them try to fit on one blanket.

"Watch Mr. Jones's ankle!" Alicia cried as Bethany nearly sat on it.

Claire laid a blanket next to Caleb, and Alicia helped Mark settle his wheelchair so that it wouldn't roll. Then Claire laid the other blanket in front of the one that Dakota and the children were on.

"Here now, I've made more room for everyone. Children, slide down onto this blanket a little." The children dutifully obeyed, and Dakota stretched out a bit.

Alicia and Claire passed around plates for everyone, and once they had blessed the food, they all began to eat hungrily. Alicia and Claire had both brought baskets full of fried chicken and biscuits.

"Hello, Claire," Dana greeted as she walked over to them. Dakota recognized her voice and looked over to see her and her uncle begin a conversation at the other blanket. He hastily wiped at his mouth with his napkin and subconsciously ran a hand through his hair.

"Dana, Dr. Clarke, how nice to see you," Claire warmly greeted.

"It's nice to see you too. How is little Emily today?" Dana asked.

"She's much better. The cough is nearly gone. Thank you again for your help."

"It's my pleasure."

"You seem to be enjoying your time in Darby," Alicia observed. Dana's eyes swept the open countryside—the rolling hills, fields of wildflowers, and nearby trees.

"Oh yes," she said with feeling. "After leaving the city, I wasn't sure how well I would adapt to life in a small town, but I love it. It's beautiful country, and the people of Darby are wonderful."

"Well, we're certainly glad to have you. Your uncle really needs you." As if on cue, Dr. Clarke began to ask the ladies about their health, and Dana looked over to see Dakota surrounded by children. She laughed quietly and walked over.

"It looks like this is the fun blanket," she said cheerily. Her eyes locked with Dakota's, and for a moment time stood still.

"Miss Clarke! Miss Clarke!" Dana was vaguely aware of someone calling her name. She felt her sleeve being pulled, and she shook her head to clear it. She glanced down and saw little Daisy pulling on her arm.

"What is it, sweetie?"

"Sit with us." Daisy pulled her down, and sat on her lap.

Dakota's eyes never left her. He had wanted an opportunity to speak with her, and suddenly here she was, sitting on their blanket. He opened his mouth, but words wouldn't come. He quickly closed it again.

Emily began talking to Daisy, and Dana leaned over to speak with Dakota.

"Will is looking good. How is he?"

Dakota swallowed. *Pull yourself together*, he chided. "He's back to his old self. We're all grateful to you and your uncle."

"It wasn't just us, Dakota," she said sweetly. Dakota's heart nearly melted. "You are really the one who saved him. You got him to my uncle quickly despite your sprained ankle, and you put that poultice on it. Where did you learn that?"

Dakota supposed that being from the city they wouldn't use such an old-fashioned remedy. "You pick up things like that. You have to learn how to survive," Dakota answered honestly without revealing too much. Dana nodded thoughtfully.

"How is your ankle?"

"It still hurts a little," he answered truthfully. "But I'd say it's getting better."

"I'm glad," she said warmly. Her eyes locked with Dakota's, and he noticed she was beginning to blush. "Well, I should go," she said hastily. "There are a few other people I'd like to say hello to before Uncle and I return home."

She bade good-bye to the children and gently removed Daisy from her lap. Dakota couldn't stand as he would have liked, but he extended his hand. Dana looked at him and took the proffered hand. Dakota didn't let go of her hand right away, even after she was up. They stood hand in hand, staring into each other's eyes for a few seconds before Dakota let go.

"Thank you," she said softly. Dakota loved the pink blush that stained her cheekbones.

"You look like an angel today," he said equally soft. A gentle smile curved the corners of her mouth, and she thanked him and slowly walked away. Dakota's eyes remained glued to her until the children forced him to pay attention to them. They wanted to play a game. Dakota thought a game might be just the thing to still his pounding heart.

CHAPTER 6

Caleb stood up and rubbed the small of his back, trying to ease the tension from his muscles. He loved running the ranch, but he didn't enjoy the bookkeeping end. He rose from the chair in his office and went to the window. The sun shone brilliantly, and there wasn't a cloud in the sky. Caleb hated being indoors on days like this one, but he had no choice. There was business that he needed to tend to. He opened the window and closed his eyes against the warm breeze that blew in the room. He took a deep breath then turned to resume his deskwork.

He took a step closer to his desk and stopped when the sounds of laughter and a familiar deep male voice wafted into the room. Caleb couldn't tell what exactly was going on, and curiosity drove him back to the window. He looked around until his eyes settled on where the noise was coming from.

His children were sitting on logs, their eyes glued to Dakota. Dakota held something in his hand, and Caleb leaned forward, squinting to make out what it was. It looked like something carved out of wood. If Caleb wasn't mistaken, it was a large fish and a man. He stretched as far as he could out the window to hear what Dakota was saying.

"But Jonah ran away from God and got on a large ship to sail away." Caleb saw Dakota pick up a carved boat and put the man on it. He moved it, giving the appearance that waves were making the boat go up and down. "What do you think happened?"

Cameron knew the story, so he didn't say anything. He looked over to his brother and sister, whose brows were furrowed in concentration.

"Did the ship sink?" Will asked.

"No."

"Did an angel come?" Daisy suggested.

"No. There was a great storm that came, and everyone was terrified." Dakota made a sound like thunder and dramatically moved the boat. "The other people on the boat threw Jonah overboard, and do you know what God did?"

The children shook their heads, eyes wide.

"God provided a great fish to swallow Jonah." He took the carved fish and put the man in front of it as if the man were in the belly of the fish.

"He swallowed Jonah?" Daisy asked incredulously.

Dakota nodded. "You see, God didn't want Jonah to die. He had a purpose for Jonah. Jonah disobeyed God, but God loves and forgives us. He gave Jonah a second chance, and so three days later the fish spit Jonah out."

"I'll bet Jonah did what God said after that," Will said.

"He sure did. Jonah went to Nineveh to warn the people of God's wrath and to turn away from their sin. The people of Nineveh believed what Jonah said and turned to God and away from their sin. And do you know what God did?"

"He forgave them," Cameron stated. He sat tall, proud to already know the story. Dakota gave him an approving smile.

"Yes, God forgave them. He gave the city of Nineveh a second chance, just like he gave Jonah a second chance."

Will shuffled his feet in the dirt. "I reckon I've had more than one second chance." Dakota laughed.

"We all have, little man," he said as he tousled Will's hair. "You children better go get washed for supper, or your mama will have my hide."

The children stood to do as they were told.

Daisy slipped her arms around Dakota's waist. "Thank you, Mr. Jones." Dakota patted her head, and Cameron took her hand. Dakota watched them walk away then began to put his carvings in a satchel.

Caleb leaned back in from the window and stood to his full height. Dakota seemed to be a natural at telling children about the Bible. And those carvings! When had Dakota made those? Caleb scratched his beard as an idea began to form. *Of course,* he thought. *Why haven't I thought of this before?*

He ran out of his office and out the side door into the yard before Dakota had time to get away. Dakota had just put the last carving in his bag when Caleb ran up to him.

Dakota's eyes showed concern. At this time of day, the Carter family was always preparing for the evening meal. "Is anything wrong, boss?"

"No, son, not at all," Caleb said as he slapped the younger man on the back. "I've just had a wonderful idea." Caleb sat down on the log next to Dakota. "Dakota, I couldn't help but overhear you telling my children about Jonah."

Dakota's face turned a shade of red.

"Now don't be embarrassed, son. The children loved it. And those carvings give it a nice touch. Sort of brings the story to life. A thought occurred to me, and I want you to hear me out. I think you should be the new Sunday school teacher for the children."

Dakota's eyes widened. "Me?"

"Yes," Caleb answered with a chuckle.

At first Caleb thought that Dakota was going to argue, but the longer Dakota thought about it, the more the idea began to grow on him. Caleb noticed a myriad of expressions cross Dakota's face from disbelief, to uncertainty, and finally to acceptance.

"Perhaps," Dakota said slowly. "Perhaps I should do it."

Caleb studied Dakota for a moment. "You know, I've been watching you, and your love for telling people about the Bible is evident. I've overheard the other hands talking about you telling them stories from the Bible, and I've seen you with my children. I do have one question, though. How did you learn so much about the Bible?" Caleb knew that Dakota spent the last ten years of his life in prison. He should have come out a hard man, but instead he was kind, sensitive, and knowledgeable.

Dakota smiled slightly as memories flooded back. He was pretty good about not thinking about life in prison, but sometimes the memories came back whether he wanted them to or not. He remembered that he had only been in prison for a month. He was sixteen and scared for his life. There was many a time when he didn't think he would live to see freedom. The other men were rough and angry with filthy language and eager to get in a fight. Dakota always tried to keep to himself. He felt relieved when he learned that his roommate was an old, senile professor and not a rough outlaw.

But one day when Dakota had laundry duty, another inmate came by just as Dakota was pulling a shirt out of the water, and it splashed on the criminal. Dakota shuddered as he remembered the outrage in the man's face. He seemed to grow two feet taller to Dakota's frightened mind, and his eyes were enraged. Dakota didn't understand; it was only a little water.

"I'm sorry," he said meekly. This reminded him of how his father or brothers would act toward him. He wondered if the day would ever come when he didn't feel intimidated.

"You're sorry?" the man bellowed, grabbing Dakota by the shirtfront and lifting him in the air. "You're gonna pay for that."

"Enough," a man said as he rushed toward them. The inmate dropped Dakota in disgust, and he landed hard on his backside.

"Aw, Chaplain Simmons, you know I was just joshin' with the kid." Dakota turned wide eyes to the chaplain, who calmly eyed the inmate.

"I know nothing of the sort, and neither does this young man. The splash of water was an accident. Now move along." The inmate eyed the chaplain angrily. Dakota flinched, wondering when the inmate would hit the man of the cloth, but the chaplain merely stared back emotionlessly. Finally the inmate stormed off, and Dakota heaved a sigh of relief.

"Let me help you there, son," the chaplain said as he extended a hand to help Dakota to his feet. "I'm Chaplain Simmons."

"Rigby Buchanan," he responded quietly.

Dakota remembered that the chaplain had looked at him thoughtfully for several seconds before he spoke. "Do you know Jesus?" he finally asked.

Dakota nodded, and his eyes lit up for the first time since he came to the prison. The chaplain laughed. "I thought so. Come over here and talk with me for a moment." He motioned to a bench sitting close to the clothesline. Dakota walked over with him and took a seat.

"Rigby, this place will eat you alive if you don't keep your focus on Jesus. He's brought you this far, and he will see you through this prison sentence, but you're going to have to keep your eyes on him."

Dakota swallowed and nodded. There was something in his innocent gaze that touched the chaplain's heart, and he knew he had found someone who really needed him.

"Rigby, if you're willing, I'd like to help you as you survive the prison term. I'd like to meet with you for an hour or so every day to teach you about God's Word and to pray with you."

The relief shone in Dakota's eyes as he eagerly agreed. He remembered that every day from then on for ten years he would meet with the chaplain to study God's Word and learn how to become the man God was calling him to be. Dakota knew that God sent the chaplain into Dakota's life and that, thanks to his unselfish giving of his time, Dakota would never be the same.

And as Dakota grew into a man and developed muscles, he stopped being intimidated by all the other inmates. He was champion of the underdog and took younger inmates under his wing much the way the chaplain had taken Dakota under his.

Caleb whistled when Dakota finished his story. "Well, that confirms it. You were meant for this job. You're a natural, Dakota, and your love for the Lord is genuine. I think you'd be perfect."

Dakota thought about the previous Sunday when he noticed all of the squirming children. He thought about how Will and Daisy didn't like going to church anymore. The idea bothered him greatly.

"All right," Dakota said as he stood slowly. He didn't need his crutches anymore, but he still walked with a bit of a limp. "I reckon I ought to at least try. If Pastor Tyler will let me," he added.

Caleb stood as well.

"You have to tell him."

"I know."

"Do you want me to go with you?"

Dakota thought for a moment. "No," he said slowly, "I think I'd like to do this on my own."

Caleb nodded as the two men parted ways, feeling confident that he had found the right person for the job.

The next day, Dakota stood outside the pastor's home and looked up at it. It wasn't an imposing building by any means. It was one of the smaller ones in town. But Dakota couldn't rid himself of the knots in his stomach. Aside from the Carters and Brewers, no one knew his secret. Now, not only did he have to tell Pastor Tyler who he really was, he also had to ask to be allowed to teach the children.

A shudder ran through him. Fear kept him rooted to the spot. He was afraid of rejection and of being judged.

"Dakota?" Startled, Dakota looked over to see Pastor Tyler walk around from the back of the house. The dirt on the knees of his pants revealed that he had been working in the garden.

"It's good to see you," he said as he approached.

Dakota was pleased that the pastor had remembered his name. His throat went dry, and he swallowed a few times.

"I wondered if I might speak with you for a moment?" Dakota asked hesitantly.

"Of course. Please come in." Pastor Tyler showed him in and motioned for Dakota to enter the study that he used. "Have a seat. Would you like anything to drink?"

"No, thank you." Dakota shook his head as he took a seat. He twisted his hat in his hands as the pastor went around to the other side of his desk and sat down. He leaned back in his seat and looked questioningly at Dakota.

"What can I do for you?"

"Well, there are two reasons why I came," Dakota began. "First, you know I work for the Carters." Pastor Tyler nodded. "Well, Caleb suggested to me yesterday that I should ask about being the new Sunday school teacher." Pastor Tyler's brows lifted in surprise, but there was no judgment.

Not yet, Dakota thought warily.

"You see, I've been telling the Carter children some of the stories in the Bible, and I've been using these"—Dakota opened up his bag and dumped out a few carvings on the desk—"to help bring the story to life for them. Well, Caleb figured I ought to share with all of the children and not just his," he finished with a shrug.

Pastor Tyler leaned forward in his chair and took one of the carvings. He turned it around in his hand, admiring the handiwork.

"You're very talented." He leaned back in his chair. "Tell me about yourself, son."

Here it was. The moment of truth.

Dakota twisted his hat in his hands and looked down at the floor. *God, help me*, he prayed. He took a deep breath, raised his head, and looked the pastor in the eyes.

"I had a difficult childhood," he began. "My mother died giving birth to me, and my father turned to drinking to drown out his pain. He began stealing and committing other crimes and forced his sons to join him, whether they wanted to or not. One son didn't want to and finally escaped that life." He watched Pastor Tyler's eyes grow wide. The elderly man leaned forward in his chair and looked hard at Dakota.

"Rigby?" he asked tentatively.

"Yes, sir."

Pastor Tyler jumped out of his chair and ran around the desk to Dakota. He put his arms around the younger man in a warm embrace. Dakota sat stunned as the pastor held onto him. He wasn't expecting this reaction.

"You don't know how many times I've prayed for you over the years." Pastor Tyler released him and stepped back. "I don't even recognize you anymore."

"That's good, because I don't want anyone to know who I am. Or who I was, rather."

"Is that why you changed your name?"

Dakota nodded.

"Is it difficult to adjust to being called something else?"

"Yes," Dakota admitted. "It's strange to hear people call me Dakota instead of Rigby. Though, changing my name was something I had to do. But please, except for your wife, please don't tell anyone my true identity. No one knows except the Carters and Brewers. I came here to start over, and if anyone knew the truth they would send me packing. Or worse."

"I'm afraid that's probably true." Pastor Tyler returned to his chair, sat back, and studied Dakota for several moments. "I'm proud of you, Dakota. I can see that God is shaping you into a fine man."

"Thank you." Dakota was both humbled and moved by the pastor's observation.

"Caleb is a wise man. Wise beyond his years, in fact. He wouldn't have suggested for you to teach the children if he didn't think you were right for the job. And given what I know about you, I tend to agree with him. So, if you'd like, you may serve as our new Sunday school teacher."

Dakota felt a rush of relief wash over him. He didn't realize how much he wanted to teach the children until that moment. He thanked the pastor as he stood to leave. The two men shook hands, and Pastor Tyler saw Dakota to the door.

Dakota walked the short distance from the pastor's house to the town. He walked by the livery and heard the familiar clang of the blacksmith pounding horseshoes, and saw children playing marbles on the boardwalk as they waited for their parents to finish their business in town. He walked slowly, taking in everything. In some ways, it was a completely different town than the one he left ten years ago, and in other ways, it was exactly the same.

Dakota reached the general store and stepped inside to make a few purchases.

"Hello, Levi," he greeted the shop owner.

"Good day to you, Dakota." Levi returned the greeting as another customer approached the counter seeking his help. Dakota strode down the aisles and plucked a few items from the shelves: a bar of soap, a new comb, and a sack of flour that he promised he'd pick up for Oscar, the ranch cook.

His mind wandered as he turned the corner and entered the next aisle. He wasn't paying attention and ran into something—or rather someone.

"Oh!" Dana exclaimed as she reached for her hat to keep it from falling from her head.

"Excuse me." Dakota took a step back. He grabbed the Stetson from his head. "I'm sorry, miss."

"No harm done," Dana responded cheerily as she unconsciously began to smooth the wrinkles from her dress.

Dakota stood, twisting his hat in his hands, feeling like a fool. How could he have run into her like that? "I wasn't paying attention."

"Well, to tell you the truth, I wasn't paying much attention either. All of these colorful fabrics were distracting me." Dana pointed to a wall full of bolts of fabric of all colors. "I need to find some material for a new dress I'm making. What do you think about this one?" She held up a bright orange fabric with yellow polka dots. Dakota raised one eyebrow skeptically. Should he dare tell her the truth?

Dana burst out laughing before he had a chance. "You should see your face! I was only joking. This is horrible." Dakota let out a breath. "What about this one?" The next one was a pale pink color. It was delicate and feminine, perfectly suited for her.

"I think it's right pretty," Dakota said. "Though I'm no expert on these things."

"Oh, I don't know. You've got a pretty good eye. That orange one was awful, and this one isn't. That's about all you need to know." Dakota watched her eye the material for a moment as she tried to decide. "Yes," she said. "I think this is the one."

"Can I help carry your items for you?"

Dana looked up at him and held his gaze for a moment. "That would be very nice. Thank you."

Dakota took her items and carried them to the counter for her. Once she and Dakota had paid, Dakota carried her purchases to the doctor's office.

"How long have you been in Darby?" Dana asked as they made the short walk from the general store to Dr. Clarke's.

"A couple of months."

"Me too. How do you like it?"

"It's a nice place to live. The people are friendly, the countryside is downright pretty, and the Carters are good people to work for."

"I trust they are all in good health?"

"Fit as fiddles. The boys are into everything. I don't know how Alicia keeps order." Dana chuckled. She could imagine that.

"I just came from seeing Pastor Tyler."

Dana looked up at him expectantly.

"I'm going to be the new Sunday school teacher for the children."

"Oh, Dakota, that's wonderful!" Dana exclaimed as she laid a hand on his arm. "The children need a Sunday school teacher, and I'm sure you'll do a wonderful job."

Dakota's chest puffed up at her praise. He was pleased that she had such faith in him. He only hoped he could live up to it. He glanced down at the little hand still resting on his arm. He gently picked it up and brushed a kiss along the back of it. Dana smiled shyly as he released her hand.

They reached the front door of the office much too soon for either of them.

"Thank you for your help," Dana said as she reached for her packages.

"My pleasure. I'll see you on Sunday at church." He tipped his hat and waited while Dana entered.

As Dakota left the doctor's office, his heart felt lighter than it had in a long time. Pastor Tyler gave him a welcome reception, he was allowed to be the new Sunday school teacher, and he was forming a friendship with the beautiful town nurse. He could sense deep down that God had big plans for his life.

CHAPTER 7

Sunday finally arrived, and Dakota leaped out of bed, ready to begin his new role as Sunday school teacher. He saddled up his horse and rode alongside the Carters as they headed into town.

"I'm so glad that you're going to be our new Sunday school teacher," Daisy said. Her pigtails bobbed in the wind, and a smile dimpled her face.

"Yeah, now we don't have to sit with the grown-ups," Will added.

"Can we sing 'Jesus Loves Me'?" Daisy wanted to know. She sat up on her knees and held onto the side of the wagon as she watched Dakota.

"Sure we can."

Dakota noticed Alicia take her husband's hand. Earlier that morning she told Dakota she was thankful he had come into their lives and would be able to share his gift with the other children of the town.

They pulled up to the churchyard, and Dakota tied his horse to the rail. He spotted Dr. Clarke and Dana standing off to the side visiting with some of the church family. He waited until they finished talking before approaching them.

"Good morning, Dr. Clarke, Dana." He tipped his hat.

Dr. Clarke wiped his forehead with his handkerchief. It was early in the morning yet so hot already. "Good morning, Dakota. Dana tells me that you're going to be teaching the children."

"Yes, sir," Dakota answered proudly.

"Well, I'm sure that all of the parents are grateful," Dr. Clarke said as he moved to greet some other townsfolk.

"I'd better go in," Dakota said to Dana. His gaze lingered on her for another moment before he turned to leave.

"Good luck!" she called after him.

Turned out Dakota was a natural. He led the children in Daisy's favorite song. Then he took out carvings that he had made and told the story of Zacchaeus. The children listened attentively as Dakota explained to them about how Zacchaeus wanted to see Jesus, but he was too short. Dakota made a particularly short carving of a man, which drew a few giggles. He took his carving of a tree and told the children how Zacchaeus climbed the tree so he could see Jesus. He then took the short man and made it look like he was climbing the tree.

Dakota explained to them how Jesus said he was going to eat at Zacchaeus's house.

"So what's the big deal about Jesus wanting to eat at Zacchaeus's house?" a boy by the name of Cole Johnson asked.

"Good question. You see, Zacchaeus was a tax collector, and back then, tax collectors were known for being rather dishonest. So everyone was surprised when Jesus wanted to eat with a man who wasn't very nice." A ripple of "oh's" went through the young crowd.

"What happened next?" a girl by the name of Mary Harper wanted to know.

"Well, Zacchaeus told Jesus that he would give half of what he owned to the poor and pay back those he had cheated four times the amount. Jesus forgave Zacchaeus of his sin, and Zacchaeus became a better man. You see, Jesus will forgive all of us of our sins and help us to be better people if we ask him to."

Bethany Brewer shifted in her seat. "You mean like when I'm mean to my sister, Emily, and ask Jesus to forgive me, he'll help me to be a better sister?"

"Exactly," Dakota said with satisfaction.

As everyone exited the church that morning, the children bounded over to their parents to tell them about what they had learned in Sunday school. They excitedly told them about the story of Zacchaeus and the wooden carvings Dakota had made.

Pastor Tyler walked over to Dakota, who was leaning against the porch rail.

"Sounds like the children enjoyed your teaching today."

"I hope so. I really enjoyed it. It's a nice feeling to be able to teach others about Jesus, isn't it?" Pastor Tyler nodded and looked at Dakota with a twinkle in his eye. Of course *he* would know.

CHAPTER 8

Fred Johnson, a local farmer who lived just outside of Darby, stepped into the bright sunshine and out of the two-room log home he shared with his wife and son. It was another beautiful morning. Fred enjoyed farming and life in Darby. He was a conservative man who made certain that he was the head of his household. Fred made the short walk from the house to the barn where the cow was bawling to be milked. He grabbed the bucket and stool and quickly got down to business.

"Dad!" his son, Cole, cried, bursting into the barn.

"What is it, Son?" Fred jumped up from the stool. He could tell from the look on his thirteen-year-old boy's face that something was wrong.

"We're missing three chickens," his son said, still trying to catch his breath.

"What? Does it look like there were animals out there?"

"No, sir. None of the others have been harmed. It doesn't look like there was a ruckus or anything. They're just … gone," he finished lamely.

Fred quickly strode to the chicken coop to investigate for himself. From the looks of things, Cole was right. Wild animals had not made off with three of his chickens. Which meant only one other thing: someone had stolen those chickens in the middle of the night. *Who on earth would do such a thing?* he wondered.

Darby was known as a safe town. The people in town respected a man's property, particularly his livestock. The penalty was too great.

"Did you hear anything out here last night, Son?" Fred asked.

"No, not a thing."

"Neither did I." Fred frowned. He asked Cole to finish the morning chores while he saddled up his horse and rode into town.

He had to pay someone a visit.

Sheriff Tom Holding was sitting with his deputy, Paul Vickery, when Fred Johnson angrily burst into the sheriff's office. Holding stood when Fred made his entrance, and at one look at his irate face Holding knew there was trouble.

"Sheriff, someone stole three chickens from my chicken coop last night."

Holding sat back down, and Vickery relaxed as well. He leaned up against the wall next to the sheriff's desk, and Holding leaned back in his chair.

"Why don't you tell me what happened?" Holding asked.

"What do you mean 'what happened'? Someone stole my chickens; that's what happened. They came in the night and took them," Fred answered, clearly frustrated.

"Are you sure it wasn't just some scoundrel?" Holding hoped that it was just the act of a hungry animal. It meant big trouble to have someone stealing livestock in these parts.

"Sheriff, aren't you listening to me?" Fred burst out. "It wasn't an animal. It was someone!"

"How do you know it was someone?" Vickery put in.

"Look, my son found them missing this morning. I took a look for myself, and they were gone. There was no sign of trouble or a ruckus. It wasn't animals. And if this person will steal chickens, no telling what else he'll steal. Now what are you two going to do about this?" Fred demanded.

Holding was silent for a moment. He looked over to Vickery, who nodded his head slightly. Holding stood and walked around the desk until he faced Fred.

"Fred, thanks for coming out here to let us know. We'll keep our eyes peeled and see what we can do to catch this person. Stealing is serious business. Let us know if anything else goes missing. We don't have much to go on without at least a description, but we'll put up a poster notifying the town, and we'll be on alert." Holding extended a hand to Fred.

"Thanks, Sheriff," he said as he turned to walk out the door. He wasn't going to sit by idly and watch his livestock get taken out from under his nose. He was going to sit up tonight and keep watch over his farm. No one was going to steal anything from him again.

Dakota whistled as he finished getting ready. He checked himself one last time in the small mirror that hung in the ranch hands' bunk then headed out the door. Dakota was so excited and nervous that he could barely contain himself. He had finally got up the nerve to ask permission to call on Dana Clarke, and tonight they were going to dinner at the restaurant.

He couldn't believe this was happening to him. A year ago he was in jail. Now, he was courting the most beautiful woman he had ever met. He knew that God had richly blessed him. Dakota was reminded of a verse he read in Lamentations: "It is of the Lord's mercies that we are not consumed, because his compassions fail not. They are new every morning." Dakota certainly understood that verse to be true. He was determined not to let his life go by without using it to glorify God for all that he did in Dakota's life. Dakota was truly grateful for God's compassion in sparing his life those ten years ago.

He walked to the door of the office and knocked. Dr. Clarke answered and invited Dakota to step inside. Dakota stepped in, and suddenly his stomach dropped. He wiped his sweaty palms on his pant legs.

"How are you, Dakota?" Dr. Clarke asked cordially.

"I'm fine. Thank you, sir. And yourself?" Dakota twisted his hat in his hands.

"Oh, I'm doing all right. Business is steady. I couldn't do without Dana, though. She's such a help."

As if on cue, Dana glided down the stairs. Dakota stood when he saw her. She was like a vision. She wore a light-pink cotton dress that was simple but very tasteful. It was a perfect dress for a summer evening.

"Dakota, I'm delighted to see you," Dana said pleasantly. She smiled at Dakota, and he thought he would melt into a puddle on the spot.

He cleared his throat. "Evenin'," he managed.

"Well, you two enjoy your dinner. I'll see you later, sweetheart," Dr. Clarke directed to his niece. She gave him a kiss on the cheek and then turned to Dakota.

"Shall we?" she motioned toward the door.

"Of course," he said. He fervently hoped that she wasn't able to see the flustered mess that he was. He offered the crook of his arm, which she accepted, and the two made the short walk from the doctor's office to the hotel restaurant.

Once they were inside and seated, Dakota decided that he was going to do his best to forget how nervous he was and simply enjoy being with this beautiful woman.

"Your uncle said that business has been steady." He decided that was a safe topic to open with. He was rewarded with a smile.

"Oh yes. I just love helping Uncle. The people in Darby love him and have so much faith in him. It's been very exciting to see him work and help the people alongside him," Dana answered.

Dakota smiled. Of course this angel would love her job. She was the sweetest thing he had ever beheld. She was anxious to help anyone, and her sweet disposition could put even the sickest patient at ease.

The waiter came, and they both ordered the special of the evening: fried chicken with mashed potatoes and gravy. It made Dakota's mouth water just to think about it.

"When did you know that you wanted to be a nurse?" Dakota inquired.

"A few years ago. I was at a friend's house, and her younger sister was outside playing. She ran inside in tears when a bee stung her. My friend's mother wasn't home, and so I took care of the bee sting. I love how it feels to help people, you know? At that moment, I knew that was what I wanted to do—help people," Dana answered.

"What about you, Dakota?" she asked. "Is there anything in particular you want to do? Not that there's anything wrong with being a ranch hand, of course," she quickly amended, "but is there anything else you'd like to do?"

"I don't know yet," he answered honestly. What did he want to do? He couldn't be a ranch hand all of his life. Especially if he was going to have a family someday. That idea sounded better and better with Dana's deep blue eyes looking at him.

"That's all right. There's nothing wrong with being a ranch hand, you know."

Dakota smiled at her, which she returned. He felt rescued when the waiter brought their food.

As he reached for his glass of water, the cuff of his sleeve moved a few inches up his forearm.

"What's that?" Dana asked, looking at his wrist.

Dakota looked down, and his eyes slid shut as memories flooded back to him. He was still a very young boy when his father decided that the family needed some symbol of unity. So he had the bright idea of getting the letter *B* branded on all of them—on the back of their wrists. That way, if there was ever any confusion as to who they were, everyone would see the *B* and know that they were from the notorious Buchanan family.

Dakota had hated the idea. He screamed and cried and fought, but it was to no avail. The pain was like nothing he ever felt before when his father put the red-hot iron poker to his skin. He hated that day. Now he had a painful reminder of his past that he carried with him every day for the rest of his life.

"Dakota, are you all right?" Dana asked, concern lining her voice.

Dakota's eyes flew open, and he quickly covered the *B* on his wrist with his sleeve.

"I'll be okay," he answered truthfully.

"Can you tell me about it?"

Dakota's mind raced for an appropriate way to explain without lying.

"I, uh, well..." He paused.

"Dana," he said as he reached for her hand. She took it, and he loved the way her small, delicate hand fit so nicely in his own. "I want to tell you about it one day, but not tonight, okay? My past ain't so good and brings back awful memories for me that I'm not up to talking about yet."

"Of course, Dakota," she said as she gave his hand a squeeze. He smiled at her as a myriad of emotions coursed through him. He longed to tell her who he really was, but when was the right time? The question plagued him for the rest of the night.

Dakota was cleaning out the horses' stalls when he heard his boss enter the barn.

"How's it going, Dakota?" Caleb asked.

"Fine, boss," Dakota replied. He was relieved no one was around. He needed advice.

"Caleb, I was wondering if I might have a word with you," Dakota began.

"Sure thing," Caleb answered as he sat down on a stack of hay. "Is there a problem?"

"Well..." Dakota put the pitchfork aside and took a seat himself. "I told you that I asked Dr. Clarke if I could call on Dana, right?"

Caleb nodded.

"Well, sir, we went to dinner last night, and while we were there she noticed this." He rolled up his shirtsleeve far enough for Caleb to see the branded *B* on the back of his wrist. Caleb's eyes widened.

"I thought that was just a rumor."

"No, sir. It's real. And I hate it. But it, like my childhood, was forced on me, and there was nothing I could do about it. I hate carrying this reminder with me every day. Well, anyway, Dana asked about it. I didn't know what to tell her, so I just told her that I wasn't up to talking about my past yet."

Caleb listened quietly.

"And what did she say?"

"She said that she understood." Dakota shrugged. "I left it at that, but I don't know what to do. I know I'm falling in love with her. I've never felt this way before. I don't want there to be any secrets between us, but I just don't know when I should tell her or how to go about telling her."

Caleb sat thoughtfully for a while. He knew that Dakota's past would catch up to him eventually in this town.

"This is a tough one. Have you prayed about it?" Caleb asked.

"Yes. One thing has been made clear to me: I have to tell her. The real question is when," Dakota responded.

"I'd say the sooner the better. One of these days that secret of yours is going to come out, and when it does, you don't want Dana to be caught by surprise. Keep seeking the Lord to learn when you should tell her," Caleb advised.

"Thanks, boss. Well, I'd better finish up in here." Dakota stood and reached for the pitchfork.

"You're doing a good job, Dakota." Caleb laid a hand on his shoulder. "Alicia and I are proud of you." With that, Caleb left the barn to see to other business. Dakota felt better after talking with Caleb. He made short work of the barn then moved on to complete some other chores.

CHAPTER 9

"Dad! Dad!" Fred heard Cole say. "Get up!"

Cole was shaking his father, and it took Fred a moment to get his bearing.

"Cole!" he cried as sat up with a start. "What's wrong?"

"Another chicken is missing!"

No, it's not possible, Fred thought as he got his boots on. For the past six days he had been standing guard outside his home. But after no sign of trouble, he had decided he was ready for good night's sleep. He couldn't believe something had happened. He ran outside after his son and looked at the chicken coop. There was no sign of a disturbance, but when he stood at the coop and silently counted the chickens, one was missing.

"I came out to get the eggs, and I noticed her gone," Cole recounted to his father.

Fred groaned. The one night he didn't stand guard. But he couldn't stand guard forever. This was getting out of hand. He strode to the barn.

"Where are you going?"

"To town. Tell your mother not to hold breakfast," he told Cole as he quickly saddled up his horse and rode off.

Tom Holding was just finishing his morning cup of coffee when Fred Johnson burst into the sheriff's office.

"Did it happen again, Fred?" he asked.

"Well, I wouldn't be here otherwise, now would I?"

"Why don't you calm down and tell me what happened?" Holding put down his coffee cup and leaned forward.

"I'll tell you what happened! I spent the last week standing guard outside my house watching for thieves. I never saw anyone. I haven't slept in a week, Sheriff. So last night, I decided to go on to bed. My boy woke me up this morning and told me that another chicken was missing. I went out there to see for myself, and it was true! There was another chicken missing. Now how do you account for that, Sheriff?" Fred's tone turned accusatory, and Holding inwardly groaned. Sometimes the people of this town expected him to be a miracle worker.

"I don't know what happened, Fred. I've alerted the other farmers in the area, and Vickery and myself have been patrolling—late into the night, no less. We haven't seen anything, and no one else has reported anything missing. I don't know what to tell you, Fred. We'll just have to keep our eyes peeled and stay alert." Holding sat back. He knew that Fred would not want to accept that answer, but it was all he could do.

"Some sheriff you are," Fred muttered as he stormed out the door. Vickery walked in as Fred was leaving, and Fred nearly barreled into him.

"Watch where you're going!" Fred shouted in Vickery's face as he brushed past him.

"Now just wait a minute—" Vickery started, but Holding interrupted him.

"Let him go, Vickery. He's not thinking clearly." The two stood in the doorway and watched as Fred mounted his horse and galloped toward his farm.

"Another chicken gone?"

"You got it. He wants us to miraculously produce a thief, but it just doesn't work that way. Fred knows that, but he's too angry to think rationally. We'll have to stay alert and see if we can't find some kind of lead into who is taking his chickens."

Dakota and Dana strolled hand in hand through the meadow behind the doctor's office. They had been seeing a lot of each other the past couple of weeks. Dana looked up at the stars and sighed contentedly.

"You know what I've been thinking, Dakota?" she broke the silence.

Dakota looked down at her, and his heart swelled with love. He felt like the luckiest man on earth.

"What, angel?" he asked gently.

"I think that moving to Darby was one of the best decisions I've ever made."

"I know it is." Dakota brushed a light kiss on the back of her hand. She smiled, and they continued to walk.

If only Dana were aware of the turmoil that was going on inside Dakota. He knew that tonight was the night he would tell her everything. He would tell her about his past, his real name, everything. He was scared to death to tell her the truth. What if she rejected him? The thought took his breath away. He knew he wouldn't be able to bear it if that happened. But Caleb was right. The sooner he told Dana the truth, the better off he would be.

He stopped and took a deep breath. "Dana?"

"Yes?" she said as she looked up at him with trusting eyes.

"I—"

"Dana!" a male voice shouted. It sounded like someone was running toward them. Dakota stiffened. Dana turned and felt Dakota's muscles tighten.

"Dana!" the voice rang out again.

"I'm over here!" Dana called. Dakota stood tensely until he could make out the face of the man running toward them. It was a fellow townsman. He began to relax.

"Dana," the man gasped, "the doc needs you."

"Slow down," Dana said. "Try to catch your breath. I can barely understand you."

"There's no time for that," the man said as he grabbed at Dana's arm. "You have to come right away. My wife went into labor, and she's having a really hard time. Doc said to send for you at once." The man started to pull Dana's arm. "Let's go."

It was one in the afternoon the next day before Dana got a chance to get some sleep. She gratefully fell into bed as sleep rushed in. What a difficult time the farmer's wife had. Her baby was breech, trying to be born feet first. Fortunately, her uncle was an excellent doctor with a lot of experience and was able to turn the baby around. His skill, and God's mercy, saved both the mother and the baby. Dana was relieved and glad that it was all over.

As sleep came to claim her, her thoughts drifted back to the night before. She was with Dakota. She loved being with Dakota. She loved the way her hand felt in his, she loved his strong presence beside her, and she loved the way his deep voice resonated—especially when he used his special name for her, Angel. Was she in love with him? The answer came as quickly as the question formed. *Yes.* Without a doubt, Dana Clarke was in love with Dakota Jones.

She was very serious when she told Dakota that coming to Darby was the best decision she had ever made. It was in Darby that she found independence and learned how to stand on her own two feet. It was in Darby that she was able to care for the patients of the town that her uncle loved so dearly, and it was in Darby that she met a man named Dakota Jones.

A man who had swept in and stolen her heart.

Alicia and Claire were settled comfortably in the living room of Mark and Claire's home. Mark and Claire's two girls, Bethany and Emily, were busy playing with Daisy in the girls' bedroom. Alicia's boys stayed at the ranch to help their father. Her boys loved to be with their father on the ranch. The women poured themselves some tea and sat back to enjoy a pleasant afternoon.

"Have you seen Mrs. Thorne recently?" Claire asked. Mrs. Thorne was an elderly woman in town who seemed to always look for an argument. Mrs. Thorne and Claire had their differences, though Claire's feelings toward Mrs. Thorne had softened because, despite her rough façade, she had had a difficult life and was actually kind underneath all of her prickles.

"No, not lately," Alicia replied.

"Neither have I." Claire frowned. "I hope that she's doing all right. She might be sick or something. I'll have to call on her this week."

"Claire, you've always been the sweetest person I know!" Alicia laughed. "That woman knows how to get under your skin like no one else in this town, yet you still worry about her and go to pay her visits."

"Yeah, well, she's not as bad as she seems."

"I know. She did make the cake for our weddings, remember?"

"Of course I remember! Not only that, but she served it as well!"

"How is Mark doing at the bank?" Alicia inquired.

"Fine. Everything is going well for him. With the town growing so much, business at the bank is growing right along with it. It keeps him busy, that's for sure."

"What about the paralysis?" Alicia asked tentatively. She was always a little hesitant to broach that subject.

"It's okay to ask, Alicia," Claire said reassuringly. She put a hand over Alicia's. "I think you already know that he's doing quite well. The paralysis really doesn't slow him down anymore. He is so used to that wheelchair, and the ramps throughout town really help him. There have been many modifications made to the bank building also."

"I'm glad."

"Now, on to a subject I'm much more interested in. I've noticed that Rigby, I mean Dakota, has been visiting the doctor's office a lot lately. I suppose he's been very ill recently?" Claire asked slyly.

"Ha! You know better than that. There's a certain nurse who's caught his eye."

"Indeed. I suspected as much. Especially since I see them walking around town together," Claire said with a smile.

"Yes, well, I'm worried about him," Alicia admitted as she worried her lower lip.

"Why?"

"What happens when Dana learns his true identity?"

"You mean he hasn't told her yet?" Claire didn't hide her surprise.

"Not yet. Caleb advised him to tell her the sooner the better. Dakota said that he tried the other night, but they were interrupted. The doctor needed her help with a patient. I'm concerned about how she will take the news. Her rejection would break Dakota's heart. He's in love with her. I'm sure of it."

"Well," said Claire matter-of-factly, "we'll just have to do what we've always done. We'll have to turn to the situation over to God. We'll pray for both of them and for God's will in their lives. And for understanding for Dana," Claire added.

"Absolutely. In fact, let's pray right now." The two women joined hands and raised their voices to petition God on behalf of Dakota and Dana.

CHAPTER 10

Dakota's hands trembled as he tried to straighten his tie. Tonight was the church social, and he was escorting Dana. He always felt a giddy kind of nervous before he would go to see her. He wiped his sweaty palms on his pant legs and headed out the door. He didn't want to be late.

As he walked the distance from the Blue Star Ranch into town, he wondered when he would tell Dana the truth about himself. He wanted to tell her tonight, but he wasn't sure if it would be appropriate to tell her during an event in which the entire town would be present. Why wasn't it working out for him to tell her? He closed his fists in frustration. Now that he had decided to tell her, waiting for the right moment was proving to be very difficult and trying his patience.

He walked up the steps to the doctor's office and knocked. Dana answered the door with a smile.

"Hi, Dakota," she greeted.

"You look beautiful," he said barely above a whisper.

She giggled. "Thanks."

"Well," Dakota said as he cleared his throat, "let's go." He offered Dana his arm, and they set off toward the church.

The social was held in the front yard of the church. There were many tables set up with all kinds of different foods and drinks. Clearly much preparation went into this gathering. There were a few men with fiddles and harmonicas playing off to the side, and the whole atmosphere was merry.

Dakota and Dana found a young couple they knew from the church who were sitting on a blanket under a tree. They walked over and joined them. Dakota looked around him and listened to the sounds of laughter and the happiness that was enjoyed by all this evening. He felt blessed to be a part of it. He suddenly felt an overwhelming sense of protection over this town and the people in it—all he held dear.

He knew that what his family did to innocent people like these all those years ago was so wrong. How would he act if someone like his father rode into town and tried to threaten someone he loved? He would fight; that's what he would do. Fight to the death if necessary to protect those he loved. His heart ached inside of him for all the damage that was caused by the Buchanan family.

His gaze fell to Mark; he was laughing and talking with some of the men from the church. He seemed perfectly at ease with his situation, but Dakota knew it couldn't be easy for Mark—and his family was responsible for it. The guilt seemed to creep up on Dakota when he least expected it to spoil any good thing around him. He knew if he continued to let his thoughts run along this vein that he would never have a good time at the social. He shook his head to dispel the memories and tried to focus on the party.

"We've got to take action, men," Fred Johnson was whispering vehemently to several of the other farmers.

"Now, Fred, we came here for a good time. Stop giving us all this grief about your chickens," another farmer named Ron was saying. "This is a social, and I mean to enjoy it." He turned to walk away when Fred grabbed his arm.

Ron broke free of his grip. "Watch yourself, Johnson," Ron growled in a low voice.

"Can't you see that I'm telling you this for your own good?" Fred insisted. "If we don't find who's responsible, the next chickens they take could be yours."

"What are you making such a fuss for? They're just chickens."

"It starts with chickens. Then they'll move on to our cows, pigs, and horses."

"Well, I'll cross that bridge when I get to it," Ron responded. "I'm in no mood for your games, and you're ruining the party."

Fred turned to the other farmers standing there. "Do you agree with me, men? We can't let this thief get away with this!"

"And what exactly do you propose we do, Fred?" another farmer spoke up.

"Well, I've been thinking. This thief that's taken my chickens seems to be aware of what I do. Every time I stand guard, there isn't a sign of anyone. Whenever I don't stand guard, I get up the next day and there's a chicken missing. Therefore, I think it's someone in this town who knows the area and can somehow anticipate our actions." Fred ran his hands up and down his suspenders, proud of himself for figuring that out.

"And again I say, what exactly do you want us to do about it?"

"Well, for starters, we need to examine everyone in this town. There are some newcomers we don't know very well. Where do they hail from? Are they criminals?"

"Oh Fred, come on!" another farmer piped up. "Be reasonable."

"Actually, I think he might have a point," someone else said. "It wouldn't hurt to at least keep an eye peeled and do some asking around."

"Exactly," Fred said. "For example, look around at this social. There are half a dozen people here who I don't know, and several of them are relatively new to the town. Take that Dakota Jones." He motioned with his eyes to the blanket where Dakota was sitting. "What do we know about him?"

"Oh get off it, Fred. He's the Sunday school teacher."

"All the more reason to check on him."

"I'm sure Pastor Tyler has already taken care of that."

"Well, I'm going to see for myself," Fred stated as he starting walking toward Dakota. Several other farmers followed after him out of curiosity.

Dakota glanced up and noticed several farmers walking his way. They all had their eyes focused on him. *What in the world?*

"Dakota Jones?" Fred extended a hand. Dakota stood and accepted the handshake.

"Yes," Dakota answered. "And you are?"

"Fred…" Fred's voice trailed off as he noticed a mark on Dakota's wrist. During the handshake, Dakota's sleeve moved up slightly, revealing the bottom half of a *B*. Fred jerked the rest of his sleeve up and gasped.

"*Buchanan!*" he shouted for all to hear. Dakota looked around in panic. Caleb looked up when he heard the shout, and his heart dropped. Not Fred Johnson. Of all the people to discover his identity, it shouldn't be Fred Johnson. He was sure to accuse Dakota of stealing. Or worse. Caleb quickly made his way over to the scene.

"I heard that one of you was still alive! And you dared to come back to our town." Fred still had a firm hold on Dakota's arm.

"Let him go," Caleb said authoritatively as he reached the two men. The entire gathering at the social was frozen in place and watching the scene unfold before them.

"You *knew!*" Fred hurled the accusation at Caleb. "Well, what you might not know is that your ranch hand has been stealing my chickens!" Fred's face was red with fury. "Why did you let this low life come back here? He should've hanged with his brothers!"

Fred turned at the sound of a gasp to see Dana looking pale.

"Oh yes, Miss Clarke. I'll bet you didn't know that the man you've been consorting with is one of the very brothers that put Mark Brewer in that wheelchair. Or that killed Caleb's parents or that kidnapped Alicia. Did you also know that *Dakota Jones*"—he said the name like it was poison—"isn't his real name? Tell us, boy, what your real name is." Fred smiled as he saw tears begin to swim in Dana's eyes.

She looked at Dakota, and he looked back at her helplessly.

"I can explain," he began, his eyes pleading with hers, but Fred stopped him.

"Oh, can you now?"

Dakota looked back to Fred, and his heart sank. *How can this be happening here? Now?*

"Can you explain what you're doing here? And can you explain, Caleb Carter, why you let this criminal near your family again? You must not love your wife as much as we all thought you did."

"That's enough!" Caleb roared. Dana jumped to her feet and ran toward the doctor's office.

"Dana!" Dakota called. But it was too late.

"Take your hands off of him," Caleb demanded. Fred finally released his hold on Dakota. Dakota's eyes held fear, but he never cowered. He was a large man, and Caleb thought Fred was foolish to try to take Dakota on. Dakota's strength far outweighed Fred's.

"Fred Johnson, how dare you disrupt this social with false accusations toward my ranch hand. He has *not* stolen anything from you, least of all chickens. Why in the world would he need them, and where would he put them?" Caleb fired his questions off at Fred who, for the first time, was beginning to look uncertain. Caleb was a leader in this town, and Fred was putting himself in a compromising position to challenge him in this way.

"And"—Caleb's voice lowered into a deep growl—"if you ever say anything about my family again or question my loyalty to them, you'll be sorry."

Alicia watched the whole exchange, wide-eyed. Caleb was usually so calm and laid-back; but when provoked, he would step up to the plate to defend his family.

Fred looked shaken for a moment then quickly regained the force with which he so strongly accused Dakota.

"That still doesn't mean he belongs here. He's a criminal, and he didn't pay!"

"Oh yes he did." Pastor Tyler stepped out of the crowd and stood facing Fred. "This boy stood before a judge and was punished for his crimes. He served the punishment. Justice has been done, Fred. Leave the boy alone."

"You knew too?" Fred asked in disbelief. "You knew, yet you let this person teach Sunday school to our *children?*"

Pastor Tyler looked around. The entire church family was standing there, witnessing this dreadful display.

"He is a changed man. He accepted Christ as his Lord and Savior. He is free from the bonds of his past. He served the punishment for his crimes, and now he lives his life to please God. You cannot judge this boy. And after seeing the way you've behaved, can you blame him for changing his name?" Pastor Tyler challenged.

Fred looked scathingly at the pastor and then at Caleb. "You two were wrong to allow a criminal to stay here," he said. He leaned toward Dakota. "This isn't over," he growled.

Fred then turned and stormed off with about a dozen farmers following after him.

Sheriff Holding approached them. "Rigby? Is it really you?"

"Yes, sir," Dakota answered as he hung his head.

"Pastor Tyler was right, you know. You are a changed man. One that I'm proud to know. And you did serve your punishment. You are a free man."

At this moment, free was probably the last thing Dakota felt. He felt trapped by his past and humiliated that everyone learned about it the way they did. And what about Dana? He was certain she would never speak to him again. That thought hurt him more than anything else.

"Dakota, will you excuse us for a minute?" Holding asked as he pulled Caleb aside.

"This doesn't look good. I'm concerned about what Fred and those other farmers might try to do. You know how people seem to feel like they can take the law into their own hands. I don't think Fred can accept the fact that Dakota is a free man who has already paid for his crimes."

"I know." Caleb raked a hand through his hair.

"Keep a close eye on him," Holding advised. "Vickery and I will be patrolling and keeping watch for any sign of trouble."

"Thanks," Caleb said. He walked over to Dakota. "Come on. Let's get you back to the ranch." Caleb's heart went out to Dakota. All of the color had drained from his face.

Caleb walked up to his wife, who was standing with Claire and Mark.

"Alicia, honey, I think you and the children might need to stay here in town with Mark and Claire for a day or so," Caleb whispered so that only the four of them might hear.

Alicia nodded. Caleb was right.

"Don't you worry about a thing," Mark assured Caleb. "They'll be safe here."

"Thanks." Caleb stooped down to kiss his children. He admonished them to behave and take care of their mother for a couple of days. Then he gave Alicia a quick kiss before climbing into the wagon and heading back to the Blue Star Ranch to await the trouble he was sure Fred Johnson and some of the others were bound to cause.

Dana sat alone in her room, staring out the window over the meadow. Was it only a couple of nights ago that she and Dakota had walked through that same meadow and she felt such love for him? She brushed away a tear that rolled down her cheek. The events of the evening replayed through her mind over and over.

She noticed the mark on Dakota's arm, and he told her he would tell her about it one day. Why didn't he tell her then? Fred Johnson knew exactly what it meant. Dana wasn't entirely sure herself, but she knew that it symbolized something from his past that was not good. Who exactly was Dakota Jones?

The thought plagued her, and another tear rolled down her cheek. She was in love with Dakota Jones, but apparently there was no such person. Her heart ached. Everything seemed so off balance after this evening. She wanted answers. Dakota didn't follow her when she left the social, nor did he come by to check on her. Did he simply not care about her?

Dana turned when she heard a knock at the door. She took her handkerchief and dabbed under her eyes.

"Come in," she answered.

Dr. Clarke stood in the doorway. Dana wanted to shrink away from the compassionate gaze she saw coming from her uncle.

"Hello, Uncle."

"How are you, my dear?" he said as he crossed the room to sit in the rocking chair next to hers.

"I don't know," she responded as she shook her head. "Everything that happened tonight... I just don't understand. What was Fred Johnson talking about?"

Dr. Clarke rubbed his hands together and looked down at the floor.

"Dana, dear, Dakota Jones is not who we thought he was," he began. Dana waited expectantly. "Do you remember when I told you about the five men who caused such destruction in these parts?"

Dana nodded.

"Well, Dakota was one of them."

Dana gasped. "Oh, Uncle, tell me that's not true!"

Dr. Clarke took another deep breath.

"Dana, Mark Brewer is in a wheelchair because Dakota's family shot him. Alicia was kidnapped because Dakota's family kidnapped her. The church building was burned to the ground ten years ago because Dakota's brother set it on fire. Caleb and Claire's parents were killed because of Dakota's family, as was Alicia's father."

Dana's eyes slid shut. It felt like the room was spinning. Her stomach churned, and she fought the urge to throw up.

"Dana, you need some rest. We'll finish this later," Dr. Clarke said with concern. His niece's face was ashen.

"No, please," she said as she reached for his arm. "Please continue."

"Well," he resumed hesitantly, "Dakota was only a boy of sixteen at the time. Apparently, the life of crime was forced upon him by an abusive father and brothers. There wasn't much Dakota could do. When Alicia was being held captive, Dakota led her escape and turned himself and his family in."

Dana looked up at him, and Dr. Clarke thought he noticed a glimmer of hope in her eyes.

"You mean, Dakota was just a boy when all of this took place?"

"Yes."

"And he was responsible for Alicia's escape?"

"More than that. He's responsible for her still being alive. Given his unique circumstances, the judge sentenced him to ten years of prison, which he served. He must have decided to come back here to the Carters after he was released."

Dana sat thoughtfully for a while. "Thank you for clearing up some things for me. I have a lot of thinking to do. I'm so uncertain about him. Uncle, Fred Johnson said something about Dakota not being his real name. Is that true?"

"Yes, Dana. His name is Rigby Buchanan."

With that, Dr. Clarke rose wearily from the rocking chair. He bid his niece good night and went to his own room. Dana sat staring out over the meadow. She knew her uncle wouldn't lie to her, so the story must be true. But why hadn't Dakota, or rather Rigby, told her his true identity? *How can I trust him after this?* Dana thought.

The longer that she sat in the chair looking out onto the meadow, the angrier she became. He lied to her. He wooed her with his kind words and gentle touch, and now she found out that it was all a lie. And because he didn't tell her the truth himself, she had to be completely taken off guard in front of the whole town by a raving man who exposed Dakota in front of everyone.

No, she amended, *not Dakota. His name is Rigby.* Would she get used to that? Could she stop thinking about the man that she thought she loved as Dakota? She felt that the entire courtship had been a lie now that she found out she wasn't going out with Dakota Jones but with Rigby Buchanan.

She shook her head. She needed to get some rest. She got up from the chair and slipped into bed. As sleep rushed in to claim her, she decided upon one thing. She didn't care if she never saw Rigby Buchanan again.

CHAPTER 11

Caleb and Dakota rode silently back to the Blue Star Ranch, each one deep in their own thoughts. Caleb was worried over what the next forty-eight hours might bring. He knew that Fred Johnson was a hotheaded man who would have no problem trying to take the law into his own hands. Caleb was afraid that the other farmers might go along with Fred and insist that Dakota was to blame without any evidence or a fair trial.

Dakota, on the other hand, had only one thing on his mind: Dana Clarke. How would he ever explain things to her? Would she even listen? His deepest fear wasn't for his life or the fact that Fred Johnson might bring a posse out to the ranch demanding justice be done, but that he had just lost a certain beautiful woman forever.

Caleb steered the team toward the barn, and he and Dakota climbed out of the wagon.

"John," Caleb called to his foreman, "please take care of the team then come inside. We've got a problem on our hands." Caleb handed the reins to John. He then turned and strode quickly into the ranch house with Dakota. John called to Robby, another hand who happened to be in the barn, to take care of the team, and he walked hastily toward the house.

John walked inside and saw Caleb standing in his normal place when he had something to think about. Caleb was standing in front of the fireplace, resting his forearm on the mantle staring into the fire. Dakota was sitting quietly in a chair, wringing his hands with his head down. John didn't know what to do, so he stood frozen in place until his boss looked up.

"John," Caleb began, "there's something you need to know about Dakota."

John nodded, waiting for Caleb to continue.

"You actually know Dakota from about ten years back. His real name is Rigby Buchanan."

John's mouth fell open, and he took a step backward. His eyes flew to Dakota then back to Caleb.

Caleb smiled slightly at the surprise on his foreman's face. He realized that most people would never understand why the Carters gave Dakota a second chance.

"It's all right, John. We were surprised too when he arrived at our door a few months ago."

"I don't understand, boss," John replied honestly.

"I know you don't. Let me try to explain." Caleb motioned for John to sit down. He took a chair opposite Dakota, and Caleb sat on the sofa and leaned forward. "John, ten years ago when Dakota was just a boy and he was being held in our town jail, Pastor Tyler and I would go visit him and share the good news of the gospel. During that time, Dakota recognized his need for a Savior and accepted Jesus Christ into his heart to be Lord of his life."

John glanced over at Dakota, who remained motionless on the chair with his head down. John began to feel the first pang of pity for him.

"After he served his ten years in prison, he came back to Darby. To the Blue Star Ranch. He had nowhere else to go. Alicia and I told Dakota ten years ago that we would help him start fresh if he ever decided to return to Darby. He changed his name to Dakota Jones, and he's been a good, honest worker. He's a changed man, John."

Caleb sat back and watched his foreman. He knew that John was struggling to process this information. John was a loyal employee who felt very protective of the Carters. The look on John's face registered disbelief, which eventually melted into acceptance. If Caleb could accept this man into his life, who was he not to? After all, it was Caleb's family that was hurt and Caleb found forgiveness in his heart. John knew that he could do the same.

Caleb watched as John stood and moved in front of Dakota. Dakota slowly looked up, and his eyes widened in surprise. John stood over him with an outstretched hand. Dakota grasped it, and John gave it a firm shake.

"Welcome to the family."

Dakota stared at him in confusion for a moment before realizing that John was referring to the family of God.

"Thank you," he responded quietly.

"So what's the problem?" the foreman turned to Caleb. He knew this couldn't be the only reason why the boss came back from town without his family and had seemed so deep in thought earlier.

"The town found out at the church social who Dakota really is." Caleb stood and began to pace. "Fred Johnson is accusing him of stealing his chickens. The accusation is absurd, and he has no evidence to back it up. When he realized that Dakota was actually Rigby, he was convinced that Dakota is the chicken thief, and we're afraid that he will try to take the law into his own hands. Not everyone wants to accept the fact that Dakota has already paid the consequences for his actions."

"How did Fred find out who Dakota really was?" John wanted to know. Caleb motioned to Dakota to show John his arm. Dakota pulled back his shirtsleeve just far enough for John to see the branded *B*.

"Well, I'll be," John said with some amazement. "I thought that was just an old wives' tale."

"No, sir," Dakota answered.

"Okay, boss. What do I need to do?" John didn't need further explanation to understand the weight of the situation. Dakota was in a precarious position.

"Well," Caleb began but was interrupted by someone banging on the door. The three men tensed.

"Who is it?" Caleb demanded in a strong, clear voice.

"It's Sheriff Holding and Deputy Vickery." Caleb visibly relaxed as he recognized the voice. He opened the door and ushered the two men inside. While they were making their way in, Caleb turned to John.

"Let the men know there may be trouble tonight and to stand guard. Put them in shifts. We need to know the minute there's commotion."

"You got it, boss," John answered as he turned to do as Caleb bid.

Caleb shut the door behind his foreman, fastened the lock, and then strode into the living room, where Holding and Vickery were waiting.

"I suspect there might be trouble tonight, Caleb. We wanted to be on hand in case Fred stirs up all of the other farmers and they come out here," Holding explained.

"I appreciate it, Tom," Caleb said with deep gratitude. He was worried about what Fred might do, and having the law on his side was a relief. Caleb offered them coffee, and the men continued to talk well into the night.

"Ma?" Cameron asked. Alicia was busy tucking her three children into bed in the guest room at her sister-in-law's house. Alicia pulled the blanket up and nestled Cameron securely under the covers. She looked down at him and saw Caleb's big brown eyes staring back at her. *Cameron is so like his father*, Alicia thought.

"Yes, sweetheart?"

"What if Pa needs me tonight? I want to go back to the ranch. I'm big enough now to help Pa." Cameron squirmed out from under the tight cocoon of blankets that his mother just tucked around him and sat up straight. Alicia smiled at her oldest child.

"Honey, the best way for you to help your pa right now is to stay here and help look after your little brother and sister."

Cameron frowned at his mother. That didn't seem like a good enough reason to him. He folded his arms and stared straight ahead.

"Cameron, your father wouldn't want you to pout. There could be serious trouble tonight, and your father wants to make sure that you are safe. He loves you. You're still young, Cameron." Alicia tried to explain as gently as possible to the child, but she knew that it was to no avail. Cameron wouldn't be happy if he was not with his father.

"What about me, Ma?" young Will piped in.

"You, young man, are also supposed to help take care of your sister." Alicia rearranged the covers around Will, who always seemed to squirm out of them the second the covers were in place. Alicia gazed lovingly at both boys.

"You are both such a big help to your pa and me," she said. "One day you will be able to help him with more jobs, but for now your job is to stay here and be brave and help take care of the family."

"Yes, ma'am," they said in unison.

Daisy chose that moment to climb into her mother's lap. Daisy didn't understand what was going on. Alicia wrapped her arms around the child and hugged her close. Alicia envied her childlike faith and ignorance of the bad things of the world.

"Come on, little one," Alicia cooed. "You need some sleep too." She gently set Daisy down on a pallet next to the bed her brothers shared and tucked her in tightly.

"Good night," Alicia said quietly as she started to tiptoe out of the room.

"Ma." Cameron's voice stopped her.

"Yes, Son?"

"Can we pray for Pa?" Cameron was sitting up again and looked at his mother expectantly.

"Of course. He will need our prayers." Alicia walked back over to the bed, and as she did, her heart swelled with pride. What a special child Cameron was. They all were. Alicia sat down next to Cameron, and together they prayed for the safety of Caleb and those on the ranch.

Dakota had dozed off in the living room chair when he heard shouts coming from outside. Caleb, Holding, and Vickery were already at the window looking out.

"Well, here they come," Holding said. "I guess we all knew it was only a matter of time. Rigby"—Holding paused—"I mean, Dakota, you better lay low."

Dakota nodded and stayed in his chair.

Caleb watched about twenty farmers storm onto his property with torches and guns. Leading the way was Fred Johnson. Caleb's ranch hands tried to dissuade them from coming toward the house, but his men were outnumbered. Caleb clenched his fists. This wasn't right. Fred Johnson couldn't just take the law into his own hands like this. Dakota was innocent.

"Vickery, stay here with Dakota," Holding ordered as he opened the door, and he and Caleb quickly stepped onto the porch. Fred Johnson and his men stood at the bottom of the porch steps.

"This is private property, Johnson," Caleb's deep voice resonated with authority. "You have no business here. You and your men need to leave at once."

"You know I won't be going anywhere until I get what I want, Caleb Carter," Fred retorted.

"And what exactly do you want?" Caleb fired back.

"It's not *what* I want. It's *who* I want." Fred sneered.

Caleb looked at Fred and was disgusted by what he saw—a man so bent on vengeance that he was blinded to the truth. Caleb leveled Fred with a look.

"Get off my property." His voice was as cold as steel.

"Not without Rigby Buchanan!" Fred yelled as he raised his torch. The men with him cheered and raised their torches along with him.

"Enough!" Sheriff Holding shouted over the cheers. The men quieted, and Holding continued. "Why do you want Rigby Buchanan?"

"You know why, Sheriff," Fred snarled. "He's a chicken thief. There's a high price to pay for that in these parts!"

"How do you know that Rigby stole them?" Holding returned.

"He's a criminal, Sheriff! I'm sure that no one here needs to be reminded of the damage his family did in this town." Fred glared at Caleb, who returned his look with an icy stare. Caleb clenched his fists at his side as Fred continued. "A notorious criminal is living in our town, and that's all the proof that I need!"

With that, the men cheered again.

"Dakota is not a notorious criminal." Sheriff Holding silenced the crowd once again. "He is reformed. Listen to me, everyone." Sheriff Holding tried to make eye contact with as many of the men in the group as he could. "Dakota paid for his crimes, and now he is a man of God. He's a hard worker and a good neighbor. You men have no basis for this charge. You need to return to your homes. You are all trespassing on private property, and if you don't leave, I will arrest all of you."

At that, some of the men began to appear uneasy. Some shuffled their feet, and many lowered their torches. They looked at each other trying to decide what to do. Fred noticed their indecision and angrily turned to them.

"What's the matter with all of you?" he shouted. "Do you want your chickens to be stolen next? He'll start with chickens then move on to our livestock. We have to get Rigby Buchanan!"

"Wait! Wait!"

Everyone turned toward the drive to see a young man running furiously toward the Blue Star Ranch. He finally made it up to the house and stood panting with his hands on his knees, trying to catch his breath.

"W-wait," he panted.

"Cole," Fred growled at his son. "What are you doing here? This is no place for a boy. Go home, Son."

"No, Pa. I can't."

Fred raised his brows in surprise, but before he could scold him, Cole continued, "Pa, Mr. Jones didn't steal your chickens."

"What are you talking about, boy?" Fred's eyes sparked with anger. Caleb and Holding came down a couple of steps.

"Dakota didn't steal your chickens." He hung his head. "I did."

The other farmers gasped in surprise. Caleb and Holding looked at each other. For the first time since Fred arrived, Caleb slowly unclenched his fists. He looked at young Cole, who had tears in his eyes. Fred stared at his son in disbelief.

"You see, one day when I was fishing out toward Groves, I met a boy whose Pa was killed in a hunting accident. His family was having a really hard time and was half starved. I told him I would help him out, and so I gave him some chickens. I was scared to ask you, so I thought if I made it look like someone stole the chickens that you wouldn't find the thief, and my friends would have eggs and chickens. They would eat, and you would have just lost a few chickens. I never figured on any of this happening." Cole gestured helplessly to the other farmers, who stood by listening in disbelief.

"You did *what?*" Fred bellowed. Cole took a step back and stared wide-eyed with fear at his father.

"I'm sorry," Cole said quietly. Caleb felt sorry for young Cole and decided to step in.

"Fred, what Cole has done tonight is admirable. He told the shameful truth in front of all of these people. And he kept an innocent man from being harmed." Caleb looked at the boy, who stood shaking. "Thank you, son, for coming down here to tell us the truth."

The boy just stared at Caleb and then turned back to his father. The other farmers began to disperse, feeling ashamed of themselves.

"Let's go, Cole," Fred said angrily. Fred barely glanced at Caleb and Sheriff Holding before taking off down the drive without even a word of apology.

"I'm glad that's over," Holding said as he watched them leave.

"Boss!" John shouted as he ran up to the porch. "The men are giving me a really hard time about Dakota. They've heard bits and pieces and are coming to some wrong conclusions."

"Tell them the truth, John," Caleb said. "But make sure they understand that Dakota is a good man, and he is welcome on this ranch."

John nodded and jogged back to the bunkhouse. Caleb knew that John would handle the job. He went back inside the house with Holding.

When Dakota saw them, he jumped up from his chair. Vickery had watched everything unfold from the window and turned to face the men.

"It's over, Dakota," Caleb said.

Dakota felt relief wash through him. This was one of the worst nights he could remember having in a long time. "It turns out that Fred's son took the chickens to give to a starving friend in a neighboring town. I think that most of the farmers out there felt pretty ashamed of themselves once they knew the truth."

"I'm so glad that's over," Dakota said. "Thank you all for helping me."

"Glad to do it," Holding said as he gave Dakota a slap on the back. "We'll be heading out now, Caleb."

"Thanks for coming out," Caleb said gratefully. Caleb and Holding shook hands; then he shook the deputy's hand and walked them to the door. Once they left, Caleb walked back into the living room.

"I don't know about you, but I'm plumb wore out," he said as he collapsed into a chair. He glanced over at Dakota, who had a look so forlorn that Caleb's heart turned over.

"Anything you want to talk about?" Caleb asked.

"I'm afraid that I've lost Dana forever." Dakota stared at the floor. Caleb waited patiently for him to continue. "I tried to tell her. Why didn't it work out for me to tell her the truth? Why did she have to find out like this?" Dakota raked a hand through his hair as he stood and began to pace.

"I don't know, son," Caleb answered.

"Do you think she'll even listen to me when I try to explain?" Dakota was clearly distraught.

"I don't know that either. What I do know is that you have to at least try to explain. She may need some time, but don't give up. Right now, though, you need to get some sleep. Take the guest room for tonight, and tomorrow you can return to the bunkhouse."

Dakota nodded and thanked him then slowly walked toward the guest room, his mind whirling.

CHAPTER 12

The next morning Claire and Alicia were busy feeding five hungry mouths at the breakfast table. The children were busy chatting and giggling, but Alicia was lost in her own world. She had spent most of the night tossing and turning, wondering what might be going on and worrying about Caleb. Claire wasn't pressuring her to talk, though. The bags under Alicia's eyes spoke volumes.

"Good morning, everyone," Mark said cheerily as he swiftly wheeled into the kitchen.

"Pa! Pa!" his two little girls squealed in delight. They jumped down from their place at the table to give their father a hug.

"Pa, guess what?" Bethany asked in excitement.

"What, dumpling?"

"Ma said that if we're good, she'll take us to visit Mrs. Tyler today!" Mark grinned at his wife, who smiled peacefully in return.

"Mrs. Tyler! Mrs. Tyler!" young Emily chimed in gleefully. Bethany climbed into her father's lap, and he wheeled her back to her place at the table.

"Well now, if you're going to visit Mrs. Tyler, you'd better eat a good breakfast," he said as he deposited her back into the chair. Bethany sat down with a thump and eagerly spooned up her oatmeal.

"Here you go, dear." Claire placed a hot bowl of oatmeal in front of her husband and dropped a quick kiss on his cheek. He grabbed her hand and held it for a moment and looked into her eyes. The love in his look was unmistakable, and Claire flushed slightly under his gaze. He gave her hand a squeeze then turned his attention to his nephews.

"You boys have any plans today?" Mark asked.

Cameron looked up from his bowl but didn't say anything. Mark astutely recognized the signs of a boy who was worried about his pa.

"Cameron," Alicia admonished her son, "Uncle Mark asked you a question."

"It's all right, Alicia." Mark looked at her in understanding. Alicia smiled appreciatively and sank down into a chair next to Daisy, who was getting more oatmeal on her face than in her mouth.

"Here, let me help you, dear." Alicia began to help her daughter spoon up her breakfast.

"Uncle Mark, can I go with you to the bank today?" Will asked from his seat. He just finished polishing off his second bowl of oatmeal. As much as Will enjoyed the ranch, he also enjoyed town and watching his uncle Mark work at the bank. Caleb and Alicia wondered if their younger son might not be born for ranching the way that Cameron seemed to be.

Will looked anxiously at his uncle.

"Well, I suppose that would be all right for the morning." Mark winked at his young nephew, who let out a whoop and jumped down from his chair.

"Thanks, Uncle Mark," he said as he threw his arms around his uncle.

"Aren't you forgetting something?" Mark asked him.

Will looked up curiously at his uncle.

"You need to ask your mother's permission first."

Will jumped out of his uncle's lap and ran around to his mother's chair.

"Ma, can I go with Uncle Mark to the bank this morning?" Will asked hopefully.

"I suppose so. But you have to behave and do everything Uncle Mark says."

"Yipee!" Will yelped as he jumped in the air. He dashed out of the kitchen to the guest room to brush his hair.

Alicia shook her head. She couldn't get over how a boy of six years could be so interested in an office job or understand the importance of a neat appearance.

While everyone was finishing their breakfast and small talk was taking place, a knock sounded at the door and then a deep "Hello!" resounded through the house.

"Pa!" Cameron said as he jumped from the table and ran to meet his father. Alicia sighed in relief and glanced over at Claire, who gave her an understanding smile. She rose from the table and went to meet her husband. Daisy, who smiled gleefully when she heard her father's voice, hopped down from her place and rushed over.

Caleb scooped up Daisy, gave her a big kiss on the cheek, and then sat down at the table next to Mark with Daisy on his lap.

"Good to see you," Mark said as Caleb took a seat. "Is everything all right?" Everyone leaned forward anxiously.

"Everything is just fine," Caleb answered. He looked down at his daughter, who was still in his lap. "Daisy, honey, why don't you go play with Bethany and Emily for a little while?"

Daisy shook her head no and nestled closer to her pa.

Caleb gave her a big bear hug then set her down. "Run along and play," he told her.

Daisy looked up at him for a moment; then Bethany walked over to her and took her hand. "Come on, Daisy. Let's go play with our dolls," she suggested.

Daisy smiled at the idea and skipped off with her cousins.

In the next few minutes, Caleb filled everyone in on what happened at the ranch the night before, ending with Cole's confession.

"I can't believe it," Alicia said in surprise. "I'm so glad that was resolved so quickly. Who would have thought that his own son was taking his chickens?"

"Johnson looked so mad and embarrassed. I felt sorry for Cole, though," Caleb responded. "But you know, I was so proud of the way that boy stood up in front of everyone and told his father the truth. That took real courage. And it saved an innocent man." Caleb gave Cameron's shoulders a squeeze as his son listened thoughtfully.

"At least it's over," Claire said, the relief evident in her voice. Everyone had been worried about Caleb and Dakota last night.

Caleb nodded and looked at his wife, instantly noticing that Alicia looked weary. Knowing his wife as well as he did, he could tell that she hadn't slept much the night before. Caleb stood and went to her.

"Let's get you home so you can rest," he suggested as he put his arm around his wife. Alicia glanced over at Claire.

"That sounds like a wonderful idea, but I promised Daisy that we would go visit Mrs. Tyler with Claire and her girls this morning." Alicia answered. "I'm feeling much better now that I know you're safe and all is well. Why don't you and Cameron head on back, and I'll pick up Will on my way home for lunch? He wants to help his uncle at the bank," she finished with a smile. Caleb raised his eyebrows and looked at Mark.

"Yep, he wants to be a banker like good ole Uncle Mark," Mark said as he dramatically puffed out his chest. Caleb punched him playfully in the arm.

"I think it's great that he's interested in banking. He might become a businessman one day," Caleb said thoughtfully. He glanced back at his wife and remembered her suggestion. "Well—"

"I think that's a good idea, Pa," Cameron interrupted, jumping at the chance for some alone time with his father.

"All right," Caleb responded with a grin down at his son, "it's a plan."

While Claire and Alicia busied themselves cleaning up the kitchen, the "men" all left. Mark and Will headed to the bank, while Caleb and Cameron went back to the ranch.

Shortly afterward, the ladies all headed out to see Gloria Tyler.

Dakota worked diligently all day alongside the other ranch hands. He didn't let the lack of sleep from the night before slow him down. He was too anxious to have time on his hands. He was more than relieved that young Cole showed up when he did, but what a mess! The entire town knew who he really was—that he was Rigby Buchanan, son of the infamous Buchanan family. But would the town accept that Dakota was not a criminal? That he was a changed man who already paid the price for the crimes his family committed? Would they ever understand that he was a man who had no home and no family, trying desperately to build a new life for himself? A life of integrity? A life that he could serve God and be proud of?

Dakota drove the ax down into the wood with more force than necessary and saw some of it splinter. He was cutting new posts to repair some of the fencing in the south pasture. Dakota looked in disdain at the splintered wood and wiped his forehead with his handkerchief. *Why did Fred Johnson have to find out who I was at the church social in front of everyone? Will Pastor Tyler allow me to continue working for the church and teaching Sunday school?* The questions kept tormenting Dakota as he swung blow after blow.

And, of course, there was the question of Dana. *What does she think?* Dakota stopped swinging for a second and looked out toward the direction of town. He saw nothing but fields and wondered what his precious Dana was doing right now. His biggest fear was that she might never speak to him again. Dakota knew without a doubt that he was head over heels in love with Dana Clarke. He wanted to spend the rest of his life with her, loving her and protecting her. He knew that in spite of his past he would make an excellent husband and father because, through his faith in Jesus Christ, he understood the true meaning of love. But would he ever be able to get Dana to understand that? He didn't know the answer to that, but one thing he knew for sure:

he was going to try. He wasn't going to let the most important thing in his life slip away without a fight.

He swung the ax and watched it cleanly spear through the wood.

CHAPTER 13

Dakota looked at himself nervously in the small mirror in the bunkhouse. He cleaned himself up and put on his best clothes to go to town. He was going to pay a visit to Dana Clarke. His hands were shaking as he checked the tie he had on. What if she refused to listen?

The thought was too upsetting to Dakota, so he forced himself not to think of it and instead dwell on what he might say to win her back. His mind faltered, however, and all he could think about was how disappointed Dana must be. He ran a comb through his hair and left the bunkhouse.

He slowly walked toward town and silently prayed for wisdom and the right words. All too quickly he arrived at Dr. Clarke's office. He saw lights on upstairs and stepped up to the door. He rapped on it and waited. He forced himself not to pace. Finally the door opened, and Dakota found himself looking down at his beautiful Dana. He nervously raked a hand through his hair. She closed the door behind her and stood on the porch, staring expressionlessly at Dakota.

"I, uh, came to talk to you," Dakota stumbled over the words. He looked down at her, his heart in his eyes, but his gaze was met with a cold stare.

"I'm so sorry that you found out that way," he began tentatively. "I tried to tell you before. The night that we went for a walk in the meadow, but someone called you away to deliver a baby." He stopped and looked at her. Her expression had not changed. He continued.

"I don't know what all your uncle has told you about me and my family, but I'm a changed man. Caleb and Alicia can attest to that—otherwise they wouldn't have taken me in when I came back to town. I'm a God-fearing man. I never wanted the life that my father forced me into. I hated it and left it. I paid the price for my crimes—ten years of hard labor. But God used that time to mature me and help me realize that I have potential, that I can be used by him. And ever since I was released from prison, I have done everything I can to make God proud and put together a respectable life for myself."

Dakota saw the faintest glimmer of hope in Dana's eyes, but it vanished just as quickly. The silence between them was nearly unbearable, and just when Dakota felt sure he wouldn't be able to take it anymore, Dana softly spoke.

"I don't know what you want me to say, Dakota," she began. "I mean, Rigby." She turned in frustration and paced the length of the porch. Dakota stood quietly and watched her, waiting for her to continue. "I don't even know who you are! All this time I thought you were Dakota Jones. Then I find out that you're Rigby Buchanan, former outlaw!"

"That's not who I am anymore," he protested but stopped when she put her hand up.

"No," she said firmly. "I don't want to hear it. You lied to me, Dakota, Rigby, whoever you are. I don't know who you are." She shook her head and tried to stop the tears that began to swim in her eyes. Dakota's heart turned over. He wanted to go to her and take her in his arms and whisper comforting words to her. But he stood still as Dana wiped at her eyes impatiently.

"I don't know who you are," she repeated. "I *trusted* you, and you *lied* to me. How am I supposed to get over that? How am I supposed to believe you and trust you again?"

"Just give me another chance. Please," Dakota pleaded with her. "I'll show you just how much you can trust me."

"I have to go," Dana said as she started to open the door.

"Angel—" Dakota began as he grabbed her hand.

Dana swung around to face him and yanked her hand out of his. "Don't ever call me that again!" she cried as she slammed the door behind her.

Dakota stood on the porch stunned. He felt like he had been punched in the stomach. How could he go on without the woman he loved? He slowly turned and despondently made his way back to the ranch.

The next Sunday, Dakota saddled up his horse as usual to head to the church. Caleb strode into the barn to hitch up the team to the wagon as Dakota was finishing up.

"Headed to church, son?" Caleb asked.

"Yes, sir," Dakota answered. Caleb inwardly flinched over how down Dakota sounded. His normally upbeat attitude was gone, and Caleb sometimes wondered if that was a permanent change. Dakota mounted his horse and sat for a moment.

"Something troubling you?" Caleb asked casually. He knew that Dakota was going through a difficult time.

"This is my first Sunday going to church since the social. I wonder if they will even let me come in?"

Dakota's admission tugged at Caleb's heartstrings. Dakota was practically like a son to Caleb, and he hated to see him going through this.

"I'm sure they will. Don't you worry. Why don't you ride in with us this morning?"

"Thanks, boss," Dakota said. Caleb didn't miss the note of relief in his voice. Within minutes, Caleb had the team ready to go. He helped his family into the wagon, and once they were all settled, he clucked to the team, and they started off for town with Dakota riding his horse alongside them.

Alicia tucked her arm into Caleb's and leaned over to whisper something in his ear.

"I hate to admit this, but I'm nervous about how the people at church will treat Dakota this morning. I'm afraid that some people simply won't be able to see past his family to the man he has become."

"You know I'd like to believe that our town has enough integrity to accept the fact that everyone makes mistakes and realize that people can change. But I'm concerned too. Not everyone will be willing to accept him now that they know the truth. Poor Dakota. I've never seen him like this." Ordinarily Dakota would be laughing and joking with the children on the way in to town, and today he was unusually quiet. Caleb and Alicia stopped talking when they heard Daisy speak.

"Mr. Jones, why are you sad this morning?" Dakota looked over into her innocent face. Her blond curls bounced as the wagon rolled along, and her big eyes looked up to him so trustingly.

"I'm fine, Daisy. I'm just thinking." Dakota smiled down at her to reassure her, and she grinned back up at him.

"What are you thinking about?"

"Oh, I was just thinking about church this morning. Do you like going to church?"

"Oh yes!" Daisy exclaimed as she clapped her hands together. "I like to sing 'Jesus Loves Me.'"

"That's a very nice song. And you sing it so well."

Daisy beamed at his praise. "Do you like church, Mr. Jones?"

"Yes, Daisy. I like church very much." With that, Dakota fell silent again. Caleb and Alicia exchanged a look, and Alicia sent up a silent prayer asking for help and strength to face what the morning might bring.

Caleb and Alicia pulled up into the churchyard. People were milling around outside the church building visiting. Caleb couldn't help but notice when they saw them ride up with Dakota that several people began to stare and whisper.

"Here we go," Caleb whispered to his wife as he gave her hand a squeeze. They stared into each other's eyes for a moment, reading each other's thoughts, and then Caleb jumped down and reached to help Alicia down from the wagon. Dakota tied his horse to the hitching post and lifted Daisy out of the wagon. Cameron and Will had already clambered down and ran to play with some friends.

"It'll be all right, son," Caleb said softly for Dakota's ears alone and gave him a pat on the back.

Daisy tugged at Dakota's hand. "Let's go to Sunday school now, Mr. Jones." Dakota smiled down at her slightly and then looked around him. There were dozens of people around, but at this moment he felt more isolated and alone than he had since he was released from jail. He heard the whispers, he saw the stares, and the feel of distrust in the air was palpable.

Daisy was blissfully unaware of it, and he felt a tug at his hand again. He snapped back to reality and slowly made his way toward the church. As he walked up the path, people turned to stare at him and moved away as if he had a disease. Caleb and Alicia stood with Mark, Claire, and their girls and watched in dismay at the reaction of the others. It was a reaction of fear and ignorance. They were unable to accept that Dakota had paid for his past and that he was a changed man.

Dakota went inside the church and walked to the back, where there was a small room for the children's Sunday school lessons. Normally the Sunday school room was full of chatter and laughter at this point in the morning, but Dakota didn't hear anything. He paused and took a deep breath. He slowly turned the knob and opened the door. It was just as he feared: the room was empty. Dakota felt tears sting the back of his eyes. He loved teaching Sunday school. It was important to him. It made him feel like he was making a difference in someone else's life. He forced the tears away, and Daisy looked up at him.

"Where is everyone?" she asked innocently.

"I don't know, Daisy. Maybe they are just a little late this morning," he responded, though he knew better. They weren't coming. The sting of rejection hit him hard, and he slowly sat down. Daisy sat next to him and cuddled up beside him. He could hear her softly humming "Jesus Loves Me." Dakota sat staring at the floor until he saw a large shadow fill the doorframe. He looked up to find Pastor Tyler.

"Daisy, will you go ask your mother if I can borrow her handkerchief, sweetheart?" Pastor Tyler gently asked the young girl.

"Okay," she happily obliged and skipped off to find her mother.

Pastor Tyler shut the door. He saw the misery in Dakota's face.

"You don't have to tell me," Dakota began. "I already know no one is coming. They don't want me to teach their children. They don't trust me." Pastor Tyler sat down next to Dakota.

"I'm sorry, son. I've told them that they are making a mistake and that you are an upstanding man of God. But they just don't want to hear it."

"Hasn't my life these past months proven that?" Dakota said as he stood and began to pace. "I've lived here peacefully for months, building a new life for myself. I teach Sunday school, I have a respectable job, and I help out others when they need it. Why are they going to suddenly turn their backs on me?"

"I know it's wrong and that it's not fair. You're hurting right now and understandably so. I'm hoping that once this calms down the people will see they have made a mistake. I've tried to talk with them, and I won't give up. But I'm afraid you'll have to give it some time."

Time. Dakota didn't want to give it time. The past wasn't supposed to be back to haunt him and ruin his life yet again. But here he was, standing in an empty Sunday school room in a town where he was disliked and distrusted. He sat back down and put his head in his hands.

"Dakota, you must continue to teach Sunday school. You'll at least have the Carter and Brewer children. You mustn't give up." Pastor Tyler put a hand on his shoulder. Dakota looked up at him. He wasn't sure if it would do any good, but he would try.

The music ended, and the congregation sat down. Pastor Tyler took a deep breath and made his way up to the pulpit. His eyes scanned the crowd, and he took in all of the familiar faces. Everyone was in church this morning—everyone except for Dana Clarke. Her uncle said she wasn't feeling well, but Pastor Tyler knew the real reason for her absence. He also made note of the many fidgeting children in the congregation who should be in their Sunday school class. The town looked up at him expectantly, and he began.

"Please open your Bibles to the book of John, chapter eight." He waited while the rustling of thin Bible pages turned. "In this chapter, Jesus is in the temple courts teaching the people when the Pharisees bring to him a woman who was caught in adultery. At that time, the punishment for adultery was death, and they wanted to know what Jesus thought they should do. Look with me at verses seven through eleven. The Bible says,

> So when they continued asking him, he lifted up himself, and said unto them, He that is without sin among you, let him first cast a stone at her. And again he stooped down, and wrote on the ground. And they which heard it, being convicted by their own conscience, went out one by one, beginning at the eldest, even unto the last: and Jesus was left alone, and the woman standing in the midst. When Jesus had lifted up himself, and saw none but the woman, he said unto her, Woman, where are thine accusers? Hath no man condemned thee? She said, No man, Lord. And Jesus said unto her, Neither do I condemn thee: go, and sin no more.[2]

Pastor Tyler paused and looked around. He could tell by the looks on peoples' faces that they knew where this message stemmed from. Fred Johnson looked ready to storm out of the church building.

"Friends," Pastor Tyler continued, "it is important that we take heed of the lesson that Jesus teaches us here. He is a God of love and forgiveness. Who sitting in this room is without sin? Raise your hand."

People squirmed in their seats as Pastor Tyler's gaze swept the crowd.

"And who among you has the right to cast the first stone?"

The room was deathly silent.

"Not a day goes by that you don't sin. Try as you might, you are human, and we live in a sinful, fallen world. But God offers forgiveness to every human being. None of us are worthy of the love and forgiveness that God so generously pours on us. Who are we to accept God's forgiveness yet not forgive our fellow man? We view sin on various levels and degrees. For example, I'm sure many of you would agree that stealing a horse is a worse sin than telling a lie. Not to God. To God a sin is a sin. And he forgives them all if we ask. We are also called to forgive as Jesus forgave us. Turn to the book of Matthew chapter six." Pastor Tyler paused and prayed that his message was getting through to the people in his congregation.

"In verses fourteen and fifteen, Jesus says, 'For if ye forgive men their trespasses, your heavenly Father will also forgive you: But if ye forgive not men their trespasses, neither will your Father forgive your trespasses.' You see, my friends, forgiveness is very important to God. Why do you think Jesus died such a brutal death on the cross? It was so that we undeserving human beings could have forgiveness of sins and spend eternity in heaven with God if we accept his free gift of forgiveness and salvation."

Pastor Tyler leaned on his pulpit and made eye contact with as many members of the church as he could.

"Don't let his saving work be in vain, my friends. Jesus forgives all men of all things. Who are we to do any less?"

People stood milling outside the church house, visiting after the service. Alicia and Claire talked while Caleb and Mark went to get the children.

"Hello Mrs. Carter, Mrs. Brewer." They both turned at the sound of the voice and saw Mrs. Harper. She was a kind lady about the same age as Alicia with two children of her own.

"Hello, Mrs. Harper." Alicia smiled pleasantly at her. She glanced over to see Mrs. Harper's two children playing with some others by the side of the church building.

"I know that you are a good friend of Mr. Jones," Mrs. Harper began hesitantly. Alicia felt her body tense as she waited for her to continue. "Well, I just want you to know that for me it's not a matter of forgiveness. I'm sure the boy has turned over a new leaf. But I have the safety of my children to think about. I can forgive him, but how do I know that I can trust him?"

"Oh, Mrs. Harper, of course you can trust him," Alicia said as she took her friend's hands. "I know that you don't know him as well as I do, but in the months that he has been in this town, has he ever given any of us a reason not to trust him? He is a man who truly loves the Lord. I'm confident that Dakota would never willingly do anything to hurt anyone else. He saved my life, if you'll recall. I trust my own children with him, and I would never ask you to trust yours to him if I wasn't completely confident that they would be safe."

"I feel exactly the same way," Claire chimed in. "Dakota is almost like another member of our family. You have nothing to fear."

"Thank you both for the kind words." Mrs. Harper smiled at them and then glanced behind her. "I believe you. The trouble will be convincing my husband. I must go now. Good-bye." Mrs. Harper turned and went to gather her children to go home.

"That was encouraging," Claire said as they watched her go. "But she's right. Convincing the women in this town that Dakota is trustworthy won't be the problem. It's convincing the men." Alicia nodded ruefully and looked over to see Dakota approach Dr. Clarke.

"Dr. Clarke," Dakota began as he twirled his hat around in his hands.

"Dakota." Dr. Clarke acknowledged the greeting and waited for the young man to continue.

"I'm sorry that you had to find out who I was that way. I tried to tell Dana the truth earlier, but it never worked out." Dakota's eyes focused on the ground, and Dr. Clarke felt his heart soften for the boy. As early as this morning, Dr. Clarke never wanted to encounter Dakota Jones again, but there was something about Pastor Tyler's message that gave Dr. Clarke a new perspective.

"Dakota, it's always hard to hear news like that from someone else." Dakota looked up, and Dr. Clarke studied him for a moment. "You know, you don't look anything like what you did ten years ago. I can't help but wonder if the inside of you has changed as much as the outside."

"Oh, it has," Dakota quickly confirmed. "I gave my life over to Jesus that night in the jail cell when I was only sixteen years old, and my life has never been the same since. I was never like the rest of my family, and once I became a Christian, I started living my life for God and God alone."

"I believe you, son," Dr. Clarke said.

Dakota nearly sagged with relief.

"Thank you. You have no idea what that means to me. But what about Dana? You must know, Dr. Clarke, that I have fallen in love with her. Now she won't even speak to me. What should I do?"

Dr. Clarke stood in thought for a moment. "That's a hard one, son. Dana is a woman who knows her mind. Though right now she's feeling confused and betrayed. Maybe with time she will come around. I will say this, though: if you really do love her, you won't give up."

"Thank you, sir," Dakota said. Dr. Clarke extended his hand, and Dakota returned the shake. For the first time since the night of the social, he began to feel a sliver of hope that the town would come to accept him again. He hoped that friendship with a prominent citizen like Dr. Clarke would go a long way in restoring the town's faith in him. As Dakota watched Dr. Clarke stride back toward his office, he wondered if he should even dare hope that Dana would come around.

When Dr. Clarke returned home, he found Dana in the office cleaning medical equipment. He could tell from her profile that her face was flushed as if she had been crying.

"Hello, Dana," he greeted her gently.

Dana didn't turn around. She stayed facing the wall of shelves that were full of equipment and medicines. He noticed her shoulders slightly shake.

"Come sit down," he said as he came up behind her, took her by the hand, and led her out of the office and into the parlor, where he guided her to a chair.

As Dana sat down, Dr. Clarke noticed the droop in her shoulders. He had never seen her so down before. He wanted to say something that would bring her some comfort, but he wasn't quite sure what. He cleared his throat and began to speak.

"You missed a good sermon this morning."

Dana fiddled with the rag in her hand and nodded.

"It was about forgiveness," Dr. Clarke said tentatively.

Dana looked at him wearily.

"You know that I need some time, Uncle. I need time to process and think this through."

"I know, Dana. And I'm not trying to rush you." He reached over from his chair and put his hand over hers. "But no matter our grievances, the Bible calls us to forgive."

Dana brushed away a stray curl and met her uncle's eyes. She wasn't up to this right now.

"What part are you having the hardest time dealing with?"

"Oh, Uncle." Dana stood and walked to the window, still wringing the rag she used for cleaning. "It's everything. Dakota didn't tell me who he was. Not only does he have a dark past, but he kept it all from me."

"You know, dear, there's nothing that Dakota can do about his childhood. In fact, I'm right proud of him for turning out as well as he did in spite of his childhood. Most children don't walk away from something like that and turn out the better for it. You know what was different in Dakota? What allowed him to turn his back on his past and work toward being the best man he could be in the present and future?" He waited until he had his niece's full attention before continuing. She finally sat back down and eyed him cautiously. "Jesus Christ. When Dakota accepted Jesus Christ into his life to be his Lord and Savior, he became a different man. And I think Dakota has proven that he's serious about his commitment to the Lord. Don't you?"

Dana looked down and thought for a moment.

"Of course I do, Uncle. But he's not just a friend or town's member to me. He was so much more. How am I supposed to trust him again or believe that he'll always be open and honest with me?"

"Dana, I truly believe that Dakota had every intention of telling you everything. Only Fred Johnson messed it all up. Dakota is really broken right now. Imagine having the whole town find out all of your secrets and then turn their backs on you." Dana looked up, and Dr. Clarke saw something flicker in her expression.

"Don't forget the story of Paul. He was an outspoken persecutor of Christians. But Jesus appeared to him on the road to Damascus, and that changed Paul forever. He dedicated himself to the Lord and became one of the greatest apostles in history. Jesus called Paul 'his chosen vessel' in Acts because he was going to use Paul to preach the gospel to the Gentiles. In spite of Paul's past, look at how God changed him and used him. You see, everyone deserves a second chance, my dear."

A tear rolled down Dana's cheek. She wiped it away and stood.

"I know these things in my head," she said as she looked down at her uncle. "The only problem is telling them to my heart."

As she walked out of the room, her uncle sat and prayed, wondering if anything he said resonated with his broken niece.

CHAPTER 14

A week had passed since the Pastor's sermon on forgiveness, and so far no one was changing his or her mind where Dakota was concerned. Least of all Dana.

"Why, good mornin', Dana," Mattie Thomas greeted in her chipper way as Dana walked briskly into the general store.

Dana managed a smile. She wasn't feeling chipper at all. The heartbreak she felt over Dakota Jones was worse than she could have imagined. She missed him so much but felt that things could never be the same between them. She worked day and night to put him out of her mind.

"Good morning, Mattie," Dana returned the greeting, sounding as upbeat as she could, but there was no mistaking the sad look in her eyes. "I need a few things this morning. Here's my list." She handed the list to Mattie, who took it with a smile.

"This won't take any time at all to fill. Why don't you look around for a spell while I get up everything?"

Dana nodded and walked over to the fabric. She half-heartedly eyed the material and ran a dark green shade between her fingers. The fabric was soft and inviting. She knew that Dakota would like that color on her. Dana let go of the material in disgust. What was wrong with her? Why couldn't she get that man out of her head?

"Good morning, Dana," a deep voice greeted her from behind.

Dana froze. She didn't want to turn around. She recognized the voice. She inwardly groaned then took a deep breath and turned.

"Mr. Jones," she greeted coolly. She tried not to make eye contact. She knew that if she did she would simply melt.

"Dana," Dakota's deep voice washed over her, and he took a step forward. Dana took a step back and found herself pressed against the wall with the fabric. "We really need to talk. I owe you an apology and an explanation."

"You don't owe me anything, Mr. Jones. Now if you'll excuse me." Dana tried to get past Dakota, but his full frame blocked her.

"Let me pass," she gritted between her teeth.

"Please, can we just talk for a moment?" Dana could hear the pleading in his voice. It nearly broke her already fragile heart, but she resolutely stood her ground.

"There's nothing to talk about. Good day, Mr. Jones," she said as she pushed her way past him and marched out the door.

"Dana!" Mattie called. "You forgot your order!"

"I'll be back for it, Mattie," Dana said over her shoulder as she rushed toward the safety of her uncle's office.

Dana pushed open the office door and stumbled inside. She quickly made her way up the stairs and into her bedroom. She shut the door behind her and threw herself on the bed. The tears that had been threatening came spilling forth, and she allowed herself to sob freely.

⌐◞

"Hello? Is anyone home?" Claire called as she walked into the ranch house that her brother and sister-in-law shared.

"We're in the kitchen," Alicia answered.

"Come on, girls," Claire directed to her daughters as she ushered them inside. Daisy ran out of the kitchen and into the living room to greet her aunt and cousins.

"Aunt Claire!" Daisy shouted excitedly.

"Hello, sweetheart," Claire said as she knelt to scoop up her niece. "We've come to visit you and your mother."

"Hi, Daisy," Bethany and Emily said in unison. "Let's go play dolls in your room."

Daisy squirmed out of her aunt's arms, and Bethany and Emily each took a hand and led her upstairs. Claire smiled as she watched them go then made her way into the kitchen.

"This is a nice surprise," Alicia said as she looked up from the pan of dough she was kneading.

"The girls were feeling a little restless today, so I thought a visit to Aunt Alicia's was just the thing."

"I'm glad you've come. Why don't you stay for dinner? Caleb can ride into town and get Mark."

"We'd love to." Claire smiled and tied on an apron. "Let me help you with the bread."

Alicia and Claire worked in comfortable silence. Claire brushed at a stray hair, which left a smear of flour on her cheek. She reached for a towel to wipe it off and finally asked the question that had been on her mind.

"How is Dakota?"

"Not too good," Alicia said with a sigh. "I've never seen him so down before. I really thought that Pastor Tyler's sermon would help, but so far no one seems to want to give him a chance. He's taking the rejection hard. And this thing with Dana has just broken his heart."

"You know, I think that she's as upset as Dakota is," Claire observed. "I saw her in town the other day, and she looked so forlorn. I think she misses Dakota."

Alicia stopped kneading and studied Claire for a moment.

"Do you really think so?"

"Yes. I think she's in love with him. I don't know why she's being so stubborn about this," Claire said as she worked at the dough.

"Then maybe there is still a chance for them," Alicia said thoughtfully.

"You know what I was thinking?"

Alicia recognized that tone and looked at Claire warily. She was up to something.

"I don't think I want to know," Alicia responded.

"Just hear me out. What if we have a dinner—perhaps at my house? We invite you all, and you happen to bring Dakota with you. I invite the doctor and his niece, just to be neighborly, of course," she added, and Alicia eyed her suspiciously. "And they happen to be there together. They might get an opportunity to talk. I think it's a wonderful idea."

"I don't know," Alicia said hesitantly. "It might upset them or make things worse."

"How could it make things worse?" Claire asked. "They are not speaking as it is. At least this will give them a safe atmosphere to talk if they want to."

"Perhaps we should see what Caleb and Mark think about this idea."

"Well, actually … ," Claire began.

"Claire Brewer, I know what you're thinking, and we have to tell them!"

"Why? They might not be too keen on the idea, and I really think it's worth a try. *Please?*" Claire looked at Alicia with her best pleading face.

"Don't look at me like that," Alicia warned.

"Come on, Alicia. We're doing it for Dakota and Dana's sake."

Alicia hesitated. Claire knew Alicia was uncertain but that she would go along. Claire smiled and hugged her best friend.

"This will work. You'll see," Claire said enthusiastically.

The following Saturday night, the Carter family loaded up in the wagon along with Dakota. Daisy sat in his lap and curled up against him. Cameron and Will were talking a mile a minute to their friend about the litter of kittens in the barn.

"This is going to be nice," Caleb said as he clucked to the team. He tucked Alicia's arm into his as the wagon began to roll toward town.

"Yes," Alicia said distractedly.

"Is something bothering you, sweetheart?" Caleb asked softly so no one else could hear.

Alicia shook her head. She told Claire she wouldn't say anything, but she didn't have a good feeling about this. It didn't take long before they were at the Brewer home, and everyone climbed out of the wagon.

Cameron and Will ran to the door and pounded on it with their little fists. Mark opened the door, and the boys threw themselves into their uncle's arms.

"You boys get bigger every time I see you," Mark exclaimed. "Why don't you head on in and see what Bethany and Emily are up to." Mark moved his chair to the side, and the boys raced in. He laughed and turned to see Caleb and Alicia coming to the door, and behind them he noticed Dakota carrying Daisy. His eyes widened in surprise, and he shook his head. He could recognize his wife's handiwork anywhere.

"It's good to see you, Caleb," he greeted his brother-in-law with a smile and a firm handshake. "Hello, Alicia."

Alicia leaned down and gave him a kiss on the cheek.

"How are you feeling?" she asked.

"I'm very well," he answered and then turned to greet Dakota and his niece. His gaze flickered over to meet Alicia's, and she blushed. *So she's in on it too*, he thought.

"Welcome, Dakota." Mark extended a hand, which Dakota accepted.

"Thank you for inviting me."

"How's my Daisy-girl?" Mark reached out his arms to Daisy, and she jumped in his lap and threw her arms around him.

"What a good hug!" he exclaimed. Daisy grinned and then jumped down to join her brothers and cousins.

"Make yourselves at home," Mark said as he closed the door and led everyone from the foyer to the living room. Caleb and Alicia walked in, but Dakota froze midstride as he saw who was sitting in the living room. Caleb looked down at Alicia, who looked back at him, smiled slightly, shrugged, then went quickly to the kitchen.

As they entered, Dr. Clarke stood. Dana turned and locked eyes with Dakota. Time stood still as their gaze remained fixed on each other. Dr. Clarke broke the silence.

"It's good to see you, Dakota," he said as he took a step forward and extended his hand toward the young man.

Dakota shook his head, breaking his reverie.

"I, uh ... " He took the doctor's hand. "Thanks. You too."

Mark looked over at Caleb and raised his eyebrows. Caleb understood the silent message. Their wives set this up. Caleb shook his head and looked over toward Dana, but she had slipped away into the kitchen. The men sat down and began to chat amicably, though it was evident to all how terribly uncomfortable Dakota looked.

"Why did you do this?" Dana cried in a loud whisper as she burst into the kitchen. Alicia was dipping up some potatoes, and her hand stopped in midair. Claire was reaching for the plates, and she stopped as well.

"Why in the world would you do something like this? I thought you were my friends."

"Oh, Dana." Alicia reached for Dana's hand, and they sat down at the kitchen table. "Please don't feel betrayed. It's because we're your friends that we invited you both over."

"Do you have any idea how uncomfortable this is for me?" Dana's eyes welled up with tears. It was almost Claire's undoing.

"Don't be mad at Alicia," Claire chimed in. She sat on the other side of Dana. "This was all my idea."

"No," Alicia said firmly. She would never let Claire take all the blame. "We're equally to blame. But listen to us, honey. We've watched both you and Dakota these last couple of weeks, and you're both so sad and miserable. Dakota is completely broken over what happened, Dana. You have to know that. You mean the world to him. And everyone can tell that you're hurting too. The two of you need to resolve this, and we thought that if we provided a safe atmosphere for you that it might help to break the ice."

"You had no right to get involved. This is none of your business," Dana said defiantly as she wiped away tears.

"Maybe not. But you and Dakota are our friends, and we just wanted to help," Claire added.

"You know, Dana," Alicia began, "you may think that Dakota was deliberately hiding his past from you, but he spoke with Caleb on more than one occasion over how to tell you and when to tell you. It was always his intent to tell you everything. Please don't be so angry with him. He never meant for you to feel betrayed."

"Don't let Fred Johnson have so much power that he can drive you two apart," Claire said as she reached over and patted Dana on the shoulder. "He's done enough damage. Just talk to Dakota."

Dana sniffed and daintily wiped her nose with her handkerchief. She stood and smoothed down her dress.

"Thank you both, but this is none of your concern," she said and then turned on her heel and left the kitchen. Alicia and Claire looked at each other helplessly.

The meal went smoothly enough thanks to the entertainment and chatter of the children. Dakota and Dana ate silently, neither one looking up from their plates. Alicia felt so guilty and miserable. She was sure that Claire felt the same, but she was trying to be a good hostess and spent the evening smiling and chatting. Alicia felt Caleb's gaze on her throughout the evening but was too ashamed to make eye contact with him. It was one of the longest meals Alicia had ever known, and when it was finally over she hurriedly went to the kitchen to begin cleaning up. The men went to sit in the living room, and amidst the bustle Dana silently made her way out the door.

Claire went back to the dining room to get the last of the silverware to wash and noticed that everyone was gone. She stuck her head into the living room to see if the children were in there or if they had gone back upstairs to play and noticed that Dana was missing. She went back to the kitchen, expecting to find her there.

"Where's Dana?" she asked as she looked around.

"She hasn't been in here," Alicia answered. "Oh, Claire, I feel so bad for putting her in that awkward position. What were we thinking?"

"We were thinking that it's high time they settle this," Claire responded firmly. "Those two are made for each other, and I can't stand to see that fall apart because of a misunderstanding."

"Perhaps," Alicia answered slowly. "But then maybe Dana was right. Maybe this isn't our concern." Claire looked over at her, and Alicia met her gaze. Silently they finished up cleaning the kitchen then went to join the others.

Dana walked purposefully toward home. She was so angry with Alicia and Claire. *How could they do that?*

"Dana," a deep voice called from behind. Dana groaned as she slowly turned. Dakota was quickly making his way toward her.

"Dana, I'm so sorry. I had nothing to do with that." Dakota stopped just in front of her and looked down. The moon cast a soft glow on her face, and he couldn't help but notice how beautiful she was.

"I know. What an awkward dinner."

"Dana." Dakota hesitated for a moment. He looked down at his shoes and shuffled his feet back and forth before finally looking at her again. "Can we just talk for a moment?"

Dana looked around uncertainly. She waited so long to reply that Dakota almost turned around to walk back to the Brewers.

"All right," she agreed. "But just for a moment." Dakota heaved an inward sigh of relief. The two walked silently toward the bench outside Dr. Clarke's office. They sat down, and Dana looked at Dakota expectantly.

"Dana, I know that you're feeling hurt and betrayed right now. I can't tell you how sorry I am. By now you know about my background and who my family was. What you also need to know is that I never wanted to be a part of the criminal world my father created for us. You had a childhood filled with happy memories and parents who loved you. I had a childhood of misery with no mother and a father who was a drunkard and a criminal. Yet in spite of it all, I managed to escape that life. When my father and brothers kidnapped Alicia, I let her escape."

"I know," Dana said quietly.

Dakota gently took her hand.

"And do you also know that I turned myself in? That Alicia and I both came to know the Lord on the same night? And that accepting Jesus Christ into my life has changed it completely? I've never been the same since. I spent ten years in prison, where I told as many men who would listen about Jesus. When I got out, I came back to Darby because the only people who cared about me in the world were here—Caleb and Alicia Carter and Pastor Tyler. Before I was sentenced, Alicia made me a promise. She said that when I got out of prison, I was welcome to come back, and she and Caleb would try to help me get a fresh start. And that's what I've done."

Dana sniffed, and Dakota pulled out a handkerchief from his pocket. He gently dabbed at her eyes then handed it to her.

"Why didn't you tell me?" she asked just above a whisper.

"Oh, Dana, I tried to tell you. Believe me. I tried. I was going to tell you the night you were called away to help deliver a baby. I agonized over the right time to tell you, but it never worked out." Dakota stood and began to pace the boardwalk in front of the little bench.

"It wasn't right for Fred Johnson to do what he did. To announce to the town about me. He was mad over his chickens. He falsely accused me, he's got the town angry and distrusting of me, and he's hurt the relationship I hold most dear." Dakota knelt in front of Dana. "Can you ever forgive me?"

Dana wiped at her eyes. "It's not a matter of forgiveness," she began. "I can forgive you for not telling me. It's a matter of trust."

Dakota hung his head.

"Dakota, I've never felt so betrayed in my entire life. I allowed myself to fall in love with you only to find out that you're not who I thought you were at all."

"Yes I am," Dakota said with urgency as he sat back down next to her. "You fell in love with the man I am now. I kept nothing of who I am now from you—just who I was ten years ago."

"Regardless, Dakota, I don't know if I'll be able to trust you again."

"I understand," Dakota responded sadly. Though, to be honest, he didn't really understand at all.

"I'm so sorry," Dana whispered as she rose from the bench and quickly went inside. She closed the door and leaned back against it. Her eyes slid shut. What a difficult night this had been.

She opened her eyes and wearily made her way up the stairs. She readied for bed, yet even when she slipped under the covers her mind wouldn't stop reeling. Thoughts and fears nagged at her, and she tossed and turned for what felt like hours. She replayed the evening over and over in her mind. Seeing Dakota walk into the Brewers' living room had caused her pulse to race. She hated that she still felt such powerful emotions whenever he was nearby. Deep down she wanted to believe that what Dakota told her was true. That he had always meant to tell her the truth. But she stubbornly resisted the feelings. It scared her how deeply in love she was with Dakota and how the impact of the hurt and betrayal had nearly caused her to suffocate with grief.

Dana threw back the covers and went to stand in front of the window and gazed out into the meadow. Thoughts continued to bombard her, and she knew she wouldn't be getting much sleep tonight.

Pray.

The word echoed so loudly in her heart that she actually looked around the room to make sure no one was there.

Pray.

A single tear made its way down her cheek as she realized that in her anger and grief she had not taken the time to pray and seek God's counsel. She turned from the window, walked over to her bed, and knelt. Tears spilled forth as she whispered a fervent prayer asking for God's guidance and strength. When she rose, her mind was no longer tortured by worrisome thoughts. She lay down and drifted into a peaceful sleep.

Dakota walked slowly back to the ranch. His soul cried out in anguish to God. He couldn't understand why this had happened. Everything was going so well, and then Fred Johnson ruined everything. Why did God allow this to happen? It was the thought that Dakota couldn't rid himself of. He struggled to understand what purpose God could have in allowing this to happen just when his life was beginning to feel normal and happy.

He continued on in silent prayer, asking for patience and wisdom. He didn't know how to proceed anymore. Dana had made it clear that she wasn't going to change her mind. Dana's stubbornness caused anger to rear its ugly head, and Dakota's jaw flexed. He didn't want to feel anger toward her; he wanted to win her back. But at this point, he was beginning to feel as if it were hopeless.

He walked past the main house at the Blue Star and heard the voices of children's laughter wafting down from the windows. Dakota paused and listened wistfully. That was what he wanted more than anything else. A family of his own. All of his life he had wanted a real family. A wife and children to love, support, and come home to after a long day of work. Dakota sighed as he realized that the Carters were the closest thing to real family that he'd ever had.

Dakota continued on toward the bunkhouse with a thought beginning to form in his mind—a thought that troubled him. Yet he couldn't get it out of his head. If Dana wouldn't change her mind, should he even stay in Darby? If a real family was what he wanted, shouldn't he pursue that? But the thought of leaving caused him to feel sick to his stomach. It was a lose-lose situation as far as Dakota could see. Staying would mean living without Dana and possibly missing out on a family of his own, but leaving would mean turning his back on the life he was building for himself and the only people in the world who cared about him.

The thought plagued him for the rest of the night.

CHAPTER 15

"Mr. Jones! Mr. Jones!" Dakota heard two young voices yell. Cameron and Will were running toward him as fast as their legs could carry them.

"What is it?" he asked as he knelt down to be eye level with them.

"Will you please take us fishing today?" young Will asked, a slight lisp making *please* sound more like *pweese*.

"Well, I don't know," he began but was interrupted when the boys' father walked up.

"What's going on?" Caleb wanted to know.

"Pa, we want Mr. Jones to take us fishing," Cameron answered. He looked at Dakota hopefully. The adoration he felt for this man shone in his eyes, and it made Dakota feel both proud and humbled.

"Mr. Jones might have something else to do on this fine Saturday afternoon."

"As a matter of fact," Dakota began as he winked at the boys, "I was hoping to spend this sunny day with two of my favorite boys down at the creek."

"Yippee!" Will shouted as he jumped in the air.

"You boys better run up to the house and get your fishing gear. And if you ask nicely, your ma might even fix a picnic lunch for you," Caleb told the eager boys. They took off at a sprint toward the house. Caleb chuckled as he watched them go. "They sure are fond of you, Dakota."

"You're raising two very fine boys, sir." Dakota paused for a moment. Caleb could tell that he was wrestling with something. And he had a good idea what it was. He could tell by Dakota's face that things weren't resolved between him and Dana.

"Could I talk to you for a minute before they get back?" Dakota asked at last.

"Absolutely. What's on your mind, son?"

Dakota took off his Stetson and wiped his forehead with the bandana that hung around his neck. He shifted uncomfortably.

"I've been thinking that it might be best for me to leave Darby." Caleb looked at him thoughtfully and nodded slowly.

"I was afraid it would only be a matter of time before you decided that. I honestly thought Dana would come around."

"No, sir, she won't. She says she can't trust me anymore. I can't say as I blame her; though I am a little put out that she won't even try to see my side in all of this. If only Fred Johnson hadn't seen the brand on my arm!" He put the Stetson back on his head with more force than necessary, and Caleb saw the muscles in his jaw flex.

"I know how upsetting this is for you."

"Forgive me, boss, but I don't think you do. How can you understand? You are a well-respected citizen from a good family. You always have been. Not me. When I did start a new life for myself, it all fell apart right before my eyes. The woman I love feels betrayed. No one in town will talk to me. Only your children and the Brewer's children come to Sunday school anymore. You can't really understand that kind of rejection."

"You're right." Caleb put a hand on his shoulder. "I'm sorry, Dakota. Where would you go?"

"I don't know yet." He paused then looked at Caleb with searching eyes. "Caleb, do you think I should leave?"

Caleb took a deep breath. "You have to decide what's right for you," Caleb began carefully. "Have you prayerfully considered this? Is leaving what God is calling you to do? Or are you leaving just to run away?"

"We're ready!" Will called as he rushed toward them, fishing pole in hand.

"Thanks, boss," Dakota lowered his voice. "You've given me a lot to think on."

"I'm here if you need me."

"Do you want to come too, Pa?" Will asked as he looked up at his father.

"No, Son," Caleb got on one knee to look at his son. "This is yours and Cameron's special trip with Mr. Jones. Make sure you do as he says."

"Yes, Pa."

Caleb looked over at Cameron, who was approaching the group. "Keep an eye on your little brother."

"Yes, sir." Caleb watched with pride. His sons were chattering a mile a minute as they went off with Dakota, a man whom Caleb also thought of as a son.

"Doc Clarke!" Paul Vickery called as he burst into the office carrying a young boy.

"My uncle isn't here right now," Dana said as she came into the room, wiping her hands on the apron tied around her waist. She stopped short when she saw Vickery. "Lay him down over here," she ordered as she moved toward the nearest patient table.

"My boy is awful sick," Vickery said as he laid his eight-year-old son, Steven, on the table. Dana made note of his flushed cheeks and felt his forehead.

"He's burning up. How long has he been like this?" Dana asked as she went to get a basin of cool water.

"About an hour. He started coughing and complaining of a headache. The next thing I know he's burning up with fever."

"Steven," Dana said gently as she put a cool rag on his head, "tell me where it hurts."

"It hurts all over," he moaned.

"You'll be all right," Dana cooed softly. Steven closed his eyes. Dana walked over to her uncle's medicine cabinet and brought out a container filled with powder. She placed a small amount in a cup and added some water.

"Drink this, Steven." She put her hand behind his head and helped him take a sip. "It will help bring down the fever."

"What's wrong with him, Dana?" Vickery asked anxiously.

Dana had a good idea of what it was but wanted to wait until her uncle saw him—just to be sure.

"I'm not entirely certain," she responded. "My uncle should be here soon. In the meantime, we'll try to keep him comfortable and lower his fever." Dana placed the rag in the basin, squeezed out the excess water, and placed the cool cloth back on Steven's head, all the while praying for this boy and for her uncle's swift return.

Dakota lay down on his bunk and looked up at the ceiling. His conversation with Caleb kept running through his mind. *Have you prayerfully considered this? Is leaving what God is calling you to do? Or are you leaving just to run away?* He knew that he had not taken the time to really pray over what God wanted him to do. He was frustrated and upset over the way the town treated him, over not being able to teach more students in Sunday school, and most of all, he was upset over Dana. He didn't know how he could go on without her, but he knew that he would have to. Leaving seemed the best option for him.

He climbed out of his bunk and got down on his knees. He rested his forehead against his hands and took a deep breath. "Father God," he began, "please help me. I don't know what to do anymore. I haven't felt this lost in a long time. The pain over losing my Sunday school class and Dana is more than I can bear. I want to leave Darby. Please show me if that's what you want for me. I don't want to run away, but I don't see how I can stay here anymore. Please guide me. In Jesus's name, amen."

He slowly rose and got back into his bunk. An answer didn't come right away, but Dakota knew that God had heard his prayer. He closed his eyes as sleep rushed in to claim him.

Vickery slept at the doctor's office that night to stay close to his son. When Dr. Clarke returned earlier that day, he examined the boy and confirmed Dana's suspicion. Steven had influenza. Vickery had ridden back home to tell his wife, who had stayed home to care for their other children, and gather a few things.

They put Steven in a patient room in the back of the office and took turns wiping him down with a cool rag to help bring his fever down. They also periodically gave him quinine that they mixed in a glass of water to help reduce the fever. It was a difficult night for all of them. Steven thrashed about as the fever raged through his body, while Dr. Clarke, Dana, and Vickery all took turns wiping him down.

At one point, Dr. Clarke pulled his niece aside and whispered, "I hope no one else in town gets this." Dana nodded. The thought of an influenza epidemic was more than she could handle right now.

"Dana, you should get some rest," her uncle added. "We don't know what the next few days will bring." She agreed and went to her room, where she gratefully sank into bed and fell asleep.

The next morning Dana woke early and went to check on Steven. Vickery was asleep in a chair by the bed, and Dana quietly walked over to the young patient and placed her hand on his forehead. The fever still had not broken. Dana took the basin and left the room to fill it up with fresh water.

"How is he?" her uncle asked as he passed her in the hallway.

"The fever hasn't broken yet."

"Well, he's a healthy young boy. He's got a good chance of pulling through this." Dr. Clarke then went in to check on Steven and shut the door quietly behind him.

While Dana was filling up the basin, a knock sounded at the door. She went to open it and gasped. Levi Thomas was slumped against one of the posts on the front porch. His face was flushed.

"Miss Clarke," he said in a wobbly voice, "I ain't feelin' so good." Dana ran to him just before he collapsed on the porch. She helped him into the office, supporting most of his weight with one shoulder. She helped lay him down on a patient table and quickly went in search of her uncle. She quietly opened Steven's room and signaled for her uncle to step outside.

"What's wrong?"

"Levi Thomas just came in. He's got influenza."

"Oh no." Dana led him downstairs to the patient table, where poor Levi was groaning. Dr. Clarke gave him some quinine, and he and Dana helped Levi to a room.

"Mr. Thomas," Dana asked in a quiet voice, "does your wife know that you're sick?"

"No ma'am," Levi was barely able to get the words out. He shivered. "I didn't want her to start frettin'." Dana brought a basin of cool water over and used the rag to wipe down Levi's chest, arms, face, and neck. While she was working, her uncle spoke.

"Dana, I need you to go to the general store and tell Mattie about this. She needs to know. Get some supplies while you're there. It looks like we might have us an epidemic on our hands." Dana nodded and quickly left the room. She grabbed her shawl and headed out the door, all the while praying for God's healing hand to protect the town and the two who were already sick.

"Mattie, where's Levi this morning?" an impatient customer demanded.

Mattie looked up and smiled pleasantly. "He stepped out for a minute. He should be back shortly."

"I ain't got all day," the customer muttered under his breath as he moved away from the counter to look at other supplies.

A bell jingled, and Mattie looked up to see who was entering the store.

"Why, hello, Dana," she greeted warmly. Dana rushed up to her, and Mattie could immediately tell that something was wrong. Dana didn't offer her usual smile, and her eyes were filled with concern.

"What's wrong, honey?"

"Mattie, I need to speak with you privately." Mattie looked around the store and, seeing that no one needed her at the moment, she ushered Dana into the living quarters that she and Levi shared off to the side of the store.

"What's going on, Dana?"

"Levi came to our office." Dana watched as Mattie's eyes widened. "He's very ill, Mattie. He has"—Dana leaned in closer to whisper in Mattie's ear—"influenza." Mattie pulled back with a gasp as her hand flew to her throat.

"The grippe?"

"Yes, ma'am. We have another case that came in yesterday with it too."

"Oh, no. I have to get to Levi," Mattie began as she turned toward the stairs that led up to their bedroom.

"No," Dana said as she reached for Mattie's arm. Mattie swung around to face her.

"What do you mean *no*? He's my husband. I have to be there." Mattie pulled free of Dana's grip, and Dana quickly put herself between the stairway and Mattie.

"Please, listen to me. With two people sick already, this may be the beginning of an epidemic. If that's the case, the fewer people that are exposed, the better. Levi needs you to stay here—healthy and strong—to run the general store. Dr. Clarke and I will take good care of him." Tears welled up in Mattie's eyes.

"I just don't rightly know if I can stay away," she whispered.

"Please, Mattie."

"How is he?"

"Well," Dana slowly began, "he has a very high fever. We're doing our best to bring it down." Mattie walked over to the sofa and sank down on it with her head in her hands. Dana pulled a handkerchief out of her pocket and handed it to Mattie. She dabbed at her eyes.

"All right," Mattie finally acquiesced. "I'll stay for now."

"Thank you," Dana said as she put her hand over Mattie's.

"Take good care of him."

"We will," Dana promised. Mattie composed herself, and she and Dana walked back into the general store, where Dana made a few purchases and then quickly made her way back to help her uncle.

"Thank goodness you're here," was the greeting Dana received when she walked back into the doctor's office. She looked around. There were at least half a dozen more people who had been brought in. She placed her packages on the desk, and Dr. Clarke walked toward her.

"As you can see," he said as he gestured with his hand around the room, "we've got a full-blown epidemic on our hands. I need you to go out one more time. Tell Pastor Tyler what's going on. We'll need all the prayers we can get. The town needs to know so that people can be aware and look for symptoms. This office will have to be quarantined." Dr. Clarke shook his head. There hadn't been an epidemic in Darby in more years than he could count. Dana put her hand on his shoulder reassuringly.

"I'll be back as soon as I can."

Dana knocked on the door to the little house that the Tylers shared. Gloria opened the door, and Dana took a step back. She had been exposed and didn't want to spread the disease, especially to those more elderly.

"Hello, dear," Gloria greeted. "Won't you come in?"

"I'm afraid I can't. Is Pastor Tyler here? I need to speak with both of you."

"Certainly. Are you sure you wouldn't like to come in?"

"I'd like to, Gloria, but I really can't."

Gloria's face reflected her confusion. She left the front door open and went in search of her husband. They returned a moment later, and Pastor Tyler took a step outside toward her. Again, Dana stepped back.

"Pastor Tyler, there's an influenza epidemic," Dana wasted no time in saying.

"Oh no," Gloria breathed as she put her hands over her mouth in shock. Pastor Tyler's eyes widened.

"We need prayers, and we need you to spread the word around town. People need to be aware so they can take precautions and watch for symptoms."

"What kind of symptoms?" Pastor Tyler asked.

"Headache, feeling achy, and a fever are the main ones." Dana looked past Pastor Tyler to see that Gloria's head was already bent and her mouth moving feverishly as she silently petitioned the Lord on behalf of the town.

"I'll certainly spread the word," Pastor Tyler responded. "You and Doc take care not to get sick yourselves."

"We will. Thank you," Dana said as she turned and rushed back to the doctor's office.

CHAPTER 16

"Dakota?" Caleb called as he entered the barn. He had seen Dakota enter the barn just a moment ago.

"Over here, boss," Dakota responded. Caleb walked toward the back, where Dakota was cleaning out a stall. Dakota propped the rake against a post and wiped his forehead with the back of his hand. He looked to Caleb expectantly.

"Alicia and I need to ride in to town for a while. Daisy's birthday is coming up, and we want to get her something really special. But we don't want her or her brothers to know about it. You know what a hard time those boys have keeping secrets."

"That's for sure." Dakota chuckled.

"Would you mind keeping an eye on them while we're gone?"

"No problem, boss. I'd be happy to."

"Thanks, son," Caleb said as he gave Dakota a pat on the back. "We shouldn't be gone long."

Dakota cleaned himself up while Caleb hitched up the wagon, and soon the couple was headed toward town, leaving Cameron, Will, and Daisy in Dakota's capable hands.

Caleb and Alicia rolled slowly into town, fully enjoying the time alone together. With three young children, there wasn't much alone time for the couple. Caleb rested one arm on the wagon seat behind his wife and held the reins with the other.

"I need to get some material for a new dress for Daisy," Alicia was saying as Caleb started to bring the wagon to a stop. Alicia could tell that Caleb had not heard a word of what she just said. "Caleb? What's the matter?"

"Look over there." Caleb motioned with his head toward Dr. Clarke's office. Alicia put her hand up to shield the sun from her eyes as she looked in the direction that Caleb told her. One of the men in town was nailing a board that had the word *Quarantine* crudely written on it.

"Oh, Caleb," Alicia murmured as her hand came to her throat. She watched as a distraught mother tried to make her way into the doctor's office. Her back was to Alicia, but Alicia could tell that she was crying. Dr. Clarke was shaking his head, and Alicia caught snippets of the conversation that was taking place.

"Please let me come in and see my child," the woman cried.

"I'm sorry, ma'am, but we can't allow anyone else to be exposed."

"But that's my child in there! He needs me."

"We'll take good care of him. He needs you to be healthy when he gets well. I'm sorry, but this is the only way to prevent further spread of the epidemic."

Alicia watched with tears in her eyes as the doctor slowly closed the door, and the woman sank onto the porch steps with her head in her hands. Her shoulders shook, and Alicia turned her head in an attempt to block out the heart-wrenching scene.

Caleb clicked to the team, and they rode on. The general store was the best place to go to get information, and that was where they were headed anyway. He drew up the team outside the store, and he and Alicia watched wide-eyed. Dozens of people were hurriedly coming in and out, leaving with large basketfuls of supplies.

Caleb let out a low whistle.

"I've never seen anything like it," Alicia said as she put a hand on her husband's arm. He placed his hand over hers reassuringly.

"Let's go see what this is about."

Once inside the general store, it was hard to move around. People frantically bustled about, rudely bumping into anyone in his or her way. Caleb held Alicia's hand and guided them toward the counter. Mattie was a flustered mess. Her forehead was damp with perspiration, and a few strands of hair had freed themselves from her bun and were hanging limply around her face.

"Mattie, what's going on?" Alicia asked.

"What's that?" Mattie nearly yelled as she leaned forward.

"What's going on?" Alicia repeated, more loudly this time.

"There's an influenza epidemic."

Alicia gasped and turned frightened eyes toward her husband. She had heard of epidemics and how fatal they could be, but never had she lived in a town that went through one. Caleb squeezed her hand.

"Mattie, these people are cleaning you out," Caleb pointed out. Mattie let out a sigh.

"Caleb, I don't rightly know what to do."

Caleb looked around. His height gave him an advantage, and his gaze swept over the mercantile. "Where's Levi?" He looked to Mattie and, with one look at her face, knew the answer. Tears swam in her eyes.

"Mattie, can we talk in the storeroom?"

"Certainly," Mattie said, "but only for a moment." She glanced at the store full of panicked townspeople, and Caleb nodded in understanding. The three stepped into the storeroom, and Caleb closed the door.

"My poor Levi has the grippe," Mattie admitted as a tear fell. "Dana Clarke asked me not to come tend to him. She says I shouldn't be exposed. I can't rightly stand here knowing my Levi needs me." She wrung her hands. "I don't know what to do."

Caleb stood thoughtfully for a moment. "You don't want to run out of supplies, first off," he began. He looked around the storeroom that was still well stocked. "Tell you what, once what you have in the mercantile is gone, don't replenish it until the next day. We have to make supplies last. When today's supply runs out, close up early and open again tomorrow."

Mattie nodded, grateful for the advice.

"Is there anyone that could help you around here?" Alicia asked gently.

"Well, I suppose Carl Holding might be willing to help. With this epidemic, he probably ain't gettin' too much business at the hotel." Alicia nodded. Yes, the sheriff's brother might be just the person to help Mattie.

Pounding at the door caused Mattie and Alicia to jump. "Hey, Mattie, we need you out here!" a gruff voice yelled. Mattie looked at Caleb and Alicia helplessly.

"I have to go," she said as she started to move past Caleb.

"We'll see if we can find Carl Holding for you," Caleb told her.

"Much obliged."

Alicia watched her go sadly. She looked as if she carried the weight of the world on her shoulders.

"Let's get what we need and get out of here. I'm afraid that Daisy's present will have to wait." Caleb steered Alicia out of the storeroom, and they bought some necessities—flour, salt, beans, etc.—and climbed back into their wagon.

"We'd better make sure that Mark and Claire know and are okay," Caleb said. Alicia nodded her assent, but before going to Mark and Claire's, Caleb and Alicia made a stop at the hotel. There was no one in the lobby, and the couple walked up to the desk, where Carl Holding stood, looking grim.

"Good afternoon," he greeted.

"Hello, Carl," Caleb answered.

"So I guess you've heard the news."

"Unfortunately. That's why we're here. We've just come from the general store, and Mattie is beside herself. It seems as if the entire town is trying to buy up all of the merchandise. And to top it off, Levi has the influenza."

Carl rubbed the back of his neck. "Poor Mattie. I'm really concerned, Caleb. This could get a lot worse before it gets better."

Caleb glanced at his wife, whose face blanched in fear. "Maybe it won't spread any further."

"Let's hope not," Carl responded.

"Actually the reason we stopped by was to ask if you could lend Mattie a hand if you have the time. She mentioned that you might be able to help."

"Certainly. I've helped out there on occasion before, so I know how it works. And considering"—Carl's gaze swept the empty room—"how busy we are, I think I could leave my assistant in charge for a while."

"Thanks, Carl," Caleb said as he extended a hand.

"Take care," Carl said as he returned the handshake.

"I've got one! I've got one!" Will cried as the line on his fishing pole grew taut. In his excitement, Will began to jerk back on the pole.

"Easy does it," Dakota urged as he came over. With Dakota's help and instruction, Will reeled in a small fish. He jumped up and down in excitement.

"Look what I caught, Mr. Jones! Cameron, come see my fish!"

Cameron forced a smile and walked over. They had been fishing for the better part of an hour, and he didn't have a single bite. Now his little brother had caught a fish. He eyed it skeptically. It was awfully small. He looked up to see Dakota watching him. Dakota raised an eyebrow as if reading Cameron's thoughts and warning him against voicing them.

"Good job, Will. You caught a nice one," Cameron said stiffly.

"Thanks! Ain't it a beauty?" Will's joy at catching a fish softened Cameron, and he couldn't help but smile at his little brother.

"It sure is." Dakota tousled Will's hair. "Daisy, come take a look." Dakota looked back at Daisy, who was sitting quietly in the shade. Dakota started toward her. It was unlike Daisy to sit quietly with all of this excitement going on around her.

"Daisy, don't you want to see Will's fish too?" She shook her head slightly, and Dakota noticed that her cheeks were flushed. "Are you feeling all right? Maybe we should go back to the house."

"Okay," Daisy agreed.

"No way!" Will shouted. "I want to catch more fish!"

Dakota turned to face the boy and spoke gently, but firmly. "Will, your sister isn't feeling well. We need to go inside." Will kicked at a pebble and started mumbling under his breath. Nevertheless, he did what he was told. Dakota reached out a hand to Daisy, who took it and, on wobbly legs, tried to stand.

"Mr. Jones," Daisy said faintly before collapsing into his arms. Dakota scooped her up.

"She's burning up," he said under his breath. "Cameron, run get Mr. Carpenter. Now!" Cameron was frightened by the look he saw in Dakota's eyes. He knew that something was seriously wrong. He dropped his pole and ran as fast as his legs could carry him to find the foreman.

Dakota walked over to the stream and gently scooped up some cool water to put on Daisy's head and arms.

"Why are you doing that, Mr. Jones?" Will asked.

"Daisy has a high fever. I'm trying to cool her off to bring her temperature back down." After a minute or so, Dakota stood carrying Daisy and took long strides back to the house. Will had to jog to keep up. John Carpenter and Cameron came running toward them.

"What's going on?" John yelled as he approached.

"Daisy's awful sick. I've got to get her to Doc Clarke. Can you keep an eye on Cameron and Will until the boss gets back?"

"Sure thing. I'll get your horse saddled." John hurriedly saddled a horse for Dakota and held Daisy while he mounted then passed her up to him.

"Will she be all right?" Cameron's voice quivered.

"Don't you worry, Cameron. You either, Will. God and Doc Clarke will take good care of her. Thanks, John!" Dakota called over his shoulder as he started toward town with Daisy nestled in front of him.

"I wonder how the epidemic got started?" Claire mused as the four adults sat in the living room sipping coffee.

"I have no idea, but it scares me," Alicia answered with a shudder. She recounted the scene she witnessed at the doctor's office on their way in to town.

"I can't imagine being told that I couldn't be with my child when they were that sick," Claire said. "How could Dr. Clarke do that?"

"He's only doing what he thinks is best," Mark answered. "The more people who are exposed, the more likely the sickness will spread."

"Well, I hope you're well-stocked on supplies. The general store will be wiped out soon," Caleb remarked dryly.

"Fortunately, we just went by there yesterday, so we should be all right for a while. How long do you think this will last?" Claire asked.

"There's no way to know for sure. Let's hope not long."

"We weren't even able to shop for Daisy's birthday present as we had planned. The store was too full to move around," Alicia told them. "If this epidemic lasts too long, we may have to postpone her birthday celebration."

"Try not to worry about that," Claire patted her arm. "We'll pray that this will pass quickly."

CHAPTER 17

Dana looked around and sighed. There were over a dozen townspeople sick with influenza. There were only three patient rooms, so everyone had to share, and there were cots set up everywhere else.

Dana pushed back some loose hair from her forehead. She reached for the water bucket. She needed to go out and refill it.

"Dana," her uncle called. She turned around with her hand still on the doorknob. "Come quickly." Dana set the bucket down and followed her uncle to the back of the building where the patient rooms were. She walked in one of the rooms and gasped. Steven Vickery was sitting up in bed with a huge grin on his face. His father stood beside him and looked ready to burst with happiness.

"His fever broke a little while ago," Dr. Clarke told his niece. Dana's hands were over her heart and tears glistened in her eyes.

"Thank the Lord," she whispered.

"This will be the room where we will put those who are on the mend," Dr. Clarke added. He looked around at the other patients in the room. "We'll have to move the others to the other two rooms and the cots." Dana nodded.

"Thank you both for helping my boy," Vickery said gratefully. "As I've already been exposed to the grippe, I'd like to stay on here and help, if that's all right." The exhausted doctor and his young nurse were visibly relieved.

"Absolutely. We'd appreciate the help."

A pounding coming from the front door caused them all to turn at once. Dr. Clarke cast a wary look at his niece, and they exited the room. The pounding of Dana's heart matched the pounding on the door.

Please, Lord, not another one, Dana prayed.

Dr. Clarke opened the door and was surprised to see Mattie Thomas standing in the doorway with one hand on her hip and another holding a small, brown suitcase. She didn't look sick, but it was hard to tell.

"Why, Mattie," Dana said in surprise, "are you all right?"

"I'm fit as a fiddle. I'm here to care for my husband," she answered as she brushed past them and into the office.

"Now wait just a minute," Dr. Clarke protested. "I thought you told her to stay at home," he said in a low voice to Dana.

"I did," she responded softly.

"You both wait just a minute," Mattie retorted. "Don't go gettin' onto the girl, Howard. She did tell me to stay home. But did you really think I'd listen? Carl's helpin' out at the mercantile, and I'm going to see to my husband." She paused and looked around. "And from the looks of things, you sure could be needin' some help." Dr. Clarke saw the steely resolve in her eyes and knew that she could not be dissuaded. Besides, they could use the extra help.

"All right," he acquiesced. "Follow me." He led her to the back to show her where Levi was staying.

Dana sighed as she picked up the water bucket once again. She was relieved for the extra pair of hands. Neither she nor her uncle had slept much the past few days, and from the look of things, that wasn't about to change anytime soon. She opened the door and took a step outside just as a tall figure ran up the steps and nearly collided with her. She stepped out of the way just in time and followed him into the office. He turned to face her, and she drew in a sharp breath.

"Dakota," she breathed. Noticing the small bundle in his arms, she immediately focused on the task at hand.

"Daisy's awful sick. She's burning up with fever."

"Put her down here," Dana directed as she moved to an empty patient table in the office. She got a clean rag, and, dipping it in some water, she began to wipe down the young girl's face, neck, and arms.

"What's going on?" Dakota asked as he looked around the room.

"Didn't you see the quarantine sign on your way in?"

"What quarantine sign?"

"I guess you didn't see it, then," Dana said dryly. "There's an influenza epidemic in town, Dakota."

"Oh no." Dakota looked down at the child miserable with fever. She looked so small and helpless.

"You need to leave," Dana told him as she continued to try to cool Daisy off.

"What? I'm not leaving."

"We don't need everyone in town getting sick."

"But—"

"What's going on?" Dr. Clarke interrupted as he entered the room.

"Daisy has influenza," Dana informed her uncle. "Dakota brought her in, and I was just telling him that he needs to leave."

"She's right, Dakota. We need to keep this from spreading."

"Look, there's a good chance I might get the grippe too. Daisy was curled up tightly against me the whole way here. It seems to me that it would be safer if I stayed here where I could help out until we know for sure whether or not I'll get sick. And since no one in the town cares whether I stay or not"—he looked at Dana pointedly—"you might as well let me lend a hand."

Dr. Clarke rubbed the back of his neck. The young man had a point. "All right, son," he conceded. "Come on. I'll show you what needs to be done."

As they turned to leave, Dana lowered her head. Dakota would be confined with them in this little office for who knows how long. The idea bothered her, but there was another emotion going through her that she couldn't quite put her finger on.

Dr. Clarke showed Dakota to the room where Daisy would stay. There was a little girl lying on one bed and a little boy on another. Dakota gently laid Daisy down on an empty bed. Daisy stirred.

"Mr. Jones, I don't feel good," she said as he pulled the covers up around her.

"I know you don't, sweetheart, but Dr. Clarke will help make you feel better." He smiled down at her, and she closed her eyes as a light sleep came to claim her.

Dr. Clarke motioned to the bed next to Daisy's. "That's Mary Harper," he whispered. "She was brought in yesterday."

"I know Mary," Dakota responded. Dr. Clarke noted the sadness in his voice. "She was in my Sunday school class."

Dr. Clarke put an understanding hand on Dakota's shoulder. "And the little boy is Barry Stewart. His family is relatively new to town. He was brought in earlier this morning, and his mother was none too happy with me when I told her she couldn't stay."

Dakota nodded. "Doc, I'll be happy to look after all of them while I'm here."

"Much obliged. We sure could use the help."

"Uncle," Dana said as she burst into the room, "we've got another one."

Dr. Clarke followed his niece down the hallway and into the office, where Fred Johnson was standing next to his son, Cole. Dr. Clarke walked over to the patient table and felt Cole's forehead.

"Tell me my boy don't got the grippe," Fred demanded. Dr. Clarke looked at him wearily.

"I'm afraid so, Fred."

Dana reached for a cloth and began to wipe down Cole's head, neck, and arms.

"What can you do?" Fred asked.

"There's not much we can do. We have to try to get his fever down and make him as comfortable as possible."

Fred raked a hand through his hair. "I don't understand it. He was fine yesterday."

"It comes on quickly," Dr. Clarke answered as he mixed some quinine and water in a glass. "Fred, we have to ask you to leave."

"I ain't leavin' my boy here like this."

"Fred, it's the safest way. We've got to stop the disease from spreading. You need to leave."

Dakota entered the room just then, and Fred turned angry eyes toward him. "What's the criminal doing here?"

Dana felt a spark of anger and wanted to come to Dakota's defense. She stopped herself just before she spoke and wondered why Fred's statement prompted that kind of reaction from her. She was still angry with Dakota, wasn't she?

"Enough, Fred," Dr. Clarke said in an authoritative tone. Fred raised his eyebrows in surprise. "Dakota's not a criminal. And he's here helping us out."

"You keep him away from my boy!" Fred shouted angrily. He took a threatening step toward Dakota, who stood his ground and never broke eye contact with the angry father.

"Deputy!" Dana called in a loud voice. Vickery made his way into the room and quickly sized up the situation.

"How can you let him stay here?" Fred demanded of Vickery.

"He's an upstanding citizen, Fred. Which you would know if you gave him half a chance. He's taking good care of the patients."

"Stay away from my son," Fred growled in a low voice.

"Leave." Dr. Clarke turned from the patient table to face Fred. "Get out now. We'll take good care of Cole." Fred kept eyes full of hatred trained on Dakota, and Vickery came forward to escort him out. Fred broke free of Vickery's hold on his arm.

"I'm going. But if anything happens to my boy, I'm holding you"—he directed a finger at Dakota—"personally responsible."

Vickery slammed the door shut behind him.

"Dakota," Dr. Clarke began rather hesitantly, "you know there's one more bed in the room with the other children."

"Of course," Dakota wasted no time in responding. "You know I'll take good care of him despite his father." He picked up the boy and carried him to the back room and laid him on the fourth bed. He then began to go from child to child wiping them down, trying to ease the discomfort of their fever.

Caleb and Alicia rode back onto the ranch at a leisurely pace. They had enjoyed their visit with Mark and Claire, but the epidemic weighed heavily on their minds—especially Alicia's.

"Caleb, I'm worried," she confided. Caleb took her hand and entwined their fingers.

"Remember what the Bible says about worrying. 'Who of you by worrying can add a single hour to his life?'" he quoted.

"It's from Matthew. I know, Caleb. But I'm a mother. I worry about our children. We didn't even get Daisy's birthday presents."

"Dr. Clarke and Dana are good at what they do. This town is in good hands. And let's not forget that God is the great physician." Alicia nodded, grateful for Caleb's calm. Alicia leaned over close to her husband and breathed in his scent. He made her feel safe, like everything would be all right even when things seemed so uncertain.

As their wagon came in view of the ranch house, they saw Cameron and Will bound out of the house, down the porch steps, and toward the wagon.

"Something's wrong, Caleb," Alicia said in a worried tone. He pulled back on the reins as the boys reached the wagon.

"Daisy," Cameron panted. Alicia came up out of her seat.

"What's wrong, Cameron?"

"Dakota had to take her to Dr. Clarke's. She's was burning up with fever."

"Oh, Caleb," Alicia murmured. Caleb looked up and saw John approaching.

"I guess Cameron done told you about Daisy," John confirmed.

"Cameron, Will, please go back in the house," Caleb directed.

"But, Pa—"

Caleb raised a hand to stop their protests. "Do as I say."

As the boys grudgingly walked back to the house, Caleb leaned down and said to John, "There's an influenza epidemic in town, John."

John's eyes widened. "I'm sorry, boss."

"Caleb, I have to get to her. We have to go back to town right away," Alicia cried as panic began to overtake her. Caleb nodded his assent.

"John, can you keep an eye on the boys for a while longer?"

"Sure thing, boss."

"Thanks. Oh, and don't mention the epidemic to them. I don't want them scared." Caleb clicked to the team, and they turned back toward town.

Dana was making her rounds through the office. So far, only Steven's fever had broken. She had never been through an epidemic before and was a bit frightened by it, but she tried not to let it show. She certainly couldn't let the patients know, but she also didn't want her uncle to know either. He thought of her as a strong, capable woman, and she didn't want to disappoint him. They had already lost six patients to the disease, and Dana didn't want her uncle to know the toll it took on her.

She walked by the room where Daisy was and stopped at the doorway. There were three other children in there, and Dakota was going from one to another with a cool rag. She cleared her throat, and Dakota looked up.

"How is she?" she asked as she walked into the room.

"Her fever is still high."

Dana and her uncle had put some supplies in each room so they wouldn't have to keep running back and forth. She reached for a glass and the quinine bottle and put a little of the powder in the glass then filled it with water.

"Here, sweetheart," Dana cooed. "Try to drink some of this." She helped Daisy raise her head and take a sip of the water.

"Try to get her to keep taking sips. I'll mix up some for the other patients in here as well." Dana mixed some quinine in three more glasses and set them down on a little table in between the beds. She raised her forearm to her head to push back loose hairs and wipe away the perspiration. As she turned to leave the room, she felt a hand rest on her arm.

"Dana, are you all right?" Dakota's deep voice nearly melted her heart. Oh, how she loved to hear him say her name. She shook her head to dispel the thoughts.

"You're not? Okay, you need to lie down over here for a while," Dakota said in a worried voice.

"No, no. I'm fine," Dana said, slightly amused. Dakota had completely misread her headshake. He eyed her warily. "Trust me. I'm not sick," she said in a convincing tone. Yes, she was exhausted, but she knew she didn't have the grippe.

"Have you gotten any sleep?" Dakota asked the question so gently, and when Dana looked up at him, she could see the love in his eyes. Unbidden, tears filled her eyes. "Dana, why don't you come sit down over here for a bit." Dakota led her to a chair in the corner. "I can take over for you for a while."

"No, please," Dana said, refusing to sit down, "I'm fine. I have to go. Thank you, though." Dana nearly ran from the room, but instead of going to check on other patients, she went upstairs to the comfort of her room. She threw herself across the bed as a few tears slipped down her cheeks. She didn't want to be having feelings for Dakota. She kept trying to convince herself that she couldn't trust him, but something deep down seemed to be gently whispering to her that she could.

Pounding at the front door awoke the young nurse. Dana sat up with a start, realizing that she had dozed off. Feeling guilty, she rose and went downstairs, where Dr. Clarke was talking to another distraught mother. Only this time, Dana knew well who it was.

"Please, Dr. Clarke, I've got to see my baby!" Alicia cried as she tried to make her way in. Dr. Clarke stepped outside and firmly closed the door behind him. Dana couldn't resist going up to the door to hear what her uncle was telling Alicia.

"Alicia, please try to understand that I'm only trying to do what's best for you and this town."

"Keeping me from my child when she's ill is not what's best for her," Alicia's voice rose in exasperation. Dr. Clarke looked at Caleb, hoping to find some support.

"Caleb, please, it's not that I am trying to keep you from your child. I'm trying to keep the epidemic from spreading. You haven't been exposed, and so the best thing for you to do is let us care for Daisy so that when she recovers she has healthy parents to return home to."

Caleb was torn. He understood both Dr. Clarke's and his wife's point of view. Daisy was his child too.

"Dr. Clarke, what do you think is best for our Daisy?" Caleb asked.

"I think it's best for you to leave her in our care."

"No!" Alicia shouted. Caleb tightened his arm around her and tried to soothe his near-hysterical wife.

"Honey, if Dr. Clarke thinks that's best—"

"She's my child, and I know what's best for her," Alicia interrupted. The door behind Dr. Clarke opened, and Dakota stepped out. Alicia turned accusatory eyes toward the doctor.

"You let him stay, but you won't let her own mother stay? What kind of doctor are you?"

"Alicia!" Caleb said in surprise. "Honey, please try to calm down. I'm so sorry, Dr. Clarke."

"Alicia," Dakota tried to explain, "I've been exposed. There's a good chance I'll get the grippe. It's safer for the town if I stay here so that if I have it, I won't spread it. And as long as I'm fit, I'll be helping tend to the patients. Especially Daisy," he added.

Alicia seemed to consider this. But only for a moment before she turned desperate eyes to her husband.

"Caleb, I think I should stay." Caleb looked over at Dr. Clarke and Dakota, who both shook their heads. Caleb had to agree with them. Daisy was in good hands, and Caleb didn't want another member of his family to get sick.

"Tell you what. Why don't you stay here in town with Mark and Claire? That way you'll be close by if they need you."

"What? Are you honestly telling me that I shouldn't stay with my child?" Caleb had never seen Alicia this wild and desperate before. It broke his heart, but deep down he felt like it was the right thing to do.

"I'm saying that Dr. Clarke is right. You shouldn't be exposed. They are working as hard as they can to stop the epidemic from spreading and healing those that are sick. We all have to do our part. Dakota is here with Daisy, and he'll keep an eye on her. You know how fond of him she is."

Tears flooded Alicia's eyes. She was outnumbered and wouldn't be able to see her little girl. It didn't seem fair. Defeat washed over her.

"I'll be at Mark and Claire's," she said in a low voice, not bothering to hide her anger. "Promise you'll come and get me if you need me for anything or if my baby gets worse."

"You're doing the right thing, Alicia. Your other children need you too. Thank you."

Alicia glared at the doctor then turned to Dakota.

"Daisy adores you. Take good care of her."

"You know I will."

Alicia turned sharply on her heel and stormed toward the wagon. Caleb turned to follow her, but Dr. Clarke reached for his arm to stop him.

"Caleb," he said in a low voice, "we've already lost six patients. Most of them were elderly and simply couldn't fight off the disease. Can you send word to the blacksmith? We need coffins." The doctor broke eye contact with Caleb and looked down. The full severity of the epidemic began to dawn on Caleb for the first time. He swallowed and nodded.

"Sure thing, Doc."

Dr. Clarke nodded weakly then slipped back inside the office with Dakota.

Caleb climbed up in the wagon and started the team toward the ranch.

"Where are we going? I'm staying with Mark and Claire."

"I know, sweetheart, but you'll need to pack a few things." Alicia nodded absentmindedly. She put her head in her hands and cried all the way to the ranch.

Caleb couldn't bear to tell her that six people had already died of the grippe. He would take her back to Mark and Claire's and then go find the blacksmith on his own.

CHAPTER 18

Claire woke up with a start.

"What is it, honey?" Mark mumbled in his sleepy state.

"I thought I heard something." Claire sat quietly for a while, trying to see if she would hear it again.

"It must have been a dream. Go back to sleep," Mark told her.

"No, listen. There it is again." Claire sat up, and the sound came again within seconds. It was the sound of someone crying.

"Poor thing," Claire said as she pushed back the covers. "I'm going to go check on her." Mark nodded and turned over. Claire slipped on her robe and tiptoed down the hallway. She stopped in front of the door to the guest room, where she could distinctly hear Alicia's muffled sobs. She knocked softly and opened the door. One look at Alicia's tear-stained face nearly broke Claire's heart.

"Please don't cry," Claire said as she sat down next to Alicia. She put her arms around her sister-in-law as Alicia's tears flowed freely. "I'm sure Daisy will be all right."

Alicia sniffed and pulled away from Claire. She used her handkerchief to dab at her eyes and blow her nose.

"Oh, Claire, I just want to see her. I want to be there to help take care of her. It's not right for them to keep me from her."

"I understand."

"Do you? How would you feel if it were Bethany or Emily?"

"I would be just as upset as you are. But, honey, Dr. Clarke is right. When Daisy gets better, she will need you to be well."

"Oh, Claire, I made such a spectacle of myself." Alicia groaned as she put her head in her hands.

"What do you mean?"

"Do you remember that earlier today I told you about a mother who Dr. Clarke refused to let be with her child and the way she carried on in front of everyone?" Claire nodded. "Well, I did that, only I was much worse. I'm so embarrassed."

"Don't worry about it. You're a mother. I'm sure anyone who saw will understand." Alicia nodded and sniffed again. She hoped Claire was right. But most of all, she hoped Daisy was all right.

"Do you think Daisy will understand why I'm not there?" she asked anxiously.

"I'm sure Dakota, Dr. Clarke, and Dana will all assure Daisy that you wanted to be there and they wouldn't let you. Please try not to worry. The best thing we can do for her is pray." Claire took Alicia's hands and led them in a prayer asking God to heal Daisy and all of the others who were sick.

It was the middle of the night, and Dana stepped out the back door and felt the cool air on her face. She dumped out two buckets of water and walked around to the well to pump some more. She couldn't get Dakota's face out of her mind. Or his words. *Since no one in the town cares whether I stay or not...* The phrase kept repeating itself in her mind. The way he looked at her when he said it was so resigned. She knew she had hurt him by staying away all this time. But she didn't quite know what to do. Part of her longed to trust him again. To go back to the way things were before she found out that he was Rigby Buchanan. She loved the way he looked at her and treated her like she was the most precious thing on the planet.

But another part of her was scared. Scared to trust him and to be hurt. The hurt that she felt the night Fred Johnson told the town who Dakota was was something that Dana never wanted to feel again. A sob caught in her throat. *What am I going to do?* she thought.

"Hello." Dana turned to find Dakota standing only about a foot away. His nearness took her breath away. She turned back around and started to pump water.

"Here let me." He gently moved her hand away and made swift work of the task. Dana watched his arm muscle tighten and flex under his shirt.

Dana took a deep breath then finally spoke. "I'm sorry about the way Fred treated you today. It was wrong."

"Thank you," he answered quietly as he finished filling up the buckets.

"Dakota, I—" Dakota turned to face her, and she stopped, uncertain how to continue. "You said something when you arrived. You said that no one in town cares whether you stay or not." She looked down and shuffled her feet. Dakota held his breath.

"I, um, well, I just wanted to let you know that I don't think that's true."

Dakota reached for her hands. "Dana, can you find it in your heart to give me a second chance?"

Dana reached up and ran her hand down the side of his face. It was rough with stubble, but Dana didn't mind. Dakota slid his eyes shut. He opened them when Dana began to speak.

"I want to, Dakota. I really do. But I still feel so uncertain. I need more time."

Dakota nodded. "Take all the time you need." He squeezed her hands before letting them go, and they walked together back into the office.

The next morning things were about the same. It was decided that Vickery's boy, Steven, was well enough to go home but that Vickery would remain to help care for the other patients. So far no one else had come to the office with symptoms of the illness, and Dr. Clarke and Dana both breathed a sigh of relief.

There were still nine people sick, though, and their care took up everyone's time.

Dr. Clarke and Dana stood together going over their inventory as Mattie came rushing into the room.

"Dr. Clarke, come quick!" she yelled in a panic. Dr. Clarke and Dana raced down the hall and into Levi's room, where he was wildly thrashing about.

"Dana, get Vickery and some quinine," Dr. Clarke ordered. Vickery ran into the room, and the two of them tried to hold Levi down. Dana quickly mixed the quinine and brought the glass over to Levi. More of the liquid ended up on the floor rather than in Levi's mouth, but still they tried. He finally calmed enough that Dr. Clarke and Vickery could let go, but he still thrashed about the covers while the fever raged through his body.

"Doctor, isn't there anything else we can do?" Mattie asked, wringing her hands.

"We have to try to keep his fever down."

Mattie grabbed the cloth and dipped it in some water and laid it on Levi's forehead as she talked to him in a soothing voice. Dr. Clarke mixed some more quinine.

"Have him take a sip every half hour or so," he said as he handed Mattie the glass. He walked out of the room, signaling for Dana to follow him.

"I'm really concerned, Dana," he said in a low voice. "Levi's not as young and strong as some of the others. If his fever doesn't break soon, well..." His voice trailed off, and he walked away. Dana covered her mouth with her hand, horrified by what her uncle was implying.

Dana walked into Daisy's room. She was sleeping peacefully.

"She looks just like a china doll, doesn't she?" Dana whispered to Dakota.

"That she does."

"How is she?" she asked as she put a hand on the young girl's forehead.

"She still has a fever," Dakota answered, and Dana nodded.

"But it's not as high as it was. That's a good sign. I'm going to go get her some broth. Try to get her to drink some if she awakens. She needs fluids. How are the others?"

"Mary seems to be a little better, but Barry and Cole are the same."

Dana nodded. "I'll bring some broth for them too."

"Wait," Dakota said as she turned to go. He walked over to her and dropped his voice to a whisper. "How's Levi?"

Dana sighed and looked away. "He's getting worse. My uncle is afraid for him, Dakota."

He nodded. "I'll be praying."

Levi made it through another night, and Mattie never left his side. Dana stood in the doorway and listened as Mattie sang her favorite hymn to him, her rich alto filling the room.

"I was once lost, but now am found. Was blind, but now I see."

"That was wonderful, Mattie," Dana said as she stepped into the room and crossed over to Levi's bed. She reached over to feel his forehead. "His fever is still high. I've brought you some broth." She set it down on the table next to Levi's bed. "If he wakes, try to get him to drink some."

Mattie nodded. Dana noticed the fear in the older woman's eyes and patted her on the shoulder. There were two other patients in the room with Levi who seemed to be holding their own pretty well. Dana left and walked across the hall. She stopped in the doorway and watched as Dakota gently spooned up broth for Cole. The boy ate several bites before he slumped back onto the pillows.

"Good job. Rest now," Dakota said in a quiet, reassuring voice. Dana wondered if she really saw a smile flicker across Cole's face or if she just imagined it. Cole closed his eyes and appeared to be resting comfortably. Dakota then moved to Mary, who was also able to eat a few bites.

"Thank you, Mr. Jones," she said in a weak voice.

"You're welcome. Try to sleep now." Dakota brushed back some hair from her forehead, and her eyes slid shut.

Dana cleared her throat. Dakota turned, and she walked into the room.

"I believe you may have missed your calling."

Dakota smiled.

"You're very good with the children."

"Thanks. I just love helping people," he answered humbly with a shrug. He moved to Daisy's bed. He sat down, and her eyes fluttered open.

"Mr. Jones, where is Ma?"

Dakota took the little girl's hand. "Your Ma wanted to be here with you so much. But Dr. Clarke doesn't want her to get sick too. So she's waiting for you at your Uncle Mark and Aunt Claire's house so that when you're all better she can take you home."

"Oh," she murmured. Her eyes started to close again.

"Daisy, honey," Dana said. "Before you go back to sleep, can you try to drink some of this broth?" Daisy managed a small nod, and Dakota spooned up a few bites for her. Once she finished, she closed her eyes to sleep some more.

"It's good for them to eat," Dana said as she rose from Daisy's bed. "You're doing a good job." Dakota smiled in appreciation as Dana went to check on other patients. Once she had left the room, Dakota reached for a cloth and pressed the cool dampness against his forehead.

CHAPTER 19

Alicia restlessly paced her sister-in-law's house. She couldn't get Daisy out of her mind. How was she doing? Did her fever break? Was she worse? Then her thoughts would turn to the Blue Star Ranch, where she knew that her husband was caring for their other two children. She thought of Cameron and Will often and prayed for their safety, along with Caleb's. She prayed that they wouldn't get the influenza and that she would be returning to them soon with Daisy healthy and in tow.

The thoughts and questions swirling through her head were driving her crazy. *Why hasn't there been any news?* There was no news from the doctor's office about anyone. Then a thought hit Alicia. *The general store.* If there were any news to be had, it would be floating through the general store. Alicia grabbed a shawl and began walking.

There were still swarms of people coming in and out. Alicia briefly wondered how long the supply in the storeroom would hold out before the town bought out all of the merchandise. She slipped in and saw Carl at the counter.

"Hi, Carl," she greeted as she approached. Carl looked calm and in control in spite of the busyness going on.

"Hello, Alicia. How is Daisy?"

Alicia wrung her hands. "I don't know. I haven't heard any news at all. I was hoping to find some news here."

"The only thing we know is that Steven Vickery's fever broke, and he was sent home. Paul Vickery is still helping out until the epidemic is over. We also know that several of the more elderly patients didn't make it." Carl shook his head sadly then turned to help a customer who needed some supplies. Alicia slowly backed away from the counter.

She had hoped to hear more news than that, but it was better than nothing. She was relieved that Paul's son was going to be fine. She prayed that Daisy was doing better.

"Alicia." She turned to see Mrs. Harper and her husband coming toward her. Mrs. Harper carried a basketful of supplies and sported a worried look. "I heard that your Daisy got the grippe." Alicia nodded solemnly.

"So did our Mary."

"I'm so sorry," Alicia responded as she put a hand on her friend's arm.

"What we want to know," her husband interrupted in a gruff voice, "is iffen that criminal can be trusted to help care for our young'uns?"

Alicia looked taken aback. She raised her chin and looked him squarely in the eye. "Mr. Harper, your children are in the best hands in Darby, and I know that for a fact. Dr. Clarke and Dana are medical professionals and extremely good at what they do. And as for Dakota"—her voice lowered in anger—"he's one of the finest men I know. He would never judge you the way that you are trying to judge him right now. He was forced into crime as a child for goodness' sake!" Alicia said in exasperation. *Why can't anyone in this town understand the truth?*

"Don't change the facts."

"Oh, really," Alicia retorted. "What exactly are the facts, Mr. Harper?" Mrs. Harper was red from embarrassment and tugged on her husband's arm in an effort to get him to end the conversation and leave the store. He brushed her arm aside as he answered the question.

"The facts are that he was a criminal. And you can't deny it. It's in his blood, and I, for one, don't think that he can be trusted."

"Let me fill you in on a few more facts," Alicia's eyes sparked in anger. "He was a boy forced into a criminal life. Did your pa ever try to get you to steal?" Mr. Harper's eye contact wavered for a split second.

"He saved my life and risked his own to do it. He gave his life over to Jesus Christ and has never been the same since. He has changed for the better, and everyone in this town knows it whether they want to admit it or not. He has helped everyone in this town who needed it without a thought of being repaid. He saved my Will when a snake bit him, and he saved my Daisy by getting her to the doctor in time when she came down with the grippe. Dakota was the one who realized she was burning up with fever and rushed her to Dr. Clarke's. He himself is at risk of getting influenza because he cared for my little girl." Alicia's voice broke as tears sprang to her eyes.

Mr. Harper shifted uneasily. "I'm sorry, ma'am. I didn't mean to upset you. I just don't know if he can be trusted."

"Mr. Harper, you know the story of Paul in the Bible. God changed him, and he changed Dakota. I have complete confidence that Dakota will do all he can to help our children. I trust him implicitly."

Mr. Harper tipped his hat and turned to leave the store without another word. Alicia had no idea if anything she said resonated with the man.

"I'm so sorry, Alicia," Mrs. Harper hastily apologized as she hurried after her husband. As they left, Alicia looked around and realized that they had caused quite a scene. Every eye in the store was focused on her. She quickly turned to leave the store and hoped that her words about Dakota would help soften the town's attitude.

"Dr. Clarke!" Mattie's piercing scream woke everyone in the office. Dr. Clarke, Dana, and Vickery rushed into the room while Dakota stayed behind to help the children settle back down.

Dr. Clarke raced to the side of Levi's bed and felt his wrist, searching for a pulse. Mattie sank into the chair by the bed and stared in horror.

"I dozed off for a piece, and when I woke up"—she gestured helplessly toward her husband—"he wasn't breathin' no more." Her voice broke, and Dana put her arm around Mattie's shoulders.

Dr. Clarke confirmed the worst. "He's gone, Mattie."

"No." Mattie sobbed in hushed tones in her hands. "No, no, no. Not my Levi." The sound was heart wrenching, and Dana's eyes flooded with tears. Dr. Clarke pulled the sheet up over Levi's head and signaled for Vickery to step into the hallway with him.

"We need to get word to the blacksmith that we need another coffin."

"I'll take care of it," Vickery responded.

Dr. Clarke walked wearily back into the room, where an inconsolable Mattie sat and cried. Dana looked helplessly at her uncle. She felt so badly for Mattie Thomas, and there was nothing she could do.

"Leave me alone," Mattie ordered quietly.

"But Mattie—" Dana began to protest. Mattie raised her hand to cut Dana off.

"Please."

Reluctantly, Dana and her uncle left the room and from the doorway could hear Mattie whisper words of love to Levi and how they would see each other again one day. Dana's shoulders sagged as she walked into the room where Dakota was caring for the younger patients. Fortunately, they had all fallen back to sleep.

"Come sit down." Dakota gently guided her to a chair. He kneeled in front of her, and she nodded, confirming his unspoken question. He covered her hand with one of his own, and they remained that way for several moments.

"Oh, Dakota," she said softly so as not to wake up the other patients, "it was so awful. Mattie is beside herself."

"I know," Dakota whispered as he stroked her hair.

"I don't ever want to go through an epidemic again."

"Why don't you try and get some rest?" Dakota suggested.

"No," Dana said as she pushed herself out of the chair. "I couldn't possibly rest now." She walked through the room by all of the beds and began to check foreheads. She stopped when she came to Cole and looked up at Dakota.

"Dakota," she whispered. He couldn't tell if her excited tone was out of worry or relief. He walked over and felt the boy's forehead.

"His fever broke," Dana said.

Dakota sighed in relief. "Thank the Lord."

Dakota sat on the side of Cole's bed and tried to swallow. The ordinarily involuntary act took great effort on Dakota's part. His throat burned.

"I think I'm going to get a glass of water. Would you like anything?"

Dana eyed him warily. "Are you all right?"

"Sure," he replied, trying his best to sound convincing. "I'm just thirsty."

"Okay. Some water would be nice." Dakota went to get the water, and the two adults spent the rest of the night hours moving from bed to bed tending to the patients.

In the morning, Cole was moved to the recuperating room, where Dakota spooned up some broth for him to eat.

"I can do it myself, Mr. Jones," he managed weakly.

"Are you sure?"

"Yes, sir." Dakota watched as the boy delicately lifted the spoon up to his mouth. He slurped the broth, and, amazingly enough, not a drop spilled.

"Good boy."

Cole smiled at Dakota's praise. "Mr. Jones," he began tentatively. Dakota waited silently for him to continue. "I owe you one heap of an apology. I'm so sorry about all the trouble I caused you. I know you ain't bad, and I tried to tell Pa, but he don't want to listen to me."

Dakota nodded thoughtfully. "I accept your apology, son."

The look of gratitude on Cole's face brought a smile to Dakota's lips. Cole looked back down at his bowl of broth.

"I'll be all right in here by myself, Mr. Jones. The others still need you."

Dakota nodded and rose from the side of the bed. He turned as he reached the door and looked at the boy. "You know, Cole, you're growing into a fine young man." Cole beamed, and Dakota left the room to check on Daisy. He reached the room and leaned against the doorway. He was beginning to feel lightheaded.

"Oh, Dakota, this is the day for miracles!" Dana exclaimed when she saw him in the doorway. She lightly clapped her hands and giddily turned back on one heel to face Daisy's bed. "All of the children's fevers have broken! Can you believe it? Not just Cole, but Mary, Daisy, and Barry. It's too good to be true. And it's all thanks to the good Lord and your fine care." Dana continued to gush, not noticing that Dakota wasn't all right.

"That's wonderful," he answered weakly. She turned to face him and really looked at him for the first time. Her eyes widened as she recognized the signs. He was leaning on the doorframe for support, his face was flushed, and his pupils were dilated.

"Dakota," she ran over to him.

"Dana, I—" he began but couldn't finish, as he began to collapse.

"Vickery!" Dana called. Vickery rushed in and helped Dana get Dakota to Cole's old bed.

"He's burning up," Dana said anxiously as she felt his forehead. "Vickery, the other children's fevers have broken."

"All of them?" Vickery asked in disbelief.

"Yes, all of them."

"Well, I'll be. The Almighty sure is watching over us."

"Yes, he certainly is. Vickery, please take the other children into the recuperating room with Cole. Try to get them to eat some broth. I need fresh water in here." Dana rose to get the water, while Vickery began moving one child after another.

"What's going on?" Dr. Clarke asked as he passed his niece in the hallway. He noticed Vickery carrying Daisy to Cole's new room.

"I have good news and bad news." Dana continued to walk as she talked and her uncle followed her. "All of the children's fevers have broken."

"Wonderful," Dr. Clarke sagged with relief. It was a doctor's worst nightmare to lose a patient. He had already lost too many. Dr. Clarke followed his niece outside, where she headed straight to the water pump.

"But the bad news is that Dakota is ill. I have a feeling he's been ill and was trying to hide the symptoms and simply couldn't hide them any longer. He collapsed, and Vickery helped me get him to a bed. He's burning up." Dana began to pump water into a bucket.

"I'll go check on him," Dr. Clarke said, his voice lined with concern.

As Dana was coming back through the house with fresh water, she heard a rap at the door. *Oh, no,* she inwardly groaned. *Please, Lord, no more. Please.* She slowly reached for the doorknob and hesitantly turned it. She swung the door open and saw the blacksmith standing at the door.

"Sorry to bother ya, miss, but I brung the coffin that yer uncle ordered."

"Thank you. I'll let him know it's here."

He tipped his hat and walked away. Dana closed the door and leaned back against it. While the children and the other patients were doing well and seemingly on the road to recovery, they were still in the midst of a nightmare. Levi was no longer with them, and Dakota was in serious condition. Dana closed her eyes and took a deep breath. She sent up a prayer asking God for strength and healing. She poured the water from the bucket into a pitcher; then she quickly mounted the steps to get the water to Dakota.

"Uncle, I brought the water." Dana set the bowl and pitcher down on the table next to Dakota's bed. Dr. Clarke stirred some quinine in a glass with water and tried to help Dakota take a sip. It was all Dakota could do to lift his head.

"He barely took any," Dr. Clarke murmured for Dana's ears alone. "He's very sick, my dear."

Dana sat on the other side of his bed and began to wipe down his forehead. "Uncle, the blacksmith dropped off the coffin."

"All right. I'll go let Mattie and Vickery know," he said tiredly as he rose from the bed and exited the room.

Dana sat with Dakota and watched as his breathing became labored. His fever was precariously high, and Dana worked tirelessly to make him more comfortable. She constantly wiped his face, neck, and arms and would give him a sip of the medicine as often as she could.

By that evening, Dakota was delirious with fever. He convulsed on the bed, and Dana and Vickery tried to hold him down. He started mumbling in his state of delirium. He wanted to get up and take care of Daisy, and Dana would quietly assure him that Daisy was doing well and was getting healthier by the minute. He tossed back and forth and would talk about needing to be at the ranch. Dana was endlessly patient and continued to gently reassure him that everything was all right.

By nightfall, Dana was exhausted and the only one in the room. She collapsed into a nearby chair and closed her eyes for a moment. Her uncle and Vickery were tending to the other patients who were eating more and feeling stronger. Mattie left when Carl Holding and his brother, Sheriff Tom Holding, came by for the coffin. Dr. Clarke asked the Holdings to pass the word along that everyone was going to be fine. Everyone, that is, except Dakota. He remained dangerously ill.

"Dana," his deep voice called out to her and broke her reverie.

She got up and quickly moved to his bed. She took his hand in hers and said quietly, "I'm here."

"Dana," he called her name again, and Dana realized he didn't know what he was saying. She put the cloth into the bowl, wrung out the water, and laid it on his head. She picked his hand back up and stroked it.

"It's going to be okay," she whispered.

"Dana."

Every time he said her name, it broke her heart. His deep voice was weak and gruff. She looked down at the hand that she continued to stroke and marveled at how nice it felt in hers. She realized with a start that she hadn't left Dakota's room all day. With all of the other patients, she always took time to eat and rest for a spell. But her uncle brought her something to eat tonight. She couldn't bear to leave Dakota. Then it hit her. She was still in love with this man.

Tears swam in her eyes as she began to pray. "God, please forgive me for how I've acted toward Dakota. He and his friends tried to tell me that I was making a mistake, but I'm too stubborn for my own good sometimes. You are a God of forgiveness and second chances, and it was wrong of me not to have faith that you really have changed Dakota. Everything in his actions have proven that he's a man of God. I know that I have hurt Dakota. Please give me the chance to make it right with him. Please don't take him from me. Please." The last word was spoken in a pleading whisper as she lowered her head and allowed the tears to fall.

"Dana," she heard her name murmured again and looked up.

"I'm here." She stroked the side of his face. "I'm here."

"Dana." His voice was getting softer. Dana leaned forward to hear him, and her eyes widened when she heard the next word that was spoken so softly it was barely audible. *Angel.*

Dana squeezed his hand and closed her eyes. How she longed for him to wake up so she could tell him how sorry she was. But her next thought took the breath right out of her. *Have I realized that I'm still in love with him only to lose him?*

CHAPTER 20

Dr. Clarke decided that it was safe to release all of the patients, save for Dakota. Concerned parents and loved ones came to pick up their patients. Dr. Clarke reminded them that they were still weak and healing but that they no longer posed a threat of spreading the illness. When the Harpers, Stewarts, Johnsons, and Carters came to pick up their children, they all tried to express their gratitude to Dr. Clarke. He raised his hand to stop them.

"Don't be thanking me," he was quick to set them straight. "Oh, I did my share of caring for your young'uns, but the one you really need to thank is Dakota Jones. I had many other patients to care for, but Dakota never left the sides of the children. He worked night and day to bring their fevers down and help them get well."

The children all spoke up at that moment confirming the doctor's words, and Dr. Clarke noticed some uncomfortable parents shifting uneasily. He supposed they were feeling just a bit guilty over the way they treated the man who helped saved their child's life.

News of Dakota's grave condition quickly spread throughout Darby. He was the only patient left at the doctor's office. Pastor Tyler called a special prayer meeting for him that night. He was uncertain as to how many people would actually attend, and that evening he stood anxiously by the door of the church ready to greet all who entered.

Not surprisingly, the Carters and Brewers were the first to arrive.

"I think this is a fine idea, Pastor," Caleb commended as he shook the Pastor's hand on the way in.

"It's the least we can do after the way he cared for our children during the epidemic," Alicia added as she ushered in her three children. Mark and Claire followed with their two children, and they all sat in the front with Gloria.

Minutes passed. No one else arrived. Saddened, Pastor Tyler looked down and shook his head. He turned and walked toward the pulpit.

"Looks like it will just be us," he admitted, feeling defeat wash over him. He had hoped this would be a turning point with the members of the town. He looked down at the Bible in his hands, and as he looked up, his eyes widened. Everyone in the room turned toward the door to see dozens of townspeople starting to arrive. Pastor Tyler, Caleb, and Alicia walked to the door and looked out at the scene. Caleb squeezed Alicia's hand, and tears stood in her eyes.

"It's about time," she whispered. Pastor Tyler, Caleb, and Alicia watched in awe as the townspeople poured in. It seemed as if the entire town of Darby showed up to petition the Lord on Dakota's behalf. Alicia was overwhelmed with joy. This was an answer to prayer in itself. The hearts of the members of the town of Darby were beginning to soften toward Dakota Jones. Alicia smiled and joined Pastor Tyler and Caleb in greeting the people as they filled the church to standing room only.

Two days passed, and the fever continued to rage through Dakota's body. Through it all, Dana never left his side. He was in and out of consciousness, and she would feed him spoonfuls of broth whenever he was coherent enough to accept the liquid.

She spent endless hours wiping him down in an attempt to lower his fever and spoke quiet words of comfort and assurance to him.

"Dana." She turned at the sound of her uncle's voice. He came up behind her and laid his hands on her shoulders. "You need to rest."

"I can't leave him, Uncle."

Dr. Clarke nodded thoughtfully. His niece was having a change of heart about Dakota Jones. At one point that would have bothered him. He didn't like seeing his niece so hurt the way she was when Fred Johnson told the town who Dakota was. But before the town learned his true identity, Dr. Clarke had respect for Dakota. And as he watched Dakota care for the children through the epidemic without a thought for his own well-being, he realized that Dakota was a man to be held in high esteem. His conduct was worthy of respect, and Dr. Clarke secretly felt ashamed that he had ever doubted Dakota.

"I still love him," Dana whispered. Her uncle reached over and patted her arm.

"I know you do, sweetheart."

"Do you think that's unwise of me?" Dana's voice pleaded with him to reassure her that Dakota was a good man. Dr. Clarke smiled.

"No, child. We were wrong to pass judgment on him. He's a fine man."

Dana breathed a sigh of relief. "I'm glad you feel that way. I feel exactly the same. I just hope I get a chance to tell Dakota."

"I heard the town held a special prayer meeting for Dakota the other night."

"How kind of them," Dana was touched over their concern.

"Try to get some sleep, my dear," Dr. Clarke said as he rose and exited the room. Dana remained in the chair, and her eyes slid shut as sleep rushed in.

Dana's eyes fluttered open. She wasn't sure how long she had slept, but she was sure of one thing: a noise woke her up.

"Dana," Dakota softly groaned.

"I'm here." Dana moved quickly from the chair to the side of the bed and took Dakota's hand. "I'm right here." He squeezed her hand slightly.

"I'm thirsty." Just speaking the words seemed to be an effort for him. Dana handed him a glass of water, and he carefully took a sip. She reached over and felt his forehead, and her eyes lit up.

"Dakota, your fever has broken!" she exclaimed.

"I'm mighty glad to hear that," he responded weakly as he fell asleep once again.

When he woke a few hours later, Dana was still by his side. He managed a weak smile at her before telling her that he was a mite hungry.

"That's a good sign, Dakota. I'll be right back with some broth." Dana hurried down the stairs and spooned up some broth and put a piece of bread on a tray to take to her patient. When she returned, she noticed that Dakota had attempted to sit up a little.

"Here you go," she said as she sat down on the side of the bed, placing the tray in front of Dakota. "This will help you regain some strength."

"Good thing," he grumbled good-naturedly. "I feel as weak as a kitten." He tried to pick up the spoon to feed himself, and as he lifted the spoon to his mouth, his hand was shaking so badly from weakness that most of the broth ended up back in the bowl.

"Here, let me," Dana said as she gently removed the spoon from his hand, dipped up some broth, and fed it to him. Dakota took a sip, his eyes never leaving hers. Dana reached out a hand and ran it softly down the side of his face. His eyes slid shut, and he placed his hand over hers. He opened his eyes and searched her face and knew he saw something different in her eyes. Something had changed while he was ill. She had a peaceful glow about her, and his heart leaped for joy at the thought that she might have changed her mind about him.

"I don't know that I want to regain my strength," he joked. He still held her hand. "All this fussin' is mighty nice."

"Well, you may get your wish—at least for a while." Dana smiled at him and then spooned up more broth. "You've been very sick. It's going to take you a while before you're going to feel back to normal."

He nodded and continued to eat. He knew he had been terribly ill. He had never felt so miserable in his life.

"Dakota, how long did you know you had influenza?"

He looked up at Dana sheepishly. "I knew for a day or two. I was trying to hide it so that I could take care of the children."

"Well, you'll be glad to know that they are all home and well on their way to being good as new. You did a fine job, Dakota. But I still wish you had told me you were ill. If I could have started treating you right away, the influenza might not have hit you so hard. We were afraid we might lose you." Something in her voice gave Dakota pause. He looked up from his broth and saw tears standing in her eyes.

"Dana?" he prompted as he took her hand.

She lifted his hand up and touched it to her cheek. Her eyes slid shut.

"I was so frightened," she whispered as she opened her eyes to look at him. She saw nothing but love and tenderness in his gaze, and it caused her tears to fall. He cupped her face, and with his thumbs, he gently wiped away the tears.

"You asked me if I could find it in my heart to give you a second chance. I don't know why I didn't see it sooner. I guess I just couldn't see past my hurt. God gives us second chances every day, and it's clear that he has shaped you into an honorable man. I'm so sorry," Dana said the words that had been weighing on her heart. "I never should have doubted you, Dakota. I don't know how I could have been so blind."

Relief flooded Dakota's entire being. How he longed to hear her say those words. He had prayed for so long that Dana would forgive him and learn to trust him again. It was too good to be true!

"You don't know how long I've wanted to hear you say that. If my getting the grippe helped bring us back together, then it was well worth it." His voice was hoarse with emotion. "I love you, angel." He spoke the last word so sweetly that it melted Dana's heart.

She squeezed his hand as she looked deeply into his eyes and responded, "I love you too."

CHAPTER 21

A week passed, and the town of Darby was beginning to feel a sense of normalcy again. The town seemed to breathe a collective sigh of relief that the epidemic was over. All of the patients had returned to their homes, leaving Dr. Clarke and Dana time to get some much-needed rest. They were also able to take inventory and order more supplies. The epidemic had left them dangerously short on quinine.

Dakota returned to the Blue Star Ranch and, at Alicia's insistence, was asked to remain in one of the upstairs rooms where she could monitor his recovery. He tried to convince her that it wasn't necessary, but she wouldn't take no for an answer. She wanted to repay him for the care that he gave Daisy. He turned his head as a knock sounded at the door.

"Dakota," Alicia said quietly as she peeked her head in.

"It's all right. I'm awake."

"I've brought you some lunch," Alicia said as she carried a tray over to him. She sat down on the edge of the bed and put the tray in front of him. He sat up straighter.

"Much obliged. You know, I really think I oughta be in the bunkhouse with the others." Dakota felt a little guilty over being in the main house. All of the other ranch hands were in the bunkhouse and hard at work while he lay in a room in the boss's house.

"Nonsense," she said as she waved her hand as if to brush the comment aside. "You're not leaving this house until I'm convinced that you are back to normal."

Dakota shook his head as a small smile teased the corners of his mouth. He knew there was no use trying to change her mind.

"Well, how are you feeling, son?" Caleb asked as he entered the room. He came up behind his wife and laid a hand on her shoulder.

"I'm much better, boss."

"You look much better," Caleb remarked as he noted that Dakota was regaining some color.

A crash downstairs, followed by Will yelling something at his older brother, caused Alicia to hurry down the stairs to see what the commotion was all about.

"Those boys are always into something," Caleb said with a chuckle. He sat down on the spot that his wife vacated. "I know it's none of my business, but can I ask you a question?"

"Of course."

"Now, mind, you don't have to answer if you don't want. I'm just curious." Dakota watched him, waiting for him to continue. "You were there in that little office with Dana Clarke for many days. Was it rough?"

Dakota's eyes lit up, and Caleb had his answer.

"It was awkward at first," Dakota admitted. "But the more we worked together, the more she began to soften toward me. When I was so sick, she never left my side. She's finally forgiven me."

A grin nearly stretched off Caleb's face. "So I guess this means you'll be reconsidering your plans to leave Darby, huh?"

Dakota's ears burned in embarrassment as he thought back to a time not too long ago when he was ready to leave Darby because no one would accept him and Dana wouldn't forgive him.

"Guess so," Dakota answered sheepishly. Caleb laughed and patted him on the shoulder. He stood, ready to leave the room.

"Take it easy, son. We'll see you at supper." Dakota watched as Caleb left the room. He finished his lunch, read from his Bible for a while, and then dozed off.

Alicia was busy working on preparations for the evening meal when a knock sounded at the door. Caleb and the boys were still outside, so she wiped her hands off on a towel and made her way to the door with Daisy coming along beside her.

"Come in," she said as she swung the door open. Claire stepped in, gave her a hug, and then picked up her niece. Mark wheeled in next with Emily on his lap, and Bethany brought up the rear. Alicia hugged her nieces and brother-in-law and invited everyone in.

"Thanks for inviting us to supper," Claire said. "It's been too long since we were all together." The Carters and Brewers ate together at least once a week, but with the epidemic, it had been a while since everyone from both families had been together.

"How are you feeling, Daisy?" Claire asked.

"I feel good," she answered energetically.

"Mark, I'm afraid that Caleb and the boys are still out on the ranch somewhere," Alicia said apologetically.

"Don't worry about it," Mark responded graciously. "I'm sure these girls won't mind keeping me company."

With that, Alicia and Claire made their way into the kitchen. As they finished the preparations, sounds of laughter from the living room wafted in.

"Mark is really good with the children," Alicia remarked. Claire beamed at the compliment. She was proud of her husband.

"Daisy looks well."

Alicia dipped up the roast in a bowl as she responded. "Yes, she's back to her old self again. Dr. Clarke said it's not as difficult for children to bounce back from illnesses."

Claire began to set the table. She placed the plates in front of the chairs and looked up when Alicia handed her a tenth plate.

"It's for Dakota," Alicia answered the unspoken question. "He's been eating in his room since he returned, but I thought it might be nice if he joined us tonight."

"How is he doing?"

"He's better. He's regaining more strength each day. He won't be able to stay confined in that bed for much longer. I think he's already a bit put out with me for making him stay there now," Alicia said with a grin.

"Better safe than sorry. A relapse would be awful."

Alicia poured some milk in the children's glasses and set them on the table.

"Were he and Dana able to reconcile since they spent so much time with each other?" Claire asked. Alicia looked thoughtful for a moment.

"He hasn't said anything to me, but he looks happier now. So I'm hopeful."

Alicia heard the front door open, and, judging by the excited chatter of her boys, they were glad to see their uncle and cousins.

"Perfect timing." Alicia went upstairs to get Dakota, and Claire went into the living room to get the others.

At first Dakota was hesitant about joining the family for a meal, but Alicia's persistence won out. As Dakota sat and watched the families laugh and talk with each other, his mind couldn't help but wander to the future. *Will Dana and I ever marry? Will we have children as happy and settled as the Carter and Brewer children?* These thoughts tumbled around in his mind until the sound of Mark's voice pulled him from his reverie.

"So Dakota, would you mind telling us what it was like being on the frontlines during the epidemic?"

Dakota wiped his mouth with his napkin.

"Not at all," he responded. He then proceeded to recount how he found Daisy and took her to the doctor's office and had to convince them to let him stay. He told them about how hard everyone worked to provide round-the-clock care to all of the patients. Sometime during the story, Daisy climbed up into

Dakota's lap and put her little arms around his neck. Dakota returned the hug as he continued to tell them about the fear they all felt watching everyone suffer. Daisy remained in his lap, and Alicia and Claire exchanged a glance. As mothers, the thought of anything happening to any of their children was enough to make their hearts stop.

"We're all mighty glad that you were there," Mark said. "I don't know how we'll ever convey the depth of our gratitude." Murmurs were heard as the other adults agreed, and color began to rise in Dakota's cheeks. He didn't enjoy all the attention and praise.

"I was just trying to help. The good Lord is the one who brought them all through," he said humbly.

Alicia and Claire rose to clear the table as the men moved to the living room. Dakota tried to excuse himself to go back to his room. He felt uncomfortable intruding on their family time, but Caleb told him that unless he felt like he needed to rest, everyone hoped that he would join them. So Dakota remained. The children all went upstairs to play, leaving the adults alone to talk for a while.

Alicia and Claire made short work of the dishes and soon returned to the living room to join the men. They were all startled to hear a knock at the door. Caleb rose to see who it was.

He opened the door and looked at his visitors in surprise.

"Dr. Clarke, Dana, please come in." He gestured with his hand for them to enter.

"I'm sorry to come unannounced," Dr. Clarke began, "but we were out making some calls and thought we'd take advantage of the opportunity to come check on Dakota's progress."

"Certainly." Caleb led them into the living room. Dakota looked up, and his eyes locked with Dana's.

Their exchange wasn't lost on any of the other adults in the room. Alicia and Claire shared a knowing glance and a smile. They had hoped the two would finally find their way back together, and from the looks of things, they were definitely on the right track.

"Dakota." Dr. Clarke's voice forced Dakota to pull his eyes away from Dana. "We came to see how you're feeling."

"I'm much better. Thank you. I'm still a little weak but getting stronger every day."

Dr. Clarke went over to him to see for himself. He took out his stethoscope and listened to Dakota's breathing and heart. His lungs were clear, and there was no fever.

"You seem to be in good shape," he announced as he patted his patient on the back.

"Won't you have a seat?" Alicia offered. "I was just about to pour some coffee. We'd love it if you would join us."

Dr. Clarke looked over at his niece, who nodded her assent.

"Thank you," Dr. Clarke said as he took a seat. Dana took a seat opposite Dakota, and the two continuously stole glances at each other.

"Doc," Caleb began, "would you happen to know how Mattie Thomas is holding up?"

They hadn't seen her since the funeral and were worried about the new widow.

"She's having a hard time," Dana answered.

"Yes, she's pretty much turned the store over to Carl Holding. She's so down. The kind of love Mattie and Levi shared is one that you never get over. I've heard talk that she's thinking about moving to Virginia to be with one of her daughters and her family."

"I can see why she'd want to move to be with her daughter. It would be so lonely otherwise. And I don't see how she could stand to stay in that house with all of the memories." Alicia shuddered at the thought. She took Caleb's hand and squeezed it. She made a note to say a special prayer for Mattie Thomas tonight.

"I think Pastor Tyler and Gloria are going to talk to her and help her as she sorts through what to do. She'll have to find a new proprietor for the general store," Dr. Clarke said.

"At least she knows she has the members of the town to lean on," Claire added. "Pastor Tyler and his wife are so kind and helpful."

Silence fell over the group, and Dakota glanced over at Dana. She smiled at him, making his heart soar. He wished he could speak with her privately but knew that wouldn't be possible tonight with everyone here. And he didn't think Alicia would allow him to walk around in the cool, night air so soon after his illness.

"You know, I've been thinking," Alicia broke the silence, "with all of the chaos of the epidemic, we were never able to celebrate Daisy's birthday."

"You're right," Caleb said in surprise as if realizing that for the first time.

"I was thinking about having a belated party for her."

"Oh, Alicia, what a wonderful idea," Claire gushed. Alicia looked over at Caleb, who smiled in approval.

"I'd like to have some of Daisy's little friends and their families over, the Tylers, and of course, our heroic doctor and his nurse."

"Please don't label me as a hero, Alicia," Dr. Clarke admonished. "I'm merely helping others the best I know how."

"I'll always think of those that saved my daughter's life as heroes." Alicia wouldn't be easily swayed. She couldn't imagine losing her precious Cameron, Will, or Daisy. "I also think it might be nice to invite Mattie. It might help take her mind off things."

"That's a lovely idea. We should probably include Mrs. Thorne too," Claire put in. Alicia nodded. The old woman could be mean as a tomcat, but Daisy seemed to bring out the soft side in her. Alicia and Claire continued to discuss plans and ideas with Dana interjecting her own thoughts here and there. They decided to have the party in a week.

The night quickly slipped by, and before anyone was ready it was time to leave. Dr. Clarke and Dana said their good-byes, and the Brewers left shortly after. Dakota tried not to feel the sting of disappointment over not getting to speak with Dana one on one but knew there would be time for that in the future.

The next Sunday, Dakota insisted upon going with the family to church. He felt he had been away too long and needed the refreshment that came with being in the house of the Lord with fellow believers. He was met with no argument. A few days before, he moved back to the bunkhouse, but only after promising Alicia that he would take it easy. He was tired of being treated like an invalid and was going stir-crazy in the house.

Dakota rode his horse alongside the Carter wagon. As glad as he was to be able to go to church, he was concerned over what his reception would be like. He didn't suppose anything would be different, and the thought gnawed at him. He wouldn't be teaching Sunday school today because he hadn't had time to prepare a lesson, but he decided that he would talk to Pastor Tyler about resuming next week—even if it were only the Carter and Brewer children in attendance. Caleb and Alicia noted Dakota's silence during the trip.

"Something troubling you, son?" Caleb inquired.

Dakota brought his horse up next to Caleb's seat, and his horse fell in step with the roll of the wagon. "I was just wondering what kind of greeting I'll get at the church today."

Caleb gave Alicia a knowing glance. "I don't think you need to worry about that." Dakota looked over at him with raised brows.

"Why do you think that?"

"Dakota, when you were so ill we feared for your life, Pastor Tyler called together a special prayer meeting, and nearly everyone in town showed up."

"Really?" he asked. After hearing that bit of news, Dakota relaxed, and for the first time he began to hope that maybe the town would see him for who he really was after all.

They pulled into the churchyard, and Dakota swung Daisy out of the back of the wagon. Cameron and Will clambered down and ran to visit with some friends. Caleb helped Alicia down from the wagon, and the four of them began to walk toward the door. As they drew closer to the entrance of the church, Mr. and Mrs. Harper approached Dakota.

"I reckon I oughta be thankin' ya," Mr. Harper said. Alicia took Daisy's hand, and the three of them continued into the church, leaving Dakota with the Harpers.

"Mary is a wonderful girl. I was glad to help."

"Perhaps we was too hasty to judge, and, well…" Mr. Harper seemed to struggle over what to say. Apparently swallowing some crow wasn't something he was used to. "Well, we just want to say that come next Sunday, Mary will be back in your class." He slowly extended a hand to Dakota, who gratefully accepted the shake.

"Thank you, sir." With that, the Harpers turned and went into the church. Dakota followed after them but didn't make it very far before he was stopped by another family. One family after another came up to him to thank him and apologize the best way they knew how. Dakota was overwhelmed at their change of heart toward him. He sent up a heartfelt prayer of thanks to God, who brought so much good to his life through the epidemic.

It seemed as if all of the families had gone inside, and Dakota brought up the rear. But he was stopped by a man loudly clearing his throat. He turned from his place on the bottom step and saw Fred Johnson with his son standing beside him.

"I owe you an apology," Fred began gruffly. "It was wrong of me to accuse you of stealing my chickens. I don't know that I'll ever really trust you, but I am sorry that I caused such an ordeal for you. You helped save my boy's life, and I'm mighty grateful."

"I appreciate that, Mr. Johnson." Dakota put a hand out that Fred reluctantly accepted. He smiled at Cole and then turned and finished climbing the stairs to go into the church building. He and Fred Johnson would never be friends, but at least they were on civil speaking terms.

Dakota went in and looked around. Families filled the sanctuary, and it did Dakota's heart a world of good to see everyone together to worship the Lord. He looked up toward the front and saw the Carters and Brewers. He thought about going up there to join them but quickly reconsidered. There was someone else he'd rather see just now. She was sitting with her uncle in their usual pew behind the Carters.

Dakota's stomach did a flip, and his pulse began to race. Dana Clarke. His angel. Dakota made his way over to them. Dana looked up and smiled when she saw him. He sat by her and tenderly took her hand in his as the service began.

Once the service was over, Dakota was invited to join Dr. Clarke and his niece for lunch at the restaurant. The threesome made their way over and in no time were seated with their orders placed.

"How have you been feeling lately, Dakota?" Dr. Clarke asked.

"I'm pretty much back to normal and doing my usual chores at the ranch."

"Don't overdo," a concerned Dana put in. Dakota gave her such a tender smile that it took her breath away. He leaned over and laid his hand on her arm.

"Don't worry about me."

"I noticed that the townspeople seem to finally be coming to their senses," Dr. Clarke remarked.

"It feels like a miracle," Dakota answered. "For so many weeks, no one would talk to me or even look at me, and this morning almost everyone stopped to speak to me. I hate that the town had to go through the epidemic, but it's amazing how God can take a bad situation and bring good out of it." He and Dana exchanged a loving glance, feeling grateful that the epidemic brought them back together.

The food arrived, and the three adults enjoyed their meal and conversation, but it came to an end much too quickly for any of them. Before they left the restaurant, Dakota had a request for Dr. Clarke.

"Sir, I would be honored if you would allow me to call on Dana." Dakota held his breath as he waited for an answer, and Dana turned hopeful eyes to her uncle.

"I can think of no finer man to call on my niece than you, Dakota." Dr. Clarke smiled at the young couple, who beamed at each other. Dakota's heart overflowed with praise to the God who so richly blessed his life.

CHAPTER 22

Monday morning dawned, and Pastor Tyler knew that a visit was in order. He came down the stairs and bid his wife good morning.

"Good morning, dear," she said in her usual cheerful voice. "Breakfast is ready." She set a plate of scrambled eggs, bacon, and a biscuit in front of both their places and they sat down. After Pastor Tyler gave thanks he forked up some of the eggs.

"You know, I've been thinking that we should pay a visit to Mattie Thomas today."

"You're right. I went by there a couple of times last week to take some meals to her and see if I could be of any comfort, but she wasn't interested in talking to me. I think in her mind she feels that I can't understand because I still have you and she doesn't have Levi anymore."

Pastor Tyler nodded. He expected her to be resistant to the help of others. Mattie Thomas was used to being the helper, not the one who received it. She was strong and proud, but right now she was broken.

"Will you go with me?" Pastor Tyler asked his wife.

"Of course I will." The two finished their breakfast, and once Gloria had finished the dishes, they walked arm in arm over to the small residence that adjoined the general store.

Pastor Tyler knocked on the door, and they waited. A full minute passed, and Gloria was afraid that Mattie wouldn't receive visitors today. Finally they heard footsteps, and the door slowly opened.

"Hello, Mattie," Pastor Tyler greeted her. "May we come in?"

The dark circles under her eyes told Gloria that Mattie hadn't been sleeping much. She had also lost a considerable amount of weight. Her face was drawn and pale. Gloria's heart went out to her. She wondered what she would be like if Douglas Tyler were to be taken from her, and she quickly pushed the thought away with a shudder. Lord willing, she would never have to find out.

"Of course." Mattie opened the door enough for her visitors to enter and closed it behind them. She led them into the living area and motioned for them to sit down. "Can I get you anything to drink?"

"No, thank you," Pastor Tyler answered for the both of them. "We missed you in church yesterday."

"Thank you," Mattie answered quietly. "You know, it's not that I don't want to be in church. I don't have nothin' against the good Lord. He saw fit to take my Levi home, and it's not my place to question it. But I'm not ready to face everyone in town yet. The looks of pity, the words of sympathy. It's too much for a body to handle right now."

"That's completely understandable. These things take time. But tell us, what can we do for you?"

"Yes," Gloria put in. "I'm worried about you."

Mattie let out a half-hearted chuckle. "Don't you be worryin' about me. I'll be okay in time."

"Do you have any plans?" Pastor Tyler asked.

"I've been thinkin' a lot on what I should do," Mattie slowly responded. "I'm thinkin' about moving up to Virginia to live with one of my daughters. My other daughter lives far out west, but Caroline isn't too terribly far away, and she and her husband and children have extended an invitation for me to come live with them."

"Is that what you want?" Gloria wanted to know.

"I don't rightly want to leave this town, but I most definitely don't want to live alone for the rest of my days managing this store. It's hard to live in this house too. There are memories everywhere I look. So, yes, I think I do want to take up my daughter's offer to live with her."

"It might do you a world of good to be with her and your grandchildren," Pastor Tyler said.

"I've never even met my grandbabies. The way I figure it, there's no need for me to stay here alone when I could be lovin' on those young'uns."

Gloria's eyes glistened. "I'm so thankful you have family to go to." She and Pastor Tyler were never able to have children, and that was always something that saddened her.

"What's going to happen to the store?" Pastor Tyler wanted to know.

"That's a good question. I reckon I'll have to sell it." She sounded sad at the prospect. Gloria reached over and squeezed her hand.

"How can we help?" she gently asked. Even with her tough exterior, Mattie was having a difficult time hiding the pain she was in.

"Well, I don't know how to go about selling the store," Mattie began. "I'm thinkin' about asking Carl if he'd be interested in buying the place."

Pastor Tyler sat thoughtfully for a moment. "He just might be at that. Carl's got a good head for business and owning the store along with the hotel might be a profitable venture for him."

"Would you like us to ask him for you?" Gloria asked.

"That's mighty kind of you, but it's my responsibility. I'll ask him about it," Mattie answered. They sat for a while longer and talked about the possibilities of Carl buying the store and Mattie moving to Virginia. For the first time since they arrived, Mattie's dark cloud seemed to lift from her just a bit.

Mattie rose from where she had knelt by the bed. Spending some time in prayer was exactly what she needed. She wanted to make sure that asking Carl to buy the store was what God wanted. She didn't like having to make the kind of decisions that Levi always handled. He was strong and confident, and Mattie was content to let him lead the way God intended for a husband to lead. But now the burden fell to her shoulders. Though she felt she had her answer. She smoothed out the folds in her dress and made her way downstairs.

As she came to the door that connected the mercantile to the living area, she stopped and took a deep breath. She never imagined she would be asking anybody to buy her Levi's store. It almost felt like a betrayal, but Mattie knew she had no choice. She also knew that Levi would want her to be happy and with family.

Mattie reached out and opened the door. It was closing time, and she watched as Carl said good-bye to the last customer and locked up behind him.

"Hello, Carl."

Carl turned and smiled. Mattie so rarely came in the store these days, and it was nice to see her. "Hello, Mattie. How are you feeling tonight?"

"I'm holding my own." She walked over to the counter and knew she would have to just blurt out what was on her mind. "Carl, I think we both know I can't run this store on my own."

Carl stopped from where he was straightening up shelves and waited for her continue.

"I also know I can't stay here without my Levi. I need to be with family and so I'm moving to Virginia to live with my daughter and her family."

"That's good news, Mattie. That will be comforting for you."

Mattie nodded and continued. "Well, I reckon I have to sell this place, and since you've been so kind to help me out I wanted to give you the offer first. Would you be interested in buyin' the mercantile?"

Carl's eyes widened. He had never seriously considered the idea. He always figured Mattie would just hire some help.

"That's a tempting offer, Mattie," he responded. "Let me think on it and I'll get back to you."

"Take your time." Mattie turned and went back to her living quarters. She shut the door behind her and leaned back against it. She felt like she had made a small step in the right direction.

Two days later, Mattie heard a knock at her front door. She opened it to find Carl Holding standing there, hat in hand.

"Please come in," she motioned with her hand for him to enter. She led him to the living area, and they sat down.

"I've come to talk to you about your offer to buy the mercantile." Mattie involuntarily leaned forward as he continued.

"I've done a lot of thinking and praying on it, and I think it would be a sound investment for me. Owning both the hotel and mercantile would be good for business, and I could hire some help. I'd like to take you up on that offer, Mattie."

Mattie felt relief wash through her. Now she could move to Virginia as soon as possible and not have to worry about the mercantile.

"Thank you, Carl," she said with emotion as she reached over and squeezed his hand. "I'm so pleased."

They spent a while longer discussing details of the price and how soon the paperwork could be drawn up. After he left, Mattie sank to her knees and prayed a thank you to the God who never leaves or forsakes his children.

Dakota's chores were done, and he wanted to be alone for a while. The weather was beckoning him outside. The birds were singing, and there was a warm breeze that gently blew through the countryside. Dakota grabbed some whittling and, in long strides, walked across the property to a small brook. He sat down on a stone beneath an oak tree and began to whittle.

He had so much on his mind; he wasn't quite sure where to begin. He decided some silent prayer time would be just the thing to help calm some of the thoughts storming around inside him. Dakota took a deep breath, breathing in the scents of the land—the green grass and flowers, the trees, the smell of horses.

He gazed across the open prairie land and then looked up toward heaven. His heart overflowed with praise as he reflected back on the last weeks.

He was no longer an outcast. God had opened the eyes of the town to see that he was a changed man. Dakota spent several minutes thanking God for his unending blessings. His thoughts then wandered to Dana, bringing a smile to his face. They were courting once again, and it made Dakota light-headed just thinking about it.

He looked around at his surroundings, and something crossed his mind that he hadn't given much thought to until now. *If I were to ask Dana to marry me, I would need a means in which to support her.* He was a ranch hand with very little money saved and no home to call his own. He knew that he could stay on as a ranch hand for Caleb, but he didn't have a desire to have a spread of his own one day. *Would I really be able to support Dana and the family we might have?*

Dakota's whittling became more forceful as the thought gnawed at him. He wanted to at least be able to provide a home for Dana. How would he do that? The whittling began to slow down until Dakota's hand had stopped midair. Once again he looked up toward heaven and prayed some more. Only this time he was asking God to show him what he was supposed to do with his life.

CHAPTER 23

Alicia slowly opened her eyes to the sound of birds chirping. Light streamed in through the window, and she raised her arms over her head to stretch. Today was Daisy's birthday celebration. She hummed as she made her way downstairs and prepared a light breakfast. They didn't need to eat too much; the party would begin at lunchtime.

She put a bowl of oatmeal and a biscuit on a tray and carried it upstairs. She opened the door to Daisy's room and smiled at the child lying on the bed. She looked like a little doll with her blond curls strewn about the pillow. Alicia walked over to her and sat down on the side of the bed.

"Good morning, sweetie," she cooed as she brushed back the hair from Daisy's face. Daisy stirred, and her eyes slowly fluttered open.

"Mama!" she murmured in a tone that told Alicia she was happy to see her mother.

"Do you know what today is?"

"My birthday party!" Daisy suddenly realized as she sat up straight. Alicia caught the tray just before it tipped over.

"Yes, it is." Alicia laughed. "And to start the day off, I've brought you breakfast in bed."

Daisy's little eyes lit up. "You mean I can eat this in here? In my bed?" She was never allowed to eat in her room.

"Yes, you can."

Daisy clapped her hands in delight.

"Try not to spill anything on your bed, and when you're done, I'll come get the tray." Alicia rose and went to get Caleb and the boys. They all got up, albeit a bit more reluctantly than the birthday girl, and made their way downstairs for breakfast.

About an hour later, the Brewer wagon rode onto the ranch. Claire wanted to help set up for her niece's birthday party. Daisy, her brothers, and her cousins all went to the barn to play with the kittens. Caleb had invited all of the ranch hands to join in the festivities, so as soon as all the necessary chores were done, everyone pitched in to help set up. There were tables that needed to be set up outside. They also planned to give hayrides, so some of the hands set about filling up the wagon with hay. The weather was cooperating beautifully, and Alicia couldn't have been more pleased.

Alicia and Claire went to the kitchen to finish last-minute preparations. The other families were all bringing a small dish to share, which eased Alicia's load tremendously. Alicia had picked some fresh apples from a nearby apple tree on their property and had dipped them in caramel for a special treat.

"The children are going to love those!" Claire exclaimed when she saw the apples. "I might want one myself."

"I made plenty." Alicia chuckled. "Take a look at the cake." Alicia lifted a lid off a platter to reveal a beautiful rectangular cake with white frosting and writing that said "Happy Birthday, Daisy" on it. Claire sucked in a breath.

"You outdid yourself!"

"Thanks. I hope Daisy will like it."

"You know she will. She's going to have the time of her life today." Claire helped Alicia take plates, cups, and forks out to the waiting tables; then they carried out several pitchers of lemonade and sweet tea. They brought the food out last—the apples, the cake, some vegetables Alicia had prepared, and a casserole. Since all of the other families would bring some sort of dish, Alicia didn't want to overdo it.

Promptly at noon, wagons began to roll onto the Blue Star Ranch. Daisy could hardly contain herself. Alicia had invited nearly every family with children, and some without, in Darby. Daisy's eyes grew wide as the presents began to pile up on a table.

"You see that?" Dakota leaned down to whisper in her ear. She nodded angelically. "All of those presents are for you."

"For me?" she whispered in awe.

"Um-hm." Dakota tried not to laugh at the expression on Daisy's face.

There were many families with little boys, and Cameron and Will enjoyed their companionship. They couldn't wait for the hayride. Caleb had also promised Cameron that there would be a short horse race for the older children. Cameron was beside himself with excitement. He couldn't wait to ride his horse. His father bought Cameron a beautiful gelding with a dark-brown coat and black mane a few years ago, and Caleb had taught him how to train the horse for riding.

Ever since the wagons began to arrive, Dakota had been watching for one wagon in particular. He finally saw it roll up onto the property and walked over.

"May I help you down?" he asked as he extended his hand to a beautiful young lady.

"Thank you, Dakota," Dana said shyly as she took his hand. He offered his arm, which she accepted, and they walked toward the festivities.

Dakota and Dana sat on a blanket that Dakota had laid out under a tree. Many families had blankets spread out. Everyone was going to eat picnic-style. Families began mingling and fixing plates of food. Dakota went to get a plate for himself and Dana.

"Miss Clarke!" Dana turned at the sound of a young voice calling her name. Daisy ran over to her and plopped down on the blanket beside her.

"Happy birthday," Dana told her.

"Thanks. Do you see that table over there," Daisy said conspiratorially as she pointed to the table full of presents. Dana nodded. "Those are all for me!"

"They are! There's so many of them!" Dana feigned shock, much to the delight of the child. "Are you going to share some of them with me?" Daisy looked deep in thought as she contemplated the question.

"All right," she slowly answered.

"You sweet thing," Dana cried as she began to tickle the little girl. Daisy's laughter rang through the air. "You don't have to share them with me. I was only kidding." A flicker of relief crossed Daisy's face as she trotted off to see more people. Dakota came back with two plates, and the couple ate and enjoyed light chatter about the party and the latest goings-on of the town.

An hour or so later, Caleb put two fingers in his mouth, and a whistle screamed through the air, getting everyone's attention. He held young Daisy in his arms.

"We'd like to thank everyone for coming today. In light of Daisy's recent battle with influenza, this birthday celebration is particularly special to our family. We're going to allow Daisy to open her presents, and then we have games for everyone!"

A cheer went up from all of the children. Daisy hopped out of her father's arms and ran over to the table spilling over with presents. She received many fine gifts, including new dresses and a small rocking chair that Caleb had made for her. Mattie Thomas brought a small drawstring purse for Daisy, which she proudly displayed on her arm. But Daisy's favorite gift came from Dakota. He had whittled her a model of the ranch. It was like a dollhouse, only it was the ranch, complete with trees and a barn. He had also whittled several horses and figures of Daisy and her family. She squealed with delight and threw her arms around Dakota's neck, thanking him profusely.

Afterward, Caleb and the ranch hands helped with the hayrides. They hitched a horse up to the wagon and rode the children around. They had a three-legged race, and, to the great surprise of their parents, Bethany and Emily Brewer won. They also had a sack race, which brought forth laughter from both the participants and the crowd to see so many fall and struggle to get up to finish the race.

Last came the highly anticipated horse race. Caleb had marked off a flat section of the property for the race. They were to race down to the trees Caleb had marked, and the first one back would win. Only the older children were allowed to participate, and Cameron eagerly mounted his horse, Felix. There were about six children in all, including Cole Johnson. Caleb had them all line up. The horses shuffled their feet in anticipation. Caleb whistled, and the boys were off.

Everyone seemed to collectively move forward as they watched, anxious to see how the race would turn out. Mark hated trying to maneuver on the uneven soil in his wheelchair. He had a hard time seeing over the crowd, and Caleb wheeled him to a spot where he would have an unobstructed view. He held his breath for his nephew, who wanted so badly to win. The riders rounded the trees and started back. Caleb and Mark saw that Cameron was in the lead but that Barry Stewart's blue roan was swiftly outpacing the gelding. In the end, Barry crossed the finish line only inches before Cameron. The crowd cheered as a smile stretched across Barry's face, but Caleb didn't miss the look of disappointment on Cameron's. He watched his son dismount and walk over to congratulate Barry. He put on a brave face and tried not to let anyone know how much he had wanted to win. Caleb nearly burst with pride over his son's mature behavior. He was growing into a man all too quickly.

"Well, how about we let the grown-ups give it a go?" Mr. Harper's voice rang through the crowd. "I've always wanted to race my mustang against your stallion, Caleb." Excited whispers made their way through the crowd as people began to warm up to the idea. Caleb rubbed the back of his neck.

"I don't know," he began. He looked over to Alicia and noted the mischievous gleam in her eye.

"Does anyone else want to participate?" Caleb asked. Several men raised their hands, and Caleb chuckled. "Well, all right, then. But this is just for fun."

"Of course," Mr. Harper agreed as the men dispersed to get their horses.

After a few minutes, everyone was in position for the race. Pastor Tyler helped everyone get lined up and then signaled for the race to begin. The horses took off at an amazing speed, and the crowd watched in awe as the magnificent animals flew down the course. Children were loudly cheering for their parents as nervous wives looked on. Mr. Harper's mustang was giving Caleb's stallion a run for his money. It was hard to tell who was in the lead. As they rounded the trees and began coming back up, another horse began to pass them both. A creamy-colored stallion rode past Mr. Harper's mustang and Caleb's black stallion.

By this time, the crowd was going wild with excitement as the creamy-colored stallion crossed the finish line seconds before Caleb and Mr. Harper. Everyone cheered and wondered who the rider of the winning stallion was. It wasn't one of the men who originally intended to race. The rider remained mounted and pulled off a hat. Auburn hair tumbled down. Caleb broke into a hearty laugh. He might have known his wife wouldn't let a horse race take place on their property without participating.

"That was fun!" she exclaimed, and the crowd burst into a mixture of cheers and laughter. Caleb rode up beside her. "Better luck next time." He let out a hearty laugh and she winked at him.

Alicia dismounted and moved to take Knight back into the barn to remove his gear and rub him down.

"I'll do that," Caleb said as he took the reins from his wife's hands. "I'm sure you're needed to help run the party."

Alicia appreciated Caleb's consideration. "Thanks," she said as she walked over to Claire to make sure that all was still in order after her little riding escapade.

"How is everything going?" Alicia asked as she reached her sister-in-law.

"I think Daisy is ready for cake," Claire answered.

"Of course. Let me go find her." When everyone was happily eating their cake, Alicia left the table and walked over to someone she had wanted to speak with all afternoon.

"Hello, Mattie." The older woman turned to face her. There was no mistaking the sadness in her eyes, but she tried to mask it with a brave smile. Alicia took her hands. "I'm so pleased you could join us today."

"Thank ya kindly for invitin' an old woman."

"Daisy loved her gift. That was very thoughtful of you."

"It seemed appropriate for a little girl."

"I think it makes her feel very grown-up," Alicia admitted with a wink. "She'll probably want to carry it with her to church tomorrow."

"I guess pretty soon I'll be doin' this kind of stuff with my own grandbabies."

"What do you mean?"

"I mean, I'm leavin' to live with my girl and her family in Virginia," Mattie said.

"This town is really going to miss you," Alicia responded. "But it will be good for you to be with your family."

"That's what I think too. Carl Holding has agreed to buy the mercantile, so as soon as all the paperwork is squared away I'll be heading off to Virginia."

"Please let me know if there is anything I can do."

"The invite to this party was more than enough." Mattie's eyes glistened. Alicia gave her a warm hug then moved off to visit with other guests.

CHAPTER 24

Dakota's pulse raced, and his palms were sweaty as he rode into town on Sunday morning. He wasn't sure if his nerves were due more to excitement or anxiety over what the morning would hold. He was about to find out if the townspeople really meant it when they said their children would be back in Sunday school. The thought made him want to shout for joy. He loved teaching the children about God's love.

He rode up to the church and tethered his horse to a hitching post.

"Good morning, Dakota."

He turned at the sound of the silky voice and found himself staring down into a pair of beautiful blue eyes.

"Mornin'," he responded huskily. He offered his arm to Dana and escorted her into the church.

"Today's the big day," she whispered. Dakota nodded. Dana could feel the tension in his arm and gave it a squeeze. "Don't worry. Everything will be fine." She took a seat beside her uncle as Dakota walked to the back of the building and through a door that would lead him to the Sunday school room.

His steps slowed as he came closer to the door. He sent up a silent prayer asking God for grace to deal with whatever lay beyond that door. As he approached, he began to hear voices. The closer he got to the door, the more voices he heard. He reached for the doorknob, took a deep breath, and slowly swung the door open.

"Mr. Jones!" Daisy exclaimed as she threw herself into his arms. Dakota laughed as he caught her and looked around in amazement. All of the children were present in Sunday school today. His gaze swept the room as he took in all of the faces that shone their happiness. It was obvious they were glad to be back in Sunday school again.

"I'm so glad to see all of you," Dakota said as he put Daisy down. "I missed having you all in Sunday school."

"We missed being here, Mr. Jones," Cole Johnson spoke up.

"Let's sing 'Jesus Loves Me,'" Mary Harper suggested. Daisy clapped her hands in excitement. Dakota asked them to all settle into their seats as they sang through the children's favorite song. Once they finished, Dakota began to speak.

"Today I want to talk to you about how much God loves all of us and how he never gives up on anyone," Dakota began as he took out some figures that he had carved and placed them on a table. The children sat in a semicircle, and Dakota sat at a chair in the center with a table in front of him. He took the figures and held them up.

"This one"—he held up a tall figure of a man—"is the father. And these two are his sons. These other people are their workers, and here are some animals." He placed them all around on the table. The children watched with fascination.

"This boy is the youngest son, and this one is his older brother," Dakota said as he pointed to the two statues. "Now the youngest son took his share of the money, and he left his family." Dakota showed the young son walking away from his family and put him on the opposite end of the table. "But he made poor decisions and lost all of his money. He had nothing left, and he had to find a way to make more money. So he began feeding pigs, which was a very lowly job in the Bible days." Dakota took a couple of figurines in the shape of pigs and showed the younger son feeding them.

"The youngest son didn't make much feeding pigs and was very hungry, and one day he decided to return to his father's house." Dakota showed him walking toward the side of the table where the father and older brother were. Dakota looked at the children. "Can you imagine how hard that must have been for the younger son? Do you think he might have been worried that his father wouldn't want him anymore or be angry with him?" Dakota saw several nods and heard a few murmurs of agreement.

"But how do you think the father reacted? When he saw his son still a long way off, he ran to him and hugged him. He was happy to see him!" Dakota took the father and showed him running toward the younger son. "The son admitted that he had sinned, but you know what the father did?" Dakota waited as eyes full of anticipation watched and waited for him to continue. "He forgave his son. He had a feast to celebrate his return." Dakota took the father and brothers and tried to arrange all the other people and animals to look like they were having a party.

"Jesus told that parable in the Bible in the book of Luke," Dakota went on to tell them. "What do you think Jesus wanted to teach us?" Little hands flew up as the children began to try for the answer.

"To be nice to everyone!"

"That everyone makes mistakes!"

"To forgive."

Dakota looked to see who had given that response. Cameron Carter looked at him, and Dakota noted wisdom in his eyes beyond his years. Dakota shook his head slightly in wonder. He wondered if Caleb realized the impact his witness for God had on his oldest son.

"That's right, Cameron. Jesus wants us to forgive, even when people do things that hurt us. He wants us to love them anyway."

"Like when my older brother ate my slice of apple pie, and I was so mad at him, I'm supposed to forgive him anyway," a child said.

"Yes, exactly. Sometimes people will do things, whether they mean to or not, that hurt our feelings or make us upset. But we still have to forgive them and love them. Just like God loves us. How many of you are perfect every day?" Dakota looked around, but not a single hand was raised. "When you do something wrong, you need to tell God about it and ask him to forgive you. And you know what? He will. He forgives you every day and loves each of you very much. God gives us all second chances every day, and it's important that we give others a second chance too." That rang all too true for Dakota. The second chance that God had given him on life all those years ago was something he still thanked God for every day. And now he had been given a second chance with Dana and the town.

The Sunday school lesson ended shortly after that, and as they left the room and joined the adults who were leaving the sanctuary, Dakota could hear the children's little voices excitedly telling their parents what they had learned about love, forgiveness, and second chances. Some parents looked sheepishly at Dakota as they realized they hadn't demonstrated that well in their own lives.

"How did it go, son?" Pastor Tyler asked as Dakota exited the building.

"Very well. It was good to be back. The children are like little sponges just ready to learn and absorb what I have to tell them about the Word of God."

"It's a wonderful thing to be able to share God's message and know that you're making a difference."

Dakota paused and looked at Pastor Tyler thoughtfully for a moment. His words kept repeating themselves in Dakota's mind.

"Are you all right?" the pastor asked.

"Yes, thank you." Dakota shook his hand and continued on his way. But the pastor's words stuck with him all day.

Dana leaned back on the blanket spread on the ground and sighed contentedly as she felt a light breeze blow through her hair. The sun radiated its warmth, and the scent of wildflowers wafted through the air.

"Let the floods clap their hands: let the hills be joyful together before the Lord,⁴" Dana's melodious voice quoting Psalm 98 broke the silence. "Isn't it amazing how even when God's people don't recognize his goodness all around, the rest of creation can't help but worship and praise him?"

Dakota sat beside her, leaning back on his elbows. "I know. The rolling hills and pasturelands are something else. Only God could create something this spectacular."

Dana was silent and slid her eyes shut. It was wonderful to have a day off to rest and enjoy the beautiful day and the company. But there was something weighing on her mind. Something that wouldn't allow her to fully relax until she had asked about it.

"Dakota?" He looked over at her and remained silent, waiting for her to continue. "Will you tell me about your childhood?" She glanced up at Dakota and saw a distant look in his eyes.

"You don't have to tell me."

Dakota took her hand and wove their fingers together. "Until now, I hadn't realized that I haven't told you about it. I want to tell you. I want you to know everything about me." She sat up straight and looked at him expectantly.

Dakota's eyes closed for a moment, and when he opened them, he began to speak softly. He started from the beginning and left nothing out. He told her how his mother died during childbirth and about the father who turned to drinking to drown his pain and never really cared for the child he held responsible for her death. He told her about his father forcing him and his brothers to become outlaws, and he told her about the horrible day when his father branded them all. He told her about the crimes they committed and about what happened in Darby ten years ago. He finished by telling her about the sentencing in Frankfort and the ten years he spent in prison.

"And then I came back here," he finished. "To start over."

Tears pooled up in Dana's eyes. She had no idea of the kind of heartache that Dakota had known. It made her feel spoiled and selfish. She had an idyllic childhood, and Dakota had known nothing but anger and abuse. And yet, the man sitting next to her was completely at peace. He held no bitterness in his heart. Only a strong desire to become the man God intended him to be. In that moment, her respect for him grew tenfold. Her heart swelled with love and pride, and she felt blessed that God had brought them together.

"I'm so sorry, Dakota."

"Me too. But it's over now, and I am not looking back. But one thing I know for sure," he said as his gaze intensified, "my children will know nothing but love. The love of his parents and the love of God."

Dana leaned over and gave him a quick kiss on the cheek. "You're a good man, Dakota Jones," she said as she began to pack up their picnic.

Pastor Tyler sat working on his sermon for the next Sunday. His study was a cozy nook of a room just off the family room in the home that he and Gloria shared. His brows were furrowed in concentration when he heard a knock at the door. He looked up to see his wife poke her head in.

"Excuse me, dear, but you have a visitor."

"Of course," Pastor Tyler responded as he rose from his desk. Gloria looked back and gestured with her hand toward the door. Dakota quietly slipped in. Gloria cast a curious look at her husband before leaving the study.

Pastor Tyler walked around his desk and extended his hand.

"Hello, Dakota. Please have a seat."

"I hope I'm not disturbing you."

"Not at all," the pastor answered as he and Dakota took seats. "What's on your mind, son?"

Dakota leaned back and took a deep breath. He wasn't exactly sure where to begin. He rubbed his hands up and down the arms of the chair. Pastor Tyler waited patiently.

"I've been trying to figure out what God wants me to do with my life. As much as I enjoy being a ranch hand, that's no way to support a family of my own. And I don't want to own a ranch. I've been praying and asking God's guidance, and I finally feel like he might have given me his answer."

Pastor Tyler leaned forward in his chair. "And what do you feel he's calling you to do?"

"You said something the other day that I haven't been able to forget," Dakota continued. "You said, 'It's a wonderful thing to be able to share God's message and know that you're making a difference.' When I couldn't teach the children in Sunday school, I was devastated. Sharing God's Word with them and helping to shape their young minds filled me with such purpose. No one ever took the time to share God's word with me as a child or show me any kindness, and I feel so blessed that God has given me the opportunity to help them in a way that I never was. Pastor Tyler, I believe that God is calling me into the ministry."

Pastor Tyler sat back, and a smile played at the corners of his mouth. He didn't speak for a while but sat looking thoughtfully at Dakota. Pastor Tyler couldn't deny the change in him from the sixteen-year-old boy he met ten years ago and the man he was today. He thought back to men from the Bible, such as Paul whose life had been completely transformed, and he became one of the greatest evangelists of all time. Pastor Tyler could see how the obstacles that Dakota had overcome would help him to become a compassionate and strong leader of the church. He nodded slowly.

"Son, if you feel that is what God is calling you to do, then that's what you should do."

Dakota looked visibly relieved. "I'm not sure where to go from here. What do I need to do? Where do I start?"

Pastor Tyler stood up and walked from his desk to a bookshelf that went from the floor to the ceiling. He searched for a moment and finally found what he was looking for. He handed a brochure to Dakota, who turned it over in his hands.

"Dakota, this brochure tells about one of the colleges in Kentucky University in Lexington. It's called the College of the Bible. Why don't you write to them and get more information? If you attend, they can teach you what you need to know to be in the ministry."

Dakota's eyes lit up as he opened the brochure and scanned the pages. "Thank you, Pastor Tyler. I'll look into it right away." He rose and bade farewell to the helpful pastor.

Gloria came in after she showed Dakota out and looked questioningly to her husband. While many things spoken between a pastor and a member of the congregation remained confidential, she thought Dakota might have come by to talk about marrying Dana. She waited to see if her husband would offer any information.

"Dakota wants to be a minister."

Gloria's eyes met her husband's for a moment, and then she spoke. "I think he would be perfect for it."

"So do I," he responded thoughtfully as he stroked his chin. "So do I."

Dakota slowly rode back to the Blue Star Ranch. He had much on his mind after his visit with Pastor Tyler. It was getting late in the day, and the setting sun sent hues of orange and red blazing across the sky. The beauty of the evening was lost on Dakota, who was busy trying to sort through his life and his hopes for the future. He knew that a long talk with God was in order to help him make sure he was staying on God's path and not doing just what he wanted to do.

His horse meandered onto the ranch property and headed toward the barn. Dakota jumped down and walked the horse inside.

"Hello, Dakota."

The deep voice startled Dakota, who was so lost in thought he didn't notice anyone else in the barn. He looked up as Caleb let out a hearty laugh.

"You should've seen your face. You would have thought I was a ghost or something." Caleb laughed.

"Sorry, boss. Guess I just wasn't paying attention." Dakota watched the even strokes of Caleb's brush as he cleaned off Midnight. "Enjoy a ride on your stallion?" Dakota asked as he began to strip his horse of the saddle.

"Oh, yes. Alicia had a hankering to ride the stallions today. I can't hardly say no to that woman," he answered with a twinkle in his eye.

"My guess is that you don't try too hard."

"I believe you've figured me out, son," Caleb said with a chuckle. "It's hard to deny the woman you love."

"She's quite a rider," Dakota remarked, thinking back to Daisy's birthday party.

"That she is." The pride in Caleb's voice was unmistakable.

Dakota led his horse into a stall and fed him some oats. "Boss, I got something on my mind. Have you got a minute?"

"Certainly," Caleb said as he put the brush away and sat down on a bale of hay. "What's going on?"

"I've just been to see Pastor Tyler. I've been thinking a lot about my future. I really enjoy working here as a hand, but, well, I don't know that it's what I need to do the rest of my life. Especially if I want to support a family." Caleb nodded encouragingly, and Dakota continued. "I've been praying about it, and I believe that God is calling me to be in the ministry. I intend to pray over it some more, but Pastor Tyler thought it was a good idea and even gave me this brochure on a college that might help me learn what to do." He handed the brochure to Caleb who looked it over.

After several moments of silence, Caleb spoke. "Dakota, I think this a fine idea. If this is what God is calling you to do, then you need to pursue it. God didn't give you a second chance for nothing. I think he has great plans for you and your life." Dakota let out the breath he was unconsciously holding. He had been afraid that Caleb would be upset with him for wanting to leave.

"Thanks, boss."

"Anytime." Caleb patted him on the back as he left the barn to join his family for supper.

Dakota finished up with the horse and went to the bunkhouse. He went inside and looked around. None of the other ranch hands were back yet, and Dakota was grateful for the solitude. He knelt by his bed and began to pray.

"Father God, please guide me in my future. Please show me what you would like for me to do with my life." Dakota continued to ask for God's wisdom and guidance for the next hour. When he rose, his heart felt lighter than it had in a long time. He knew without a doubt that God was calling him into the ministry. His heart filled with joy at this new sense of purpose he felt for his life.

There was one thing left he needed to do: talk to Dana.

CHAPTER 25

Dana sat in a rocking chair on the front porch and breathed deeply of the evening air. This had been one of the busiest days they had had since the influenza epidemic. They spent most of the previous night with a woman in labor who delivered a beautiful baby boy early that morning. Then there was a broken leg that needed to be mended, but the break was so serious that it required surgery. Among that was the normal flow of people with ailments such as coughs and bee stings.

Once the day ended, Dana made a cup of coffee and took a book outside to try to wind down. On the truly busy days when she should be the most exhausted, she found that it was harder for her to go to sleep. And so she rocked away, enjoying the coming of dusk and her book.

Footsteps coming up the stairs onto the porch caused Dana to stifle a groan. She wasn't up to seeing another patient today. She set her book in her lap and plastered on a smile as she looked up. Her heart skipped a beat as she realized it wasn't a patient. She was looking up into the eyes of the man she loved.

"Dakota, what a nice surprise," she said as she stood to greet him. He leaned in for a kiss that took her breath away. When he pulled away, she stared at him, unable to think. He took her hand and guided her to sit back down in the rocking chair, and he took the matching one that was next to it.

"I hope I always have that effect on you," he said after a moment. His light laughter helped bring Dana back to her senses. Her cheeks blushed a bright pink.

"How was your day?" Dakota asked.

"Crazy," Dana responded as she rolled her eyes. She told him about everything that went on at the doctor's office that day, and Dakota whistled. "It's a good thing all days aren't like this, or I don't think I could make it," she finished dryly.

"You're one of the strongest women I know. You could do it." While Dana appreciated his vote of confidence, she was doubtful.

"What about your day?" Dana returned the question. She saw a look she couldn't quite identify in Dakota's eyes and grew concerned. "Is everything all right?"

"Everything is fine. It's better than fine, actually. God has shown me his purpose for my life." Dana leaned forward in her chair. Dakota's words had her full attention. He took a deep breath before he continued and kept his gaze steady on Dana's to gauge her reaction. "Dana, I believe that God is calling me into the ministry."

Dana didn't skip a beat as she took both of his hands in her own. "I can see that, Dakota. You have such an amazing testimony. God is going to use your life in a powerful way." Again, Dakota felt relief. The assurance of his decision seemed to be coming from all sides.

"I'm glad you feel that way. I talked to Pastor Tyler today, and he gave me this brochure about a college I can go to that will help me prepare." Dana took the brochure Dakota gave her and quickly scanned it. "I plan to send them a telegram tomorrow and get more information. I've saved some money, and I think if I can work and go to school at the same time that I'll make it."

"This is really great, Dakota." Dana managed an encouraging smile, willing herself not to cry. How would she say good-bye to him for the years it took him to complete his training? What if he met someone in Lexington?

"Dana." His serious voice broke through her tormenting questions, and she looked at him. His eyes captured hers, and she lost herself in his gaze. His eyes told how much he loved her. It was enough to shatter what was left of her breaking heart. "Dana, I don't want to go alone." His words gave her pause and caused her heart to nearly thud out of her chest. *What does he mean by that?*

"Dana, you know all about my past, and you know the man I am today. I vowed long ago never to treat anyone, especially women and children, the way that I was treated. I ask God every day what I did to deserve having you in my life. Your love is more than I could have hoped for. I don't want to begin this new chapter of my life without you. I want you to go to Lexington with me. As my wife."

Dana's eyes glistened with tears. The heart that was about to shatter only moments ago now bubbled over with hope and love. Hope for the future and love for the man in front of her. Dana laughed and nodded her assent.

"Of course." She giggled as Dakota gathered her in his arms.

Dakota was good on his word and sent a telegram to Kentucky University the next day. It took a couple of weeks before he got a response, and he was beginning to wonder. But the reply didn't come in a telegram. It came in the form of a letter.

"Mr. Jones! Mr. Jones!" Cameron yelled as he and his father rode onto the Blue Star, and the boy saw Dakota standing near one of the corrals. "You got a letter!" Dakota walked over to the boy, who excitedly handed him a thick envelope.

"It says it's from Kentucky University. Open it, son," Caleb said.

Dakota tore into the envelope and pulled out a letter. He quickly read it and relayed its message.

"It says that they are sending me an application, and I need to fill it out and send it back in for consideration of admission. I'll fill this out tonight and mail it back tomorrow." He beamed as he headed back toward the corral. Another step in the right direction.

The next day he took the completed application to the post office and mailed it. He sent up a prayer asking God to go before the application and, that if it was his will, to let Dakota get accepted.

In the meantime, he and Dana had preparations to make. The wedding was set for two months from now, in early September, and Dakota was trying to find odd jobs here and there along with his work on the ranch to make some extra money. Dana was consistently busy at the doctor's office, and when she wasn't there, she was poring over preparations for the wedding. Alicia, Claire, and Gloria were a great help to her. Dana's family was set to come into town a week before the wedding. Dana didn't know who was more excited over that: herself or her uncle. Howard Clarke could barely contain his excitement over the prospect of seeing his brother, Dana's father, again.

"Do we need to go to the general store to look for material for a dress?" Alicia asked Dana. Alicia, Claire, and Dana were seated around the table in Claire's kitchen going over some details.

"No, I'll be wearing my mother's dress. She's bringing it with her when they come."

"That's so nice. I wasn't able to wear my mother's gown. I'm hoping to pass mine on to Daisy."

"Do you have any brothers and sisters who are coming to Darby?" Claire asked. Dana took a sip of coffee and set the mug down.

"Oh, yes." She nodded. "My parents are coming along with my two younger brothers and younger sister."

"I'll bet you've missed them while you have been here," Alicia added.

"You have no idea," Dana said with a laugh. "You don't realize how much people mean to you until you're separated from them. When we were growing up, it wasn't always easy being the oldest. There always seemed to be so many responsibilities. And younger siblings can be such pests sometimes," she added.

"Not me," Claire said as she crossed her arms over her chest, pretending to be put out.

"That's not what Caleb says," Alicia retorted with a smirk. Claire playfully slapped her on the arm. "I'm only kidding." Alicia laughed.

"Are any of your siblings interested in the medical field?" Claire wanted to know.

"Well, my brother Stan wants to be a doctor like Uncle. My other brother and my sister aren't interested. My sister can't stand the sight of blood."

"I couldn't do it." Alicia had to agree with Dana's sister.

All three heads turned as they heard someone knocking on the door. The sound became more urgent, and Claire swiftly rose to answer it. Alicia and Dana followed. Dana briefly wondered if everything was all right at the doctor's office. Claire opened the door a little ways to see who it was and then swung it open. Dana's breath caught.

Dakota stood panting with his hands on his knees, trying to catch his breath.

"Dakota, are you okay?" Dana asked as she put her arm around his shoulders. He nodded as he waved an envelope in front of her.

"Is it from Kentucky University?"

He nodded. Dana's eyes grew wide with excitement. "Well, what did they say?"

"I haven't opened it yet." Dakota's face held a mixture of apprehension, curiosity, and excitement.

"Well, open it!" Alicia exclaimed as she clapped her hands together in front of her chest. Everyone held their breath as Dakota slowly opened the large, white envelope. He pulled out a piece of paper and quickly scanned it. Dana's questioning eyes never left his.

"I got in!" he shouted as he grabbed Dana and whirled her around in the air. Alicia and Claire both let out shouts of excitement. They all made spectacles of themselves jumping up and down on Claire's front porch.

"I'm so proud of you," Dana said after the commotion died down. Claire invited everyone inside, and they all made themselves comfortable in the living room.

"We all are," Alicia added. She couldn't wait until Caleb found out the news. He would be fairly bursting with pride.

"May I see the letter?" Dana asked. Dakota handed it to her, and she read through it. When she was almost to the end of the letter, she stopped and looked at him.

"Dakota, it says that you have to be in Lexington a week from tomorrow."

"What?" He took the letter from her, and his eyes skimmed the page until they landed on what Dana saw. "You're right. It says I have to be in Lexington by next Sunday to begin orientation the following week."

Alicia's gaze went from Dana to Dakota and back to Dana. Both looked surprised, but Dana looked crestfallen. Alicia knew that Dana was wondering how this would impact plans for their upcoming wedding.

"All right." Alicia decided to take charge. Everyone turned to look at her, and she smiled encouragingly at the young couple. "We have to change things up a bit. We can move the wedding up to this Saturday. That's not a problem." She reached over and patted Dana's hand. "Dana, let's go telegram your family and see if they can come this week. Then we need to go see Pastor Tyler." Relief shone in Dana's eyes as she looked gratefully at Alicia.

"Thank you," she said. She reached over and took Dakota's hand. "I was afraid after I read that letter that—" She left the sentence unfinished as she looked at everyone and shrugged.

"Don't you worry," Claire added. "This is a good thing. Dakota is accepted into college, and you and Dakota can begin your lives together sooner than you planned."

Dakota squeezed her hand, giddy with excitement. "Come on. Let's go send that telegram and see Pastor Tyler."

CHAPTER 26

Two days later, an excited Dana stood on the train station platform, shifting her feet as she waited for the train to arrive. Her uncle and fiancé stood with her, and Dr. Clarke couldn't stop himself from pacing back and forth. After what seemed like hours, they could finally see a train in the distance. Dana grabbed Dakota's hand and squeezed. A smile threatened to burst from her face. This would be the first time she had seen her family in almost a year.

Steam blew from the train as the whistle pierced through the air. Dakota rested his hand on Dana's arm to keep her from bouncing up and down. He had never seen her so excited before. He, however, was filled with trepidation. *What will they think of me? What's more, what will they think of their daughter marrying a former outlaw?* He took a few deep breaths to try to calm his racing heart.

The train finally chugged to a slow stop, and both Dana and Howard craned their necks in eager anticipation of the first glimpse of their family. A man with a cane stepped down first, followed by a couple with a young child. A few more passengers descended, and then Dakota heard Dana take in a sharp breath. He looked up and saw what had to be Dana's family coming off the train steps.

Dana ran over to them and threw herself in her mother's arms almost before she had a chance to reach the platform. Howard's face lit up when he saw his brother, and he strode over to greet him. Dakota stood awkwardly off to the side, waiting for Dana to bring them over. He looked over at them and inwardly sighed. They were from Richmond and looked every bit like city dwellers. Dakota couldn't think of a word to describe Dana's mother's dress other than *fancy*. It was a beautiful shade of green, long and flowing, with a high lace neck. Her father wore a dark suit complete with a derby cap. Her brothers and sister were dressed similarly. Dakota looked down at his clothes. They were his Sunday best, but they looked awfully plain in comparison to the Clarkes'.

Dana finally began to guide them toward her waiting fiancé. Dakota took a deep breath. This was it. The moment he had both looked forward to and dreaded. Dana walked up with her arm looped around her mother's. She stopped in front of Dakota.

"Mother, I'd like you to meet my fiancé, Dakota Jones. Dakota, this is my mother, Judith Clarke." Dakota stuck out a hand and was surprised when he felt Judith draw him into a warm embrace. He returned the hug and finally felt himself begin to relax.

"I'm so happy to meet you, Dakota," she gushed. "I couldn't wait to meet the man who won my daughter's heart." Her warm expression quickly put Dakota at ease. She smiled easily, revealing a row of pearly white teeth and dimples on both sides. Her light-brown eyes sparkled as she spoke. Dakota liked her already.

Howard and his brother walked up next. Dana grabbed her father's hand and pulled him over.

"Father, I'd like you to meet Dakota Jones."

"Glad to know you," Nelson Clarke responded.

Dakota extended his hand, and Nelson returned the shake. "Likewise," he responded. Dana's father was more intimidating in appearance than his wife or brother, but Dakota could tell he was a good and gentle man. Dakota could finally breathe easily again.

Dana's brothers and sister approached as Nelson and Howard went to retrieve the luggage.

"Stan, Patrick, Laura, this is my fiancé, Dakota Jones," Dana made the introductions. A round of hellos went around. They were all younger than Dana but not by much. Stan would soon be finished with medical school, Patrick was halfway through law school, and Laura was beginning her studies to become a teacher. Laura shared her mother's dimples, and Stan and Patrick favored their father. Both brothers were tall with dark hair and pointed features.

Once Nelson and Howard loaded the luggage into the buggy, they all headed toward Dr. Clarke's office.

"Hope you don't mind staying in the patient rooms," Dr. Clarke said as they rolled through town.

"As long as there aren't patients in them," his brother responded dryly.

"Thankfully, things are pretty slow right now," Dana put in.

"Not like when you had the epidemic," Judith said as she put an arm around Dana's shoulders.

"That was awful." Dana shuddered.

"You'll have to tell me all about it, Uncle," Stan said. "I'm almost finished with medical school, you know."

"I know, and I'm proud of you. Have you thought about where you'd like to practice?"

"I haven't decided yet. I don't know if I want to stay in the city or go somewhere smaller."

"Well, you know you're always welcome to join me in Darby if you'd like."

"This is such a pleasant little town," Laura said as her eyes swept over the town. The rows of shops and the boardwalks in front of them were bustling with people. She noticed how many of the passersby would stop and talk to one another. "Everyone seems so friendly."

"You pretty much know everyone in a small town," Dana said. "It's actually really nice. I like that part of being in a small town much better than the city."

Howard pulled the horses to a stop in front of his office. His brother looked over the white two-story building and gave Howard a slap on the back.

"You've done pretty well for yourself, big brother."

"Thanks."

"We've got some snacks and lemonade waiting inside," Dana added as she looped one arm through her mother's and the other through her sister's and led them inside. The men all grabbed a bag and followed them in.

Dana showed them to the rooms they would be staying in, while Dr. Clarke proudly showed his brother his office and his equipment.

"All up to date and state of the art," he added.

Stan joined them and looked around. "This is a nice spread, Uncle. It's better than I expected for a country doctor."

"Stan," his father admonished. Stan's face began to redden in embarrassment.

"I'm sorry, Uncle. I didn't mean that the way it sounded."

"It's quite all right, young man. You're in that fancy school and in those fancy city hospitals. And doctors out here don't get paid much like the city doctors do. I would be surprised myself if I were you."

Stan smiled in gratitude, relieved his uncle understood his thoughtless remark.

The group gathered around the table in Howard's small kitchen and enjoyed sandwiches and lemonade. It was a bit cozy. The kitchen wasn't designed with eight adults in mind, but it didn't bother anyone. Dakota sat back and observed this new family he was marrying into. They all seemed to adore each other, and Dana was glowing with happiness. It was a far cry from the family he knew growing up.

After their snacks, Dana, her uncle, and Dakota gave the family a tour of the town. They were proud of the way that their family seemed to appreciate the fresh air and friendly atmosphere of their small town. They had a nice dinner at the restaurant and finally started back for Dr. Clarke's office.

As they were walking along and chatting, Nelson Clarke took Dakota's arm, and they began to walk at a slower pace, trailing behind the others.

"I wanted a moment to speak with you," Nelson said to Dakota, who suddenly felt his palms beginning to sweat.

"Certainly, Mr. Clarke," Dakota said, trying not to show his nervousness.

"First of all, please don't call me Mr. Clarke. I would like for you to call me Father, just as Dana does. And Judith and I would like for you to think of us that way, as mother and father. You're part of our family now, and we love you and would like to think of you as a son."

Dakota stopped and stared at him. His eyes widened as he processed what the man had just told him. Dakota was so moved he was unable to speak.

"I know what a hard life you've had. Dana told us about your past and your family. But that's what it is—the past. You're part of a new family now, one that loves you. If you'll allow us the privilege, you'll have a mother and father, two brothers, a sister, an uncle, and a wonderful wife. You're free to start over, and we'd like to be a part of it. Oh, and the family's talked it over, and we won't mention your past unless you'd like to talk about it."

Emotion swelled up inside Dakota, and he fought back tears. All his life he had dreamed of a family that would love him, and suddenly here it was. He never expected this kind of reaction from Dana's family. Such open acceptance of him was unheard of.

"You don't know what this means to me," he said slowly then added, "Father."

"I know what it's like to be loved, and it hurts Judith and me that you haven't known that for the majority of your life. But that's all going to change. You and Dana will build a new family together. Dana adores you, and you will have children together, and you can raise them in a home filled with love."

"Thank you." Dakota was so moved, that was all he could manage to say. Nelson patted him on the back, and they continued walking toward the doctor's office.

The two walked into the living area of Dr. Clarke's office, and Dana turned from talking with her mother and sister to glance at her father and Dakota. She noticed that Dakota seemed more at ease, and the two were talking like they were old friends. Something had happened while they were outside. She didn't know what transpired between the two of them, but she was grateful for whatever it was. She smiled as warmth radiated through her body. Her family was here, and they accepted Dakota with open arms. She walked over to Dakota and her father and looped her arm through her fiancé's. Her eyes momentarily locked with his before he continued on with his conversation with her father. She had never been happier.

The next day the Clarke family loaded up in Dr. Clarke's buggy to visit some of the people who were helping Dana prepare for the wedding. The first place they went was to Pastor Douglas and Gloria Tyler's home. Gloria's warm smile greeted them as she ushered the guests in and served them cool lemonade. The men took a tour of the church building, while the women sat in the kitchen discussing flower arrangements. Gloria's specialty was flowers, and Judith and Laura were impressed with her ideas. She wanted to line the pews with white satin ribbon and have a flower arrangement at the head of each pew.

Next, they dropped by the Brewers. Mark was working at the bank, but Dana wanted her family, especially her mother and sister, to meet Claire. Finally they made their way to the Blue Star Ranch. As they drove onto the property, Dakota felt a sense of pride as he noticed the look of admiration in the eyes of Nelson and his sons. Caleb Carter kept up the ranch well, and Dakota was proud to be a part of it. Caleb and Alicia came out when they heard the jingle of the buggy and pleasantly welcomed Dana and

Dr. Clarke's family to their home. Caleb took the men on a brief tour of the ranch, while the women sat on the porch with Alicia.

"Since Dakota's not here, I suppose I'm allowed to ask this," Laura began tentatively as she looked from her mother to Alicia. "Did his family really kidnap you, and did he really save your life?" Alicia's eyes widened in surprise, but only for a moment. She smiled at the young innocence in Laura's eyes. Laura was at an age where it was easy to be fascinated by stories of outlaws and heroes.

"Yes, he did," Alicia answered. She gave a brief synopsis of the story as Laura's captivated eyes never left her face.

"Oh my," Laura breathed as she put her hands up to her face. "He was very courageous to do that."

"It's amazing how God can change a person's life for the better," Judith added. "We're so pleased that Dana will be marrying such a fine man." Alicia sat back in her rocking chair and sighed contentedly, happy to see that Dana's family felt no judgment or ill will toward Dakota.

Later that afternoon, Caleb and Alicia stood on the porch and waved good-bye to the visitors. Caleb's arm rested around Alicia's waist, and he pulled her close.

"I'm so happy for Dakota," he said softly. "The Clarkes are good people. He'll finally have the family he's always dreamed of." His voice broke, and Alicia looked up at her husband. She put both arms around him and leaned her head against his chest.

"It's going to be sad to see him leave," she responded.

"Yes, but I have no doubt that God has mighty plans for him in Lexington."

CHAPTER 27

The day of the wedding was glorious. The bright-blue sky held hints of white as small clouds formed overhead. Gloria outdid herself with the flowers, and the moment Alicia stepped into the church, her nose was assailed with the fragrance of roses. Alicia, the Brewers, and all of their children sat near the front. Caleb was Dakota's best man.

Caleb stood next to a nervous Dakota and laid his hand on his shoulder.

"Who would've thought ten years ago that I would be standing as your best man?" Caleb whispered with a laugh. "Just goes to show that you never know what to expect."

"I'm glad you're here with me. I'll never forget the kindness you and Alicia have shown me. I wouldn't be here if it weren't for you." Dakota's eyes revealed the depth of his sincerity, and Caleb nodded humbly.

The sound of music caused everyone to turn as Dana swept up the aisle on her father's arm. The breath went out of Dakota as he stared at the most beautiful creature he had ever beheld. The ceremony went by in a blur, and before Dakota knew it, Pastor Tyler was pronouncing them husband and wife. He gathered his beautiful bride in his arms and gave her a delicate kiss before proudly escorting her back down the aisle.

The reception was a small affair in the Tyler home for family and close friends only. The couple didn't have much time before they had to board the train for Lexington. The Clarke family, the Carters, Brewers, and Tylers all went with the newlyweds to the train station to see them off.

Dakota made a difficult round of good-byes to the people who helped him build a new life. He shook the pastor's hand and gave his wife a momentary hug. He did the same with Mark and Claire. When he turned to face Caleb and Alicia, he couldn't stop the tears from filling his eyes.

"I don't know what I would have done without you," he said huskily. He blinked hard, bidding the tears away.

"You've been such a blessing to our family." Alicia reached up to hug him. "Please write to us and let us know how you and Dana are doing. You know you're welcome back anytime." Dakota nodded and faced Caleb. He held out his hand, but Caleb grabbed him in a steely embrace instead. Dakota knew that this man, his greatest mentor, would be the hardest to say good-bye to. He stepped back and took a deep breath.

"Words won't adequately express how much what you and your family have done mean to me. You befriended me, gave me a job, and had faith in me when no one else did. If it weren't for your friendship and support, I probably wouldn't be going into the ministry."

Caleb was humbled by Dakota's little speech. To think that he had any part in furthering God's kingdom was enough to bring him to his knees in gratitude and humility.

"You're a good man, Dakota Jones. We're going to miss you around here," Caleb extended his hand for a final farewell. Dakota took it, and Caleb leaned forward and said quietly, "I love you, son." Dakota was filled with so much emotion that all he could manage was a nod. He worked to compose himself then turned to the Carter children.

He knelt down in front of little Daisy, who was sniffling into the handkerchief her mother gave her. "I'm going to miss you, Daisy. You be a good girl, and I promise I'll write." Daisy gave him a tearful smile then threw her arms around him. Dakota squeezed her tightly then turned to face the boys. "Take good care of each other and your mother and Daisy," he admonished. "I'll write to you both, too." The boys nodded, bravely trying to hide the emotions that they felt were too girly. They were heartbroken that their favorite ranch hand was leaving. He gave them each a hug and then stood to his full height and put his arm on his wife's elbow.

After a tearful farewell to her family, Dana boarded the train with her new husband. They stood at the end of the train car, holding onto the rail and waving at their family as the train began to slowly pull away from town.

Dakota put his arm around his new bride and spoke softly against her ear.

"You know, the first time I saw you was on a train."

"It was?"

"We were on the same train the day you arrived in Darby. I thought the same thing I think now—that you are the most beautiful woman in the world. Little did I know that we would be leaving Darby on the same train."

Dana giggled as she snuggled closer to her husband. "Only this time we're leaving as husband and wife."

"I don't know what I did to deserve you and this new life God has blessed me with, but I know that I'll spend the rest of my days taking care of you and serving the Lord."

Dakota and Dana Jones walked hand in hand in the train car and took their seats. Dakota put his arm around his wife and sighed contentedly. He looked out the window as the steady roll of the train took them toward their new life—a life full of hope and promise.

DEAR READER

What fun it has been for me to visit with the Carters and Brewers again! And it's been exciting to see how God worked in Rigby, a.k.a. Dakota's, life. You know, forgiveness is a powerful thing. It can help mend a wounded relationship, heal a bitter heart, and show others the power of the cross of Christ. There is no one better in history that exemplified forgiveness the way that Jesus Christ did. Because of Christ's redeeming work on the cross, we are forgiven! It says in Acts 13:38-39,

> Therefore, my friends, I want you to know that through Jesus the forgiveness of sins is proclaimed to you. Through him everyone who believes is set free from every sin, a justification you were not able to obtain under the law of Moses.[5]

That's a powerful thing. If you ask Christ to come into your heart and forgive you of your sins, he will.

It's not always easy to forgive others sometimes, though, is it? When someone really hurts you, it's hard to put that aside and have a forgiving heart. But holding a grudge only hurts the one holding it. Ask God to help you forgive, and he will. Forgiveness isn't a feeling; it's a conscious decision that you have to make. I urge you to choose forgiveness.

Dakota was given a second chance at life in this story. It took time, but by the end, he was finally accepted by the town. God gives all of us second chances every day. I'm thankful for the forgiveness and second chances that he's given me!

God bless you all.

Until next time,

Julie Bell

DISCUSSION QUESTIONS

1. Do you think that Rigby did the right thing in changing his name? Why or why not? Do you agree with the comparison he made with Saul in the Bible?

2. Mark Brewer's life was changed forever because Rigby's family made a wrong decision to rob the bank and shoot him. But he told Rigby that it was in the past. How easy is it to forgive someone completely and move on with life? Has something happened to you because of someone else that permanently changed your life? How did you handle that?

3. Dakota waited too long to tell Dana about his real identity. Should he have tried to wait for the perfect moment, or should he have told her that first night in the restaurant? Is there something in your life that you need to be honest with someone about? If so, what is holding you back from telling that person?

4. Fred Johnson wrongfully accused Dakota of stealing his chickens. Fred and several other farmers decided to take the law into their own hands even though Dakota had already been punished. Why is it difficult for people to give second chances? Why should we give second chances?

5. When the town learned of Dakota's true identity, people kept their children out of Sunday school because they didn't trust him. Dana stopped trusting him. How easy is it to lose someone's trust? What does it take to earn it back? Is there something you need to do in your life to earn back someone's trust?

6. Pastor Tyler gave a sermon on forgiveness in an attempt to help the members of the town realize that their attitude toward Dakota was wrong. But even then people still didn't want to accept Dakota. Why is forgiveness so difficult? God can help you forgive. Forgiveness is a conscious decision that we make. Is there someone that you are withholding forgiveness from?

7. In an attempt to reconcile Dana and Dakota, Alicia and Claire set up a dinner where they invited them but they didn't know the other would be there. The dinner backfired on them and created an uncomfortable situation for everyone. Did Alicia and Claire do the right thing by setting up the dinner? How could they have better helped their friends? Have you ever tried to help someone and it backfired?

8. It took Dakota nearly dying from influenza for Dana to realize that she had been wrong and that Dakota deserved a second chance. Why is it that it oftentimes takes extreme circumstances for us to realize how important the people we love are to us?

END NOTES

1   Psalm 100:4 (KJV)

2   John 8:7-11 (KJV)

3   Matthew 6:14-15 (KJV)

4   Psalm 98:8-9 (KJV)

5   Acts 13:38-39 (NIV)